I0760769

WOLF CURSED

LONE WOLF SERIES
BOOK ONE

HEATHER HILDENBRAND

WOLF CURSED

Lone Wolf Series, book 1

Heather Hildenbrand

Cover: Design by Definition

Special Edition Jacket designs: Design by Definition & Malice and Mayhem Covers

Art by Samaiya

My muscles tensed until they hurt as I huddled on my sagging mattress. In the darkness of my tiny bedroom, every shadow cast felt like a threat. My thrift store dresser sat sadly against the far wall, taunting me with its larger-than-life silhouette. The secondhand mirror propped beside it offered a reflection of me that looked like something out of a horror movie looming up from my twin bed. Wild dark hair. Wide, worried eyes. But it wasn't the dresser that scared me.

A car had parked outside our trailer.

The time on my phone read two in the morning.

Considering we rarely, if ever, had guests during the day, it couldn't be a good thing to have anyone coming over this late at night. Dad would be beside himself with paranoia, and in this case, I couldn't blame him. Years' worth of his rants about "those people hunting us" had taught me it was best to keep him away from strangers.

Fat chance of that now.

The voices outside were loud as the uninvited visitors

climbed out of their car and crossed the gravel drive toward our trailer. This place had thin walls to begin with, but after a lifetime of vigilance, I'd woken the moment the headlights had pointed through my window.

Already, my heart was threatening to beat right out of my chest. Dad was always going on and on about enemies everywhere. One long look from a shady stranger, and he'd declare it too dangerous. We'd moved fourteen times just in the last five years alone. No public school. No college either unless you counted that one class I took before we went broke again. No friends. Which was honestly just as impressive as it was pathetic for a nineteen-year-old to have literally zero friendships.

"Don't let anyone get close enough to *see* you, Ash," my dad had always warned me.

I was over it. Or I had been until strangers had driven up to our doorstep in the middle of the night.

What the hell did they want?

I crawled over and peeked out of the cracked blinds covering my window. Three men were making their way to our front door. I couldn't make out their faces in the darkness, but something glinted, and I zeroed in on whatever object had reflected against the streetlight.

My breath caught.

One of them carried a metal bat.

I scrambled back, letting the blinds fall into place. This was bad.

Really, *really* fucking bad.

Footsteps sounded in the hall, and I knew from the slow, heavy rhythm they made it was my father emerging from his bedroom at the end of the hall. He stumbled once. The wall creaked underneath his weight as he caught himself.

Shit. He was drunk. As usual.

Outside, someone knocked, just a quick two-rap with a knuckle. But it sent my heart rate soaring.

"I'm comin', asshole." My dad's gruff voice was easy to hear through our thin walls.

My hands fisted around my blanket at that. I wanted to scream at him to stop. To hide.

Whoever was out there at two in the morning couldn't be friendly.

The fact that my father was actually going to answer the door was proof of how far he'd fallen.

It was all mom's fault.

If she hadn't left us seven years ago, Dad would never have gone off the deep end. He'd still be my protector. My safe place. Instead, it felt like I'd been the one protecting him these last few years. And now, he was about to open that door and invite the devil inside.

He was going to get us killed.

A pounding on the front door shook me loose of the frozen panic that gripped me. I got to my feet and rushed from my bedroom. I made it into the tiny living room just as my dad opened the front door. The smell of alcohol clung to him like a second skin, knocking me back a step.

"Whatever yer selling, we ain't buyin," he said in a sleepy, slurred voice.

Over my dad's shoulder, I counted three figures standing on our sagging porch. The one carrying the bat stood at the very back, but none of them looked like they were selling so much as *demanding*. A pair of beady eyes landed on mine. His hands were empty, but the man standing in front of the others didn't need a weapon to convey his intentions. I rushed forward, pressing my palms against the back of the door as I slammed it closed again.

Securing the deadbolt, I whirled on my dad.

"What the hell are you doing?" I hissed.

My dad swung his bloodshot gaze to mine. "Ash," he said, and a flicker of awareness shot across his slackened face.

"It's two in the morning, Dad. Those guys can't be here for a good reason."

More awareness. Then alarm.

My heart rate accelerated until it hurt my ribs.

"Should I get the go-bags?" I asked.

Dad insisted we keep a bag packed underneath the kitchen counter. If we're ever found—by whom, I still had no idea—I was supposed to run, with or without him. I never actually thought that would happen, but now I wondered if maybe Dad had been right about monsters chasing us all along.

"It's Vorack. Open the door, Joe," one of the guys outside called. Not yelling exactly. Confident. Calculating. But no volume. Like a predator who knew he'd cornered his prey.

My dad scowled as some of the panic faded from his taut expression.

"Nah, we don' need the bags," he said, unable to meet my eyes. "This is something else."

"Who's Vorack?" I whispered.

"Get the hell off my property," my dad yelled, ignoring my question.

"Not happening," the man called back. "It's time to settle your debt."

"Shit," my dad whispered, his eyes suddenly wide and no longer dilated.

"What debt?" I demanded in a heated whisper. When he didn't answer, I grabbed his shirt sleeve and forced him to focus on me. "Dad, who are those guys?"

"Jus' some guys I met at the bar," he said, waving me off.

His answer should have made me feel better. Whatever ghosts my dad was convinced were chasing us from town to town and state to state, these guys weren't it. Local bookies were not the demons my dad forced us to run from constantly. No, these guys were a very normal-looking evil; the kind my dad could have only brought on himself.

Anger eclipsed my fear, and I aimed it all at the one who deserved it.

"How much do you owe them?" I demanded, my breaths coming in short, raging bursts.

"Don' worry 'bout it," he insisted.

"Don't worry about it? There are three angry bookies outside our door in the middle of the damned night, and you want me to not worry about it?"

My dad scowled. "Ash, go back to bed. I got this."

He swayed, and I used my grip on his arm to steady him. Not easy, considering how much bigger he was than me. My dad had always been tall and built, but after years of drinking away his constant stress, he wasn't the solid wall of muscle he used to be. Instead, he was a solid beer belly with a spare tire made of fast food—and a brain with a penchant for making stupid bets.

We'd already moved once because of his stupid gambling habit and his inability to pay up. Looked like we were doing it again. This time with nothing but the clothes on our backs. At least I had sweatpants on instead of just the nightshirt I sometimes wore.

Dad, on the other hand, wore nothing but a white tank and a pair of dirty jeans. And he was in desperate need of a shower—a luxury that was probably a long way off for us right about now even if we did make it out of here in one piece.

"You're not opening that door," I told him firmly.

My dad waved me off. "Id'll be fine. I'll jus' git 'nother 'stention"

Shit. The slurring was not a good sign.

For a moment, I'd thought the danger of three goons on our doorstep in the middle of the night would sober him. But no such luck.

"Joe, I know you're in there," called the man outside. Vorack. "We can do this the easy way or the hard way."

"Dad, those guys aren't going to give you another extension," I said, half-pleading now.

Why couldn't he be stronger? Better? Why couldn't he stop letting her absence break him? Ugh. I hated seeing him let himself go. I hated my mother more for causing it.

"Go get the rifle," he said.

My jaw fell open. Was he kidding? There was no way he could shoot straight right now.

"What? No, come with me. We'll go out the back. Run to the car—"

Something hard slammed into the outside of the front door. I jumped and looked down to see a small dent had appeared on our side. I stared at it in horror. Stupid, cheap-ass, plastic door.

But really, what did I expect in a trailer? This thing was not exactly fortified against invasion.

"Joe, you can either come out or we're coming in," Vorack called.

My panic rose.

Urgency gripped me.

"Dad," I said, tugging on his arm. "We have to get out of here."

He hesitated. I could see some sort of indecision in his eyes. Like he was trying hard to access a clear thought.

"Okay," he said finally. He reached over and grabbed the car keys off the wall hook and pressed them into my hand. Then he looked at me intently, the glassy look turning fast to fear. "When I say go, run for the back door. Start the car."

"What about you?"

He reached out and pressed a warm hand to my cheek. "I'm right behind you, kid," he said.

I nodded, my chin bobbing incessantly. This would work. It had to work. Forget the bags we had stashed. We needed to get the hell out of here.

Something slammed into the door a second time.

I jumped.

"You have to be fast," I warned him.

"Kid, I'm the fastest," he shot back. It was an old argument and hardly true anymore. But I didn't say so. "Ready . . . set . . . go!"

With the car keys clutched in my fist, I took off at a barefooted sprint for the back door. My dad shuffled, but the noise was lost to the roar in my ears as panic drove me onward.

In the kitchen, I flipped the lock free and yanked the back door open only to crash into someone waiting on the other side.

Hands came up to grip my wrists, and I immediately started kicking and fighting. A male grunt sounded, and my attacker released one of my wrists to grab at his shin where my foot just landed. I tried turning and twisting away, but then a fist smashed into my cheek, and I went down to my knees as pain radiated through my skull. I blinked, my vision closing in until I saw through a narrow tunnel.

I fell to the floor and covered my face with my hands, my eyes filling with tears.

God, that hurt.

A loud crash came from the front, followed by yelling. Then grunts like the one my attacker had made. Except the voice sounded exactly like my dad's.

"You always choose the hard way, Joe," Vorack said—except this time, his voice came from inside the house.

No.

I scrambled up and rushed toward the living room only to be grabbed again before I could make it across the tiny space.

"Let me go," I demanded, twisting and kicking and scratching at the body currently blocking me from getting to my father. In the darkness, I could see the way the man's eyes lit every time I fought back. Bile rose in my throat as I began to imagine just how they planned to extract this debt my father owed.

We damn sure didn't have any money to give them. Or not enough anyway. I had no idea what Dad owed them, but judging from our middle-of-the-night visit, it was probably a lot. If not, he would have paid them already.

That meant they'd have to take payment some other way.

I fought harder.

"Got a live one, boss," said the man holding me—or trying to.

More grunts and scuffling from the living room. Something hard hit the wall, and the few pictures we had hung rattled in their frames.

"You bet the wrong house, Joe," I heard the man say.

"Screw you, Vorack," my dad said from where he'd slumped to the floor against the wall.

My heart broke at the defeat I heard in those three words.

"No thanks," Vorack said. "Your daughter, on the other hand, might have better luck with such an invitation. Might even be enough to call us even."

Horror filled me. My voice broke on my next scream.

"Don't even think about it," my dad warned.

"Bring her here, Frank."

The man holding me gave me a rough shove, and the momentum sent me sprawling onto the stained carpet. I rolled onto my side and looked over at my dad slumped against the wall by the smashed front door. The dim overhead light revealed his nose was bleeding, and both eyes were already swelling.

Vorack's other goon stood over him, brandishing the baseball bat and making sure he didn't get up.

"If you touch my daughter," my father started.

A heartache so deep I knew it would never heal ripped through me. My father's threat was empty. Everyone here knew it. Hell, he didn't even try to get up when he said the words.

"What?" Vorack taunted. "Tell me, Joe. What will you do?"

No answer.

Vorack stalked over to me and prodded me with his boot. "What's your name, princess?"

"Get away from her," my dad snarled.

"Happy to, Joe," Vorack said. "But that's up to you. Pay me, and I'll be on my way. Otherwise, I'll take what's owed by other means."

He gave me a look that made it clear he hoped for the latter.

"There's five hundred in the freezer," I blurted. "Take it and leave us alone."

My dad shot me a look.

I worked four nights a week at the diner around the corner. Just like I had in every backwoods town we'd lived in. Most of my earnings went to keeping the lights on, but I'd hidden some extra cash in a bag of frozen peas since I knew it was the only place he wouldn't find it.

It was my ticket out.

If Dad wanted to drink himself to death at a new address every three months, that was his choice. I planned to pick a spot and plant roots. Build a home. Screw whatever ghosts he was convinced were hunting us. Parting with it for Dad's bad habits was the last thing I wanted, but if it meant getting Vorack out of here, I'd let it go.

Unfortunately, Vorack merely grinned. "That's cute, princess. You think I'd get out of my warm bed at this hour for five hundred bucks?" He snorted and shared an amused look with his goons.

They all laughed and not in a fun way.

Then Vorack looked down at me again. "Try ten thousand, and that's not including interest."

I blinked.

The bit of hope I'd let myself feel drained away.

"What kind of idiot loans ten thousand to a guy with no collateral?"

The words were out of my mouth before I could think them through.

Vorack's eyes narrowed. He took a step closer, and I curled around, bracing myself for a kick or a punch or something equally painful.

He leaned down, and I squeezed my eyes shut, preferring not to see it coming.

"Take the five hundred as a down payment," my father said quickly. "I'll get you the rest tomorrow."

Vorack shook his head. "We're way past down payments, Joe."

My father didn't answer. I could hear the defeat ringing in his silence.

"Have it your way then." Vorack reached down and grabbed my wrist, squeezing painfully as he pulled me to my feet. With his other hand, he yanked my long hair back so I was forced to look up at him.

"How about it, princess?" he drawled. "Want to help save your daddy?"

Panic clawed at me as I realized my worst nightmare was about to happen. And there wasn't a damn thing I could do to stop them. The worst part was that this had nothing to do with the actual reason we'd been running all these years. All of it for nothing because, in the end, my father had fallen apart.

If I wanted to survive, it was up to me now.

Knowing it would only make things worse, I pulled my leg back and shoved my foot into his groin.

Vorack groaned and doubled over, stumbling away. "Bitch," he roared.

The guy who'd hit me, Frank, chuckled. "She sure has some fire in her."

"I like a good firecracker," Vorack said, his expression twisting to something cruel and sinister as he straightened.

He reached for me again, and this time, whatever struck him, it wasn't me.

Thunder boomed, and the trailer shook. Windows shattered, sending glass flying in all directions. I closed my eyes and shielded my face as tiny shards landed in my hair and against my forearms.

The men around me yelled and rushed at my father.

I opened my eyes and froze at the scene before me.

My father had . . . transformed into some sort of monster.

Either that, or the demons we were always running from had caught up and taken over his body.

His skin was broken open with bones sticking out at unnatural angles. Blood leaked from the wounds, but the worst was his eyes. Glowing and without a hint of humanity left, they were trained on Vorack. He hopped up onto all fours and bared his teeth—canines that had elongated to look like fangs.

Fear gripped me, unlike anything I'd felt before. My father was gone. In his place was a demon from Hell. And I couldn't be sure he didn't want to drag all of us—me included—back there with him.

2

My father—or the monster inside him—snarled while thick drool dripped from his sharpened teeth. At the sight of him advancing toward them, Vorack and his men fell over one another in their scramble to get out.

"Go," Frank screamed, shoving past the others.

Glass crunched underneath their boots, and I watched, unable to tear my eyes away, as my father—or the monster he'd become—moved slowly toward the open door. He watched as Vorack and his men raced into the yard and across the driveway toward their car.

I took a slow step backward, terrified of whatever that thing was. Fur had sprouted in some places, obscuring the protruding bones. And his mouth was elongating into a kind of snout. He looked like a demon straight out of a horror movie.

Except this was real life.

What the hell had happened to my father? And how was I going to fix him?

"Dad?" I called tentatively.

The thing swung its red-eyed gazed toward me.

Fear sent me backing away. My father—the demon—didn't move.

That was a good sign.

Recognition flared in his glowing eyes. "Ash," he said, the sound of his voice distorted.

Still, it was him. And he recognized me.

Maybe he wasn't going to hurt me after all.

I took a step toward him.

A gunshot rang out, loud and sharp enough to make me jump.

I sucked in a breath and watched as my father, or the monster that had taken him over, flew backward into the wall. He hit hard enough to leave a hole the size of his broken body before sliding to the floor. Blood poured from a hole in his chest, and right before my eyes, the demon-form receded, and my father's body and bones returned to their normal appearance.

He lay limp and still, in a growing puddle of his own blood.

"No!" I rushed forward, forgetting Vorack, forgetting the demon my father had just become. Forgetting it all.

Nothing else mattered except saving him.

"We'll be back to collect," Vorack yelled. "One way or another."

Outside, the engine revved, and Vorack's car spewed gravel as he hit reverse and drove off like a bat out of hell.

I didn't even look up to make sure they'd all gone. Instead, I collapsed to my feet beside my father and pressed my palms to the gunshot wound on his chest. Already, his shirt was drenched in blood. This wasn't good. I had to call for an ambulance.

"Dad," I called, half-sobbing. "Dad, please hang on."

My voice broke, and I started to climb to my feet, to find the phone. My father's hand shot out and gripped mine, holding me in place. His eyes flew open, and he looked up at me, his gaze intent and not at all like that of a dying, drunk man.

It was the clearest I'd seen him in months.

"Ash, listen to me. Take the money in the freezer," he said, his voice strained. "Take it and the car and go. Now, tonight. Don't wait for Vorack to come back."

"Not until you get to the hospital," I said.

"A hospital can't help me," he said, wincing and then gritting his teeth.

Every time he spoke, the blood seemed to spill faster.

"Dad, please," I said.

"Ash, listen to me. Go to Ridley Falls. Find Oscar, my brother. He'll help keep you safe. Your mother—"

He broke off, squeezing his eyes shut, and his head lolled to the side.

"Dad," I sobbed, still pressing my hands to his wound, for all the good it did.

My dad took a ragged breath and looked at me again. I could see the pain reflected in his eyes. This was costing him.

"Dad, don't say another word," I told him. "I'm going to call for help. I'll be right back. Stay with me."

"Ash." His hand gripped my wrist with not nearly the force needed to stop me. But I didn't move. I couldn't make myself walk away. In the back of my mind, I knew he wouldn't be breathing by the time I returned from making that call.

A sob built in my throat at the thought.

"Ash, I love you. I'm so damn sorry. For all of it." He sighed, and it was the saddest sound I'd ever heard. "Your mother thought it best, and I . . . all I ever wanted was to protect you. I'm sorry I wasn't strong enough. For her. For you."

"Forget Mom," I nearly screamed. "I'm here. Do this for me. Survive for me."

Stay sober for me.

It was everything I'd wanted to say for years. But I bit my lip and pleaded instead with my eyes.

With shaky fingers, he reached into his pants pocket and pulled out a familiar pendant. "Take it," he rasped.

I started to shake my head.

"Ash, I'm not asking."

"I told you I refuse to wear anything that came from her," I spat. Even now, he was trying to bring my mother into this. To make it seem like she was still a part of this family. She wasn't.

"Not for her," he insisted, shoving it at me. "For me."

I took the pendant, squeezing it inside my fist with one hand while still holding pressure to the gunshot wound on his chest with the other hand.

"It's important," he said, his eyes intent on mine now. "Put it on, and don't take it off, okay? No matter what. Promise me."

For once, I didn't argue or roll my eyes at the one thing my mother had left when she abandoned us.

"Promise, Ash," he repeated.

"I promise," I said quickly.

He reached up with his free hand and cupped my cheek, calloused fingers brushing over the bruise I could still feel throbbing from where that asshole had punched me earlier.

"No matter what happens, don't let them cage you," he whispered roughly.

Then his hand fell, and his expression went slack.

A sob ripped from my throat, and this time, I didn't bother holding it back. For a long time, I sat there, hands still pressed to a wound that couldn't be healed. Blood pooled until I was covered in it. My face swelled until it pulsed with my own heartbeat. The only heart in this room still beating.

Finally, the sky behind me began to lighten.

Something about the breaking of a new day snapped me from my grief, and I forced myself to accept what had happened—and to get up. I moved like I was in a haze. Brain fog made my thoughts fuzzy, my movements methodical.

Vaguely, I supposed I was in shock. But what could I do about that? What could I do about any of it?

On autopilot, I grabbed the cash from the freezer and a bottle of water from the fridge. Then, I snagged the car keys from where I'd dropped them hours ago.

It felt more like days. Like last night had been a nasty nightmare. Not real. But then I saw my father's body lying in the entryway, and I had to face the reality of what had happened all over again.

Pausing at the back door, I used our landline to dial emergency services and report my father's body. He would have told me not to bother, but I couldn't leave knowing he'd be lying here for who-knew-how-long before someone found him. When they asked my name, I hung up.

In the light of dawn, I stumbled my way to the aged sedan Dad had hustled from a desperate used car salesman back in Kansas City a few months ago. The air conditioning didn't work, but the windows did. I slid into the driver's seat, numb and lost.

After a long moment, I pulled out the pendant and fastened it around my neck—a white crystal carved into the shape of a crescent moon. It sat cold and still against my chest, a weight I'd long refused to accept no matter how many times Dad had tried talking me into it before.

My mother couldn't be bothered with raising me, so why should I let her off the hook by accepting her stupid necklace?

But it was different now. It was all different now.

Reeling and completely drained, I stowed the cash in the glove box and started the car. At the main road, I hesitated, trying to decide where to go. Dad's instructions rang in my mind. Ridley Falls. His brother. Oscar. Whoever the hell that was. He'd never mentioned any family before. It had always just been us. Him and me against the world. And Mom. Until she decided not to include herself.

I opened the glove box and checked the map Dad kept there. A cell would have been easier but our minutes had run out two months ago and there hadn't been money to afford more.

According to the map, Ridley Falls was nestled in the Blue Ridge Mountains of North Carolina. Right smack in the middle of nowhere from the looks of it. More rural than even this town.

That's where Dad wanted me to go?

Somewhere so remote I'd have zero chance of blending in? This from a guy who'd always insisted that I not let myself be seen for fear it would bring monsters to our doorstep.

I almost decided against it, but then I thought of Vorack and his parting promise to return. The monsters had already come to my door. They'd kicked it in and taken the one person I had in this world. If I didn't get someplace safe, somewhere off that asshole's radar, I was going to end up like my father.

And the one thing I refused to become was my parents.

With resignation and a heavy heart, I made the turn that would take me to Ridley Falls. To a family that couldn't possibly be any more terrible than the one I'd left behind.

The drive took me two days. Even that was probably impressive considering how many times I had to pull over and cry. Altogether, I made it through three states and four mountain passes—nearly all the way to Ridley Falls—before the car gave out. Steam leaked out from underneath the hood but more concerning was the thump-thump-thumping of something that went along with it. I'd ignored the noise for the last hour, but there'd been one last loud thump and then the engine had died. I barely managed to pull over to the shoulder before the tires stopped coasting.

By then, according to the last sign I'd passed, I was five miles out from the town's limits. The last car that passed was miles back, and in the fading light of dusk, the tree-lined road had a quiet sort of vibe that was comforting.

With no other choice, I stuffed the cash from the glove box into my bra, re-adjusted my sunglasses, and started walking.

It wasn't long before the night sounds of insects surrounded me and my footsteps faded into the background until all I could hear were my own thoughts and the cricket's song.

Images flashed in my mind as I followed the road. The memory of my father being shot. The way he'd transformed into some sort of demon beast.

I might have begun to believe I imagined that part if Vorack and his men hadn't fled the way they did.

A few tears slid down my cheeks as the loss hit me square in my chest. A hollowed-out hole formed where once there had been love, safety, security. My father had been paranoid, terrified, and erratic, but he'd been mine. And now he was gone. And I was alone. Surviving was all on me now.

Inevitably, my thoughts drifted to the bookie. Vorack. He'd promised to be back, and I had zero doubt he meant it. Ten thousand plus interest. I'd been in my father's toxic world long enough to know it would take twice that to get those assholes off my back, and even then, they could just as easily kill me as let me walk away.

A cool breeze whispered through the trees and down my spine, making me shudder. Suddenly, I was keenly aware of how quiet it had become. No more night sounds. No more anything. Just...stillness.

The feeling of eyes on me scraped along the back of my neck.

When I turned to look, there was no one there.

I forced myself to keep moving.

Steady pace.

No running or I'd only attract whatever predator was out here. Absently, I clutched at the pendant I wore. My last promise to my father. I wasn't about to take it off, no matter how much shit he'd put me through.

I still wasn't ready to accept he was really gone.

Or that this Oscar guy I was headed toward was my only family left.

Although, whatever awaited me in Ridley Falls had to be better than my life leading up to this. That's what I told myself as I forced one foot in front of the other.

The feeling of being watched never went away, but soon, lights from town came into view, and I relaxed. If someone or something was going to try and hurt me, they wouldn't wait until I'd strolled into public to do it.

The first building I came to was a gas station.

Pushing my way inside, I approached the clerk and waited for him to notice me. The kid couldn't have been older than sixteen and was just beginning to sprout that first attempt of facial hair.

It didn't take long for him to finish stocking the cigarettes and turn around. When he did, he stopped and stared, eyes wide.

"Are you okay?" he asked.

"Um." I glanced down and realized I still wore the same clothes—sweatpants and an oversized tee covered in blood. Shit. At least I still had my sunglasses on. "I'm looking for Oscar."

"Oscar Lawson?"

Weird. My last name was Langford. Shouldn't they have the same name? I didn't have the energy to decipher it though.

"Is there another Oscar in this town?" I asked.

"Well, no," he said after a pause, still staring at my face like he'd never seen a chick with a swollen cheek before.

I rolled my eyes. Or tried to. It hurt. "Okay, so Oscar Lawson..." I prompted when he didn't say more.

"Right. Yeah, uh, he's over at the shop."

"What shop is that?"

"Oh, uh." He closed his eyes and shook his head as if

clearing the image of, well, me. Damn. I must have looked like a hot mess. "Twisted Throttle Repair Shop. Next block up on the left. Can't miss it. Just look for all the bikes."

"Thanks."

I turned to go, and even without looking back, I had zero doubt the kid stared at me all the way out of the parking lot.

Despite the kid's instructions, I did, in fact, almost miss it thanks to what looked like some kind of tailgate party parked nearby that blocked my view. I ignored the catcalls—from both men and women—and kept my head down and my sunglasses on despite the twilight hour. The smell of cigarettes and marijuana drifted toward me. Music blared from someone's stereo—and a few girls in short skirts stood on the hood of a Jeep, writhing to the beat. Making a wide arc around the dance party, I strode past a couple making out in the bed of a pickup truck and a pyramid of beer cans poised on the hood of a Camaro.

Damn. For a Monday in a small town, this place was pretty wild.

Maybe it was a town holiday or something?

Just ahead, I finally spotted my destination.

Twisted Throttle had an aging sign hanging above a two-story building on the corner that looked old enough to be historic but was still well kept from the looks of it. And yes, there were bikes.

Except they weren't bicycles like I'd expected.

Motorcycles were parked along the curb lining the front and side of the corner lot. At least eight that I saw. With more in the back, I noticed, from my quick view of a paved lot enclosed by a chain-link fence.

A set of two large garage doors faced the side street and were currently closed up tight. On my left, the side street dead-ended into thick woods that encroached on the side and back of the building. It made the place feel secluded despite sitting on the very edge of what looked like a quaint little downtown area just past the shop. Even from here, I could smell the pine scent of the forest wafting out to welcome me.

I looked away from the call of the trees to the shop's front door and approached slowly. My exhaustion and the shock of everything that had happened muted my fear, but I knew enough to be watchful of my surroundings. A threat could be lurking anywhere.

The sign in the office window read Closed, but I grabbed the knob anyway.

Unlocked.

I pushed my way inside and inhaled the smell of oil and engine grease.

Underneath all of that, the pine scent of the woods still lingered, and I appreciated the sense of comfort it brought even if I couldn't understand it. I'd never felt comforted anywhere in my life.

Maybe it was because I'd finally stopped looking for demons and ghosts. Why should I keep worrying about being hunted down when my dad had turned out to be the beast we'd feared all along?

Absently, I reached down and brushed a hand over my right hip to be sure my shirt and pants covered the skin there. Habit. Then I plucked my sunglasses off and looked around.

"You lost?"

I looked up sharply at the sound of the voice. A guy not much older than me stood behind the counter, glaring at me. If I hadn't noticed the hostile tone, it was made plain on his face. A very handsome, very dangerous-looking face, I might add.

Wow.

Tall, dark hair, dark eyes, a chiseled jaw that probably always came across as slightly angry.

Except for right now when he looked downright enraged.

I couldn't imagine the sight of me—a complete stranger who'd never done anything to him—had sent him into a rage, but who knew. It had been a long day, and I knew my mind was still a fog after everything that had happened.

"I'm looking for Oscar," I said.

The hottie rounded the counter, and I could see his angry response right there on the tip of his tongue. But then he must have gotten a good look at me, coated in two-day-old dried blood and probably bruised to a pretty shade of purple by now, and his eyes widened—only for a second before they immediately narrowed.

"What the hell do you want with Oscar?"

The energy coming off this guy was intense and threatened to break through the numbness that was keeping me calm.

"I just need to talk to him."

My voice wobbled.

Of course it did.

His mouth flattened into a hard line. "I can give him the message."

For some reason, his continued hostility made me braver. Rather than shrinking away, I straightened and held my ground. "No thanks, this is personal."

The guy snorted. "Oscar doesn't concern himself with outsiders."

The way he said the word spoke volumes. Like being from out of town was a crime in itself.

"If that's true, he can tell me himself. Is he here or not?"

The guy gave me a once-over as if assessing whether I was worthy or not. Whatever he saw must have been good enough because he finally leaned away and, without taking his eyes off my face, yelled, "Oscar! Get your ass in here."

A second later, a muffled male voice came from out in the garage. "What?"

"Someone here to see you."

"Take care of it, would ya? This piston is being a real pain in my ass."

"Nah, this one's for you."

"What the fuck does that mean?"

"Special delivery." The angry hottie gave me a smug smile and crossed his arms, clearly content to wait for the show.

I rolled my eyes, aggravated and beginning to regret not eating all day. I hadn't been able to conjure up an appetite before, but for some reason, this asshole was clearing my head and bringing me back to myself.

The side door opened, and a guy about my dad's age walked in. He had salt and pepper coloring his dark hair, including his short beard, but his face was somehow still youthful. Maybe it was the hard set of his features or the sinewy arms that looked like they picked up more than just a bottle every night. But something about him seemed young and able despite the age his gray hair implied.

"What the hell is it?" he demanded of the asshole who looked like he was about to swallow his teeth with that smug ass smile.

Without a word, the jerk gestured to me.

"Who are you?" the older man grunted at me.

"Are you Oscar?" I asked, some of my bravado fading at the grumpy way he eyed me.

"Maybe. Who the hell wants to know?" he demanded.

His eyes cut the length of me, but he didn't react at the blood like the others had. I had to wonder how much of this sort of thing he'd seen in his life if it didn't faze him anymore.

"My name is Ash. My father was Joseph Langford." I paused, waiting for the recognition to register in his eyes.

But there was nothing.

"I believe he was your brother," I added pointedly.

Oscar's eyes narrowed. "I don't know anyone by that name."

Uncertainty rippled through me. For the first time since leaving my father's body behind, I wondered if I'd made the right choice.

What if he'd been mistaken?

What if the pain and whatever monster had infected him had made him crazy? Of course, he didn't have a brother. He would have told me—

"Did Cohen put you up to this?" the hottie suddenly demanded.

He gripped a shop rag in his clenched fist, and I shrank back at the animosity that rolled off him.

"Who's Cohen?" I asked, my voice suddenly not nearly so confident as before.

"Don't play with me," he growled. "You can tell Cohen sending some doe-eyed little ragdoll in here isn't going to—"

"I don't know any Cohen," I said, shaking my head in frustration. Grief threatened to break me down. But my anger steadied me. I held onto that.

"Right. Just like that isn't makeup all over your face. Give me a break."

Fury swelled. He really thought I'd fake bruises like the ones currently making my head throb? I reached for my cell phone—which was basically nothing but photo storage since I didn't have service—and pulled it out, sliding up and scrolling my photos until I found the one I wanted.

"Look," I snapped, holding the phone up so Oscar could get a good look.

He blinked, his eyes glancing over the picture of my dad. It was from a couple of months back. He'd been sober, and we'd gone for a drive down to the lake and back. My throat closed up just remembering it—and knowing it was our last good day together. Forever.

In fact, these photos were the only reason I'd bothered bringing the damned phone at all.

Oscar did a double-take, staring at the screen, a frown frozen on his angry expression.

"This is bull shit," the other guy went on. He was still looking at me like he was about to grab me and toss me out on my ass at any moment. "Tell her, Oscar," he added.

But Oscar hung his head and shook it slowly before waving him off. "Kai, you can go. I'll finish up here."

Kai.

The hot asshole was named Kai.

And Kai did not look happy with that order.

"Oz, you can't be fucking serious—"

"I mean it," Oscar snapped, rounding on Kai and pinning him with a glare that would have made me shit a brick. "I got this. Now go."

Kai cast me a look that made it clear he was only more pissed at being told to leave. Muttering to himself, he tossed the rag onto the counter with more force than necessary and then turned and stomped out through the side door. I could hear him slamming a few tools around in the garage, and then another door slammed, somewhere in the back.

A few seconds later, an engine revved to life.

Even then, Oscar didn't say a word. Instead, he marched around the counter and opened something down low I couldn't see. When he pulled his hand up, it held a beer.

"You want one?" he asked gruffly.

My stomach sank. I shook my head.

He uncapped it and held it out anyway. "You look like you need it as much as I do," he said. "Maybe more."

I shook my head again, bile rising. If this guy drank as much as my father, how was he supposed to help me? It felt like I'd just walked into another version of the life I'd left behind.

"I'm good," I said.

Oscar shrugged and tipped it back, emptying half the contents before he came up for air again. Outside, the sound of an engine grew louder. Closer. I turned to see a black motorcycle rounding the corner from the back alley. The rider made the turn onto the main road way faster than he should have.

Even with the helmet he wore that obscured his face, I knew it was Kai.

He didn't even look over as he sped away on two wheels.

I looked back at Oscar, unable to take the silence anymore.

"Are you going to say something?"

"My brother's name was Caleb Lawson when I knew him."

His voice was quiet, but there was an undercurrent of anger that kept me on edge, no matter how calm he appeared to me. Still, curiosity made it impossible to stay quiet.

"What do you mean 'when you knew him?'"

He sighed. "I haven't seen or heard from Caleb in twenty years."

"Why not?"

"Good question. Guess you'd have to ask him."

"Well, I can't because he's dead."

I'd meant to say the words in a flat voice. Uncaring. Untouched by it. But it was the first time I'd said it out loud, and my voice cracked on the last word.

Oscar's expression fell. For a split second, I saw the pain he carried at having lost his brother, not once but twice now. Then the neutral mask slid back into place.

His eyes zeroed in on my face knowingly. "That isn't makeup you're wearing, is it?"

"Why the hell would I fake getting the shit beat out of me?" I retorted.

He softened. Only by a few inches, but it was enough.

"What happened?"

I took a breath to steady myself, and before I knew what was happening, the truth was spilling out of me. Well, most of it anyway. There were secrets I would never utter, not for anyone. But this was close enough.

"My mom left when I was thirteen. After that, my dad became paranoid. We moved a lot, and he drank—to cope, I guess. A couple of years ago, he started gambling. Stupid stuff. Card games. Betting. Problem was he couldn't afford it. Last night, a bookie came to collect."

"Is that who did this to you?"

I nodded.

Oscar didn't respond.

My head throbbed, and my body felt like it had been hit by a truck. The last two days were catching up, and I wasn't sure how much more of this I could handle before my body simply gave out on me.

"Why did you come here?"

My temper rose at the question. The challenge in it. It was clear he didn't want me here. Which meant I would have to figure out my next move. And I'd have to do it without a car.

Shit.

"Before he died, Dad said to come find you. That you'd protect me."

Ugh. Even saying the words felt embarrassing. I hated asking for a handout.

Oscar looked skeptical. Or maybe just confused. "From bookies?"

"I don't know," I shot back. "Dad was convinced there was someone after us. It's why we moved so much."

"Your dad was special," Oscar said slowly, and something about it made me think of the beast he'd become right before...well, the end.

I didn't answer.

"How'd you get here?"

I sighed, sick of the inquisition. "My car died a few miles back, so I walked the rest of the way in. Look, if you don't want me here, fine. Just say the word, and I'll go. But I'm not going to answer any more questions like I'm some sort of criminal or imposter. I just watched my dad get murdered in front of me, and before that he— Ugh. Never mind. I'm out of here."

I started for the door, my balance wavering thanks to the exhaustion and pain I'd finally begun to feel. But I refused to stop now. I could do this. I could get a job. Find a hole somewhere to sleep. A trailer or maybe rent a room. I'd worked since I was fourteen, so that wasn't a deterrent. I didn't mind the work. It was the being alone part that would suck.

My hand closed over the knob just as I heard the words, "Hold on."

I stopped but didn't turn back.

"I have an extra room upstairs. You can have it if you want."

I turned slowly, half-convinced he was kidding.

"You're letting me stay?" I asked.

"Did the bookies get their money?"

"No."

"Do they know your name?"

"Yes."

"Then you'll stay." He pushed off from the counter and headed through a swinging door that led toward the back. "Come on. I'll show you the way up, and you can shower. I'll call a tow truck for your car."

"I – I don't really have money for—"

"Relax. Crater owes me a favor." He turned back, eyeing me where I still stood by the exit. "You coming?"

I could have said no. Actually, a big part of me wanted to turn him down and waltz out of there. To prove I didn't need some grouchy stranger of an uncle whom I didn't even know existed before now. But the sad fact was that I did need him.

And a shower sounded way too good to pass up.

Not to mention a bed. It might even have a pillow.

"Yeah," I said finally, "okay."

Too tired and broken to argue, I followed him upstairs. To an apartment above the Twisted Throttle Motorcycle Repair Shop. My new home.

4

I woke to the sound of loud machinery pulsating through the floor and groaned, pulling the pillow over my head. For all the good it did. My head throbbed with a headache worse than any I'd ever had. And my entire body felt like one big bruise.

Whatever rest and escape sleep had provided was over now.

I couldn't even appreciate the pillow or blankets—a luxury compared to my previous life. Not considering how much everything hurt. Including my ears now, thanks to the noise.

As I came awake, the nightmare of the last couple of days trickled in again. Reality was a hard punch in the gut. My eyes welled with tears as the grief and loss hit me all over again. For a long time, I laid there and just let the tears come. This hole in my heart would probably never mend. But I had to focus on the future. No matter how badly I wanted to just go back and have one more moment. One more chance at goodbye.

But that was the past. This was my life now.

Slowly, I eased the pillow away and looked around my room.

It was small. Smaller than even the one I'd had in our last trailer. But it was well-kept and with better construction, so that was something. It was also on the second floor. Apparently, Oscar lived above his garage.

The twin bed he'd offered me had a comfortable mattress, and the bathroom was clean, which was more than I expected for a grouchy bachelor like Oscar.

After a hot shower, I'd dressed in a t-shirt and sweats Oscar had loaned me and fell into bed. My eyes had shut almost immediately. Right after I'd stuffed all my cash underneath the mattress. Cliché, yes, but it worked.

Now, I was aware enough to notice the dresser and mirror across from me. And the small bedside lamp. All of them looked newer and nicer than anything I'd left behind. It wasn't the Ritz, but I didn't care about that. It was warm and safe and clean. More than I could have hoped for.

I tried not to get excited though.

Oscar might have been generous last night, but who knew how long it would be before he changed his mind. A guy like that didn't give anything for free.

The machine shut off again, and in the relative quiet, the sound of voices drifted up from the shop. All male. One of them sounded a lot like Kai. The tall-dark-and-asshole from last night.

And despite his threatening, angry demeanor, I couldn't help the heart flutter I felt at the thought of seeing him again.

Ugh.

Why did I have to feel that for *him?*

It's hormones, nothing more, I told myself.

Hell, if he wasn't such an asshole, he would have been

a great distraction from my own grief. But Kai *was* an asshole, and I wanted nothing to do with guys like that. I'd had my fair share and I was done.

So why did my heart constantly try to tell me otherwise?

In the middle of my internal argument, my stomach grumbled, forcing me to move. I couldn't remember the last time I'd eaten. Two days ago now? Three? I'd been too numb or too upset to eat much on the drive. And last night, I'd passed out before Oscar could even mention dinner.

Without a charger, my phone had died sometime in the night, so I had no idea what time it was. I left it on the nightstand and hobbled to the bathroom.

One look in the mirror, and I wasn't sure Oscar would even recognize me as the same girl he'd let in last night. My face was more swollen and an even brighter shade of purple than before. Crying probably hadn't helped, but mostly, it was the bruises. My cheek had a shine that glinted off the bathroom light where the skin had tightened and turned all sorts of crazy colors.

My hair was a hot mess, tangled and knotted after I'd slept on it wet. I poked around the cabinets and found a comb, putting it to work until I was slightly less "mountain woman" looking.

Then, I went in search of food.

The stairs let out in a back room just behind the front office. I stepped down from the last stair and froze at the sight of a strange guy. His shirt had the Twisted Throttle logo on it, and his name tag read Mick. He was poised to walk from the front office into the garage, but when he saw me, he stopped and stared. His expression morphed from surprise to horror when he saw my face.

You and me both, dude.

"Is Oscar here?" I asked.

"He ran an errand," the guy grunted and then walked out like he couldn't escape me fast enough.

"Wow, everyone's so friendly," I muttered.

But then I stepped into the main lobby area and froze. Kai stood behind the counter, staring down at some kind of spreadsheet.

"Maybe consider our lack of hospitality a sign that you shouldn't be here," he said without looking up.

"Trust me, as soon as I'm able to go, I'm gone," I muttered.

Ugh.

I'd dealt with guys like him before. The diners were full of them, especially late at night. They were always cocky and entitled, acting like the world revolved around their wishes. I'd learned a long time ago that backing down only made it worse.

He finally looked up, and when his dark eyes landed on my face, he tensed.

"What's the matter? My makeup job not believable enough for you today?"

For a long moment, he didn't answer. Instead, he simply stared, his eyes running over my body in a way that felt almost intimate. Like he was seeing every part of me, even the ones I didn't want to show him. Even in my borrowed oversized sweats, I felt naked before him.

I shuddered, and his gaze flicked back up to mine. Something flashed in his eyes. A darkness that bore the same hint of murder I'd seen in Vorack just before he'd fired the gun.

Fear coiled in my gut, and I took a step back.

He blinked and looked away.

"Aspirin's in the cabinet on your right," he said flatly.

I walked over and opened the cabinet, swiping the

bottle of painkillers with a sigh of relief. By the time I turned around again, Kai was setting a bottle of water on the counter beside me.

I took two pills and chased them with water.

Kai went back to reading over his spreadsheet, and the silence stretched until it felt awkward. I was just about to turn and head back upstairs when he spoke.

"I hope whoever did that to you got what they deserved."

Wait. Was he actually being nice?

I hid my surprise with sarcasm. "You sound almost like you feel sorry for me."

He glared, which seemed to be his permanent expression—at least, when I was around. But I couldn't help goading him. He'd been a dick this entire time, and now he wanted to show empathy? I wasn't in the mood. Probably because my head was pounding like a high school marching band. Also, for some reason, fighting with Kai helped keep the grief at bay. Anger was so much easier to feel than heartache.

"You look like shit," he shot back. "And if whoever did that comes here, looking to do it again, I don't want to clean up your blood off my floor."

"Isn't it Oscar's floor?"

He dropped the spreadsheet and walked up to me, closing the distance so fast I didn't have time to think before my back hit the wall and Kai was towering over me, invading my space.

His scent hit me.

Pine, like the forest. I hated that whatever soap he used made me kind of want to lick him. It was probably called "sexy woodsman asshole" or something.

I swallowed hard as he leaned in, his expression definitely more the 'asshole' part of that scent right now.

"Listen to me because I'm only going to say this once," he said in a quiet voice that was somehow worse than if he'd yelled. "You don't belong here. You don't know me, and you sure as hell don't know Oscar, so don't pretend to understand his business—"

He stopped short, his nostrils flaring and his eyes darkening to something like a thunderstorm. Lightning flashed—pure, raw rage—and then his expression shuttered and went blank.

"What are you?" he demanded in a quiet voice that raked over every nerve ending I had.

"Excuse me?" I asked, breathless and more turned on than I'd ever been in my life. It didn't matter that he was rude. Or hostile. Or invading my personal space for the sole reason of intimidating me.

I couldn't think straight, and even if I could, my body responded to him in ways I kind of wanted to slap myself over.

"Ugh. Forget it. This is insane." He stepped back, shoulders lowered. I didn't miss the way his hands had fisted at his sides, but other than that, he was completely devoid of the anger that had just driven him to corner me here.

With a little space between us, my breath whooshed out of me. Instead of the relief I should have felt, disappointment speared through me. And on its heels, the grief crashed in around me again. My lip trembled and I bit it to hide my display of emotion.

"I have no idea what you're talking about," I mumbled, still trying to understand what the hell he meant.

He didn't answer right away, just continued to stare at me with disbelief and those bedroom eyes that made me want to strip naked right here and—

"Impossible," he muttered into the silence, and then he

turned and slammed his way out the front door. I watched through the window as he marched around the corner and out of sight.

What in the actual hell was that?

It took my ovaries several moments to recover from the loss of everything that would not be happening next. I'd almost talked myself into giving in and using Kai as the distraction I knew he could be. Anything to not feel the loss and emptiness inside me.

Confused and already exhausted, I gave up on finding food or Oscar or anything else. Instead, I made my way back upstairs and crawled into bed, lost and hurting—in more ways than one.

Maybe fighting with Kai wasn't the best way to deal with grief after all.

Some time later, pain shot through me, and I came awake to a hand shaking my shoulder. I winced and shrank away from it. The hand disappeared.

My eyes cracked open, and I recognized Oscar leaning down over me. "Sorry," he muttered. "You were out."

He straightened and looked down at me, frowning.

"What's wrong?" I asked, alarm zipping through me.

If he kicked me out now, I had nowhere to go. And no way to get there.

"You look like hell," he said matter-of-factly.

"So I've heard." I struggled to prop myself on my elbows.

"Here." He dropped a paper bag onto the mattress next to me.

"What's this?" I asked, my nose already giving it away. The smell of bacon hit me, and my stomach cramped with hunger.

"Figured you might be hungry," he said.

And even though the words were gruff, the gesture

was kind. I grabbed for the bag, undeterred by his brusqueness.

"Thank you," I said, sitting up and pulling the brown paper open to peer inside. A wrapped breakfast sandwich and hash browns. Baby Jesus.

I reached inside and started shoving hash browns into my mouth then immediately regretted it.

"Shit, hot," I managed around a mouthful of scorching potato.

Oscar chuckled. "Orange juice is there," he said, pointing at where he'd set it on the nightstand.

I grabbed for the cold liquid and practically poured it down my throat. "Thanks." My word was muffled from the mouthful of warring temperatures.

"I made some calls," he said in a voice that had me pausing just before I could take another bite. I lowered the sandwich, heart hammering at the sad look in his eyes.

"About what?" I asked. Was he trying to get rid of me?

"Caleb—your father's body was being held by local police until their investigation was complete. I signed off for him to be transferred to a funeral home back in Reading. They're holding a small service this afternoon graveside. I thought you might want to know."

Surprise then gratitude washed over me. "I appreciate that."

"I would have brought him back here to be buried on family land, but they said his will specifically asked that he not be returned."

"He had a will?" That was news to me.

"Apparently."

Apparently was right. I had no idea. He must have felt very strongly about this place to make a will that stated he not be returned even in death.

"Did it say anything else?" I asked.

Anything about what the hell he'd made us run from my whole life.

"Not that I'm aware of."

I nodded, absently rubbing my chest as heartache panged. Not being there to say goodbye sucked. I looked down, blinking away tears. The last thing I wanted was for Oscar to think I wasn't grateful for everything he'd done.

"I have a link from the funeral service company," he went on, and my head snapped up again, my eyes wide. "They'll live stream it if you want to watch."

"Yes, I—" I swallowed hard against the lump in my throat. "I'd like that very much.

Oscar looked mildly uncomfortable, and I wondered if it had to do with the emotional moment we were having. "Eat and rest," he said, turning and heading for the door. "I'll come back later to check on you and give you the link."

"Actually, can I ask you something?" I asked.

He turned back. "What's up?"

I set the food aside for the moment, ignoring my empty stomach for a few minutes more.

"About my car," I said, unsure where or how to begin.

"Oh, right. It's parked in the back lot. I'll have one of the guys take a look at it this afternoon."

"It's here?" I blinked, surprised.

"Yeah, I had a buddy tow it in early this morning." He shrugged like it was no big deal.

Except, in my world, it was a huge deal. All of this was. I couldn't remember the last time someone had taken care of me this way. Hot tears burned my eyes, but I blinked them back.

"Thanks, look, I'll pay whatever it is."

He waved me off. "Like I said, Crater owed me a favor."

"Okay." I swallowed, trying to figure out my next words. Avoiding his eyes, I said, "Listen, I appreciate you letting me stay the night. I'll be out of here as soon as—"

"I told you already; you can stay as long as you need."

My head came up. I checked his face for some sign of a joke or a punch line.

"You're my brother's kid," he added as if that explained everything.

"You don't owe me anything," I began.

"No. But family takes care of family," he said firmly as if the phrase meant something to him.

I didn't bother mentioning I had no idea what family even was. Besides my dad, I'd never had anyone. Flings and acquaintances, sure, but no one I could count on. No one who could be considered family. After my mom left us, I wasn't sure I wanted it either. Oscar wasn't a complete asshole, like Kai, but he wasn't exactly sunshine and rainbows either.

"I don't even know what that means," I admitted.

He grunted.

"And I can't take your charity," I added.

"Not offering charity," he drawled.

My eyes narrowed.

He crossed his arms.

It felt like a standoff, except I had no idea what the stakes were.

"You know how to answer a phone?" he asked.

I nodded.

"What about computers?"

"I aced my classes and even took one college course in accounting," I said.

I didn't bother explaining my classes had all been done

on a refurbished laptop provided by the state to low-income households. A computer was a computer, right?

"Why?" I asked.

"I need someone up front to schedule and do invoicing."

"You want me to work for you?"

"Like you said, you can't take charity."

Hmm. "So, I'd earn a paycheck?"

"It doesn't pay much but yeah. Fair and square. As long as you do the job."

I looked around the small bedroom. "I can't exactly afford rent."

"You can have this room," he said. "Perk of the job."

When I opened my mouth to argue, he cut me off. "You'll pull your weight here too. Cook, clean, take care of the place. Do that, and we'll call it even."

I bit my lip, considering it.

Vorack wasn't likely to just forget the debt my father owed. Not after witnessing that monster he'd become. And I damn sure didn't want to live the rest of my life on the run from him. If I could earn enough to pay him, it would clear me. And it wasn't like I would find a better deal anywhere else.

Besides, I'd worked in diners and dives since I was fourteen. Stocking and running a kitchen was the easiest work he could have asked for.

"Okay," I said finally. "You have a deal."

Oscar grunted his own agreement, and just like that, I had a home and a job. A new life. I wondered what Kai would do when he found out. If he'd be angry. I snorted to myself. Of course he'd be angry. I couldn't imagine him any other way, honestly. Okay, that was a lie. I imagined Kai all sorts of ways. Angry and naked. Angry and kissing me. Angry and taking my clothes off.

At first, I'd considered my attraction a response to my grief. Anything to distract me. But now, I was starting to wonder if there was more to it. The thought should have scared me, but all it did was excite me in ways that were, without a doubt, going to get me into serious trouble. Story of my life.

Despite my protests, Oscar insisted I spend the entire day in bed, downing Aspirin and water until the pounding in my head and the throbbing throughout my body became manageable enough to function. After he returned to the shop and the next round of painkillers kicked in, I found myself sinking once again into a restless sleep. My dreams were horrible; nightmarish visions of my father becoming a monster and then dying and then waking up and doing it all over again.

I watched my father's funeral through bleary eyes and fuzzy thoughts. Tears ran freely down my face, but Oscar, dry-eyed and stoically silent, stayed for all of it. I was glad. Other than us watching the live stream, there was no one present. Once, I thought I saw a figure in the corner of the camera as they passed by the gravesite. A man dressed in a dark jacket and sunglasses. His haircut had reminded me of Vorack, but he was gone too fast to know for sure.

After that, I was too lost to my own grief to even care.

By the time the service ended and the live stream cut

off, Oscar was fidgeting. I told him to get back to work, and the moment he was gone, I gave in to my grief and cried myself to sleep.

Hours later, Oscar brought me dinner—another paper bag full of fast food—and even through my haze of pain and grief, I realized he needed that cooking and cleaning more than he'd let on.

The place wasn't gross, but dust motes danced in the slanted sunlight that streamed in through the windows, and the fast-food dinner seemed like a habit.

By the next morning, I woke a little less achy and a lot more clear-headed.

Oscar's bed was already empty when I stumbled to the bathroom and took a shower. But when I emerged, a couple of pairs of leggings along with a few sports bras and tank tops had been tossed onto my bed.

I looked around, listening for someone else, but the apartment was quiet. Empty.

Wrapped in a towel, I picked up the clothes and examined them. One was a button-down shirt with the Twisted Throttle logo printed on the right breast. Underneath, Oscar's name had been stitched. It would be big, but I could tie off the ends at my waist and make it work. Moving on, I studied the sports bras and leggings. They were my size, I realized with surprise. Somehow, I couldn't picture Oscar shopping for clothes in my section. Especially sports bras.

Not that I was complaining.

I got dressed and ran a comb through my hair. My face was still a hot mess, but the rest of me looked almost human again. It would have to do. I couldn't sit in this apartment alone for another day. Not when my thoughts kept drifting back to my dad.

Now that the funeral was over, all I could think about

were monsters. The one he'd become and the ones supposedly hunting us. I'd lived with his fears for so long they'd become commonplace. I'd dismissed them and learned to live with his paranoia like one would live with OCD. But now, I knew there had to be more to it.

The questions my mind made up continued to torture me. So, rather than drive myself crazy, I headed downstairs. Even another run-in with Kai would be better than sitting alone with my thoughts.

But Kai was nowhere to be seen in the front office. In fact, despite the "Open" sign lit up in the window, the place was empty.

I peered through the side door that led to the garage and saw Oscar perched on a stool beside a large motorcycle decked in chrome.

Beyond him, there was one other guy farther back. He was bent over the hood of a car. My car.

I opened the door and stepped into the garage. The scent of grease and oil hit me. I found it weirdly pleasant. Oscar looked up as I walked over.

"Morning," I said.

"I didn't think those bruises could get any worse," he said, studying my face.

I lifted my fingers to my cheek but then thought better of it. "They look worse than they feel," I said.

"Good thing." He snorted.

"How's it going with my car?" I asked.

He looked over at it and then pushed to his feet. "Let's go find out."

I followed him over.

"Drake," Oscar called out.

The guy bending over the hood straightened and turned, giving Oscar a nod. When he saw me, his perusal became more thorough. As did mine. He was a little older than me but not by much. Good-looking too. His brown eyes were sharp, assessing. His gaze lingered on the bruises I wore, and his expression turned guarded.

"This must be the niece," he said to Oscar, somehow ignoring me despite looking right at me.

I rolled my eyes. And just like that, my interest in him dried up.

"Ash," Oscar supplied. "What's the verdict?" he asked, gesturing to the car.

"She's DOA, in my opinion."

"What's DOA?" I asked.

He pretended I hadn't spoken. It was Oscar who answered.

"Dead on arrival." He grimaced. "That bad, huh?"

"From the looks of it, the thing should have been junked a long time ago," Drake said. "It's not worth the rust it's covered in. I vote we sell it for scrap metal and be done with it."

"That's not your decision to make," I said.

The guy arched a brow but otherwise didn't respond.

Oscar turned to me. "Drake's right. It would cost more to fix than the damn thing is worth. You're better off junking it and starting fresh."

"Starting fresh?" I repeated, biting back a scream.

Couldn't he see that's what I'd already done? It wasn't like I'd had a choice either. But without a car, I was completely and utterly stuck here. At the mercy of guys like Kai and Drake and Oscar.

Not a single friendly face in sight.

My dad might have been a drunk and paranoid, but he didn't talk to me like he wanted to shove me into a ditch somewhere.

"Whatever, fine," I said.

"Drake will take care of it and settle up with whatever

we get for the scrap," Oscar said, totally clueless about my looming breakdown.

"I'm on it, boss," Drake said.

"Good." Oscar turned to me. "I need to call a customer, but then you and I can go over some training in the front office." Oscar looked at me for confirmation.

"Okay," I said, already counting down the hours until I could crawl back into bed.

"I'll be there in five," he said and then strode away, already pulling out his phone.

I started to head back to the office to wait, but Drake stopped me.

"Does Kai know you're sticking around?"

I turned slowly, wary and angry. "I can't see how it's any of his business."

Drake snorted. "Everything that happens in this town is his business. Especially outsiders."

"You do know this is a free country. People can come and go as they want. Unless you have some law against visitors?"

He chuckled as if I'd said something funny. "Believe me, laws are not our thing around here. We do things our way. And that means keeping the town clean from people who don't belong."

My face heated with anger. "Good thing it's not up to you," I snapped. "Tell Kai to kiss my ass."

"Babe," he said, grinning in a way that felt a little unhinged. "Be careful what you wish for."

I walked away, forcing myself not to turn around or quicken my steps despite the ripple of fear at showing him my back. Something about Drake felt dangerous. Hell, they all felt dangerous. And I'd seen my fair share over the years too. Between the kind of people Dad brought around and the customers I'd waited on at work,

I recognized toxic when I saw it. But these people were something else.

What was with the guys in this town thinking they could order me out of it? I'd be damned if it was going to work.

Oscar spent an hour going over the computers and invoicing system and the scheduling calendar he used to book jobs.

"How are you doing?" he asked at the end of it. "I mean, you know, with everything."

If the question hadn't stirred my grief up, I would have laughed at the discomfort he wore as he spoke. Oscar and feelings didn't mix well.

"I'm good," I told him.

He studied me as if trying to decide whether I meant it. Finally, he nodded. Then he deemed me ready and left me alone.

The work helped distract me, and by lunchtime, I actually felt like I had it under control. A few calls came in from people asking to schedule maintenance on their motorcycles, and I used the cheat sheet Oscar had given me to slot them the proper time in Oscar's schedule. He was busy, booked out for more than two months, and most of his other techs were the same. Did everyone in this town ride a motorcycle?

Outside, I saw plenty of cars passing by on their way farther into town, so I knew there were other vehicles. But by the end of the day, I was convinced that either Oscar was the best around or all motorcycles broke down once a week.

A few of the customers asked my name, some even asking me to repeat it or being obviously nosy and asking how I knew Oscar. I didn't give them more than the professional basics, but I had a feeling a town this small would probably allow them to find out what they wanted to know soon enough.

By closing time, the sun had dipped behind the building, casting the street and sidewalk out front into long shadows. Oscar had sent everyone else home, and the phone had stopped ringing almost an hour ago. When the clock struck six, I walked up and switched the Open sign to Closed.

I was just about to turn the lock when a figure darkened the doorstep on the other side. Unlike the other day, he was dressed in a plain tee that was fitted enough to reveal a lot more of him than I'd seen the first time. Broad shoulders, tanned arms tatted with a sleeve of symbols that I'd missed the other day, and a jawline that I was already seeing in my daydreams.

Kai.

I swallowed hard, my stomach flip-flopping with nerves.

He pushed his way in without waiting for me to invite him.

"We're closed," I said, retreating under the pretense of grabbing my pen from the counter.

A pen.

Like it was some necessity of my job to hold a pen in my hand. Like that would somehow protect me.

"I work here," he said flatly.

Right. Shit. I tried not to think about what that meant for tomorrow. Or every day after that. Working under the same roof didn't seem like a safe option, not with how much animosity he held toward me.

"You weren't here today," I pointed out.

"I took the day off. Not that it's any of your business. Is Oscar here?"

"In the garage."

He marched past me and out the door, taking the cloud of tension with him. Alone, I let out the breath I'd been holding and prepared to head upstairs. My head was throbbing after a full day on my feet. But the sound of voices kept my feet firmly planted.

Evidently, these walls were thin.

"You gave her a job?" Kai demanded in a voice almost as angry as he'd used with me.

"Watch your tone," Oscar snarled with slightly less volume. "This is my shop last time I checked. Which means I make the decisions around here."

"You know the rules, Oz." Kai's voice quieted, but the hardness remained.

"She's family. That counts for something."

"She's an outsider. You're putting us all at risk."

"She's an orphan who just got the shit kicked out of her by some deadbeat assholes. What am I supposed to do?"

Kai didn't answer. I could picture the scowl he was probably wearing though. Lust pooled low in my belly. I seriously needed to work on that. I'd never had a thing for the rude asshole before. Not like this anyway. Even the jerks I'd hooked up with in the past had been passably polite to me. It was kinda embarrassing how attracted I was to a guy who hated me. And really annoying.

"This is a dangerous game you're playing," Kai finally said.

Oscar grunted. "Don't I fucking know it?"

"Why's her last name different?"

"No clue. Caleb wanted to disappear—that much I know. I guess he decided to be thorough about it."

"What's the story with the mother?"

"She left a few years back, apparently. No word since."

"Any idea who she was?"

"None. Caleb kept a lot of secrets."

Kai snorted. "Yeah, and one of them is standing in your front office."

There was a pause.

"Does she know?" Kai asked.

"I don't think so."

"What about her?" Kai asked. "Her old man was one of us."

"I don't know. Something's off. I can't get a scent. It's like she's just human."

I blinked, confused. Of course I was human. What the hell else did he expect? But then I thought of my dad. The weird beast he'd morphed into right before he'd died. Did Oscar and Kai know something about it? And did that have anything to do with Kai's question the other day?

What are you?

It hadn't made sense, and I'd nearly forgotten about it in favor of all of the other fantasies I'd been having since. But now, it seemed important.

Before I could decide what it all meant, I heard Oscar again.

"I know that look. What's your instinct tell you, kid?"

I stilled. It was a weird way to phrase it, but I understood what it meant. Oscar wanted to know what Kai honestly thought about me. And even though it shouldn't have mattered, I wanted to know what his answer would be.

"She's different," he said, and I huffed. The vagueness of his words only frustrated me more. He cleared his throat, clearly not willing to elaborate.

"She's harmless," Oscar said.

"Look, the fact is it's just as dangerous for her as it is for us."

"I'll take responsibility," Oscar said.

Kai snorted. "You sure that's a job you want? Something tells me that girl finds trouble wherever she goes."

"She's family," Oscar repeated and then after a pause, "If you won't give your blessing, I'll go to the council."

Kai growled, a sound of frustration. "The council already knows, Oz. You had her working your phones today, apparently. Without a single heads up to the rest of them."

"Shit," Oscar muttered. "Now what?"

"Keep her out of the woods. Hell, keep her inside these walls if you can. And I'll do my best to keep the others off your back. But you need to find a way to get rid of her."

"I can handle the others," Oscar said.

"Yeah, that's what I'm afraid of."

I barely registered footsteps signaling the conversation had ended before the door swung open and Kai stepped back inside the office. Our eyes met, and I had zero doubt he knew I'd been eavesdropping. Instead of calling me out for it, he sniffed then wrinkled his nose as if something had disgusted him.

"You really shouldn't be here, Ashes," he said then started for the exit.

Ashes?

"That's what Drake said."

He stopped and stared at me. "When did you talk to Drake?"

"He looked at my car. Then he told me I needed your permission to live in this town."

"And what did you tell him?"

I couldn't help the smirk that spread as I remembered my words. "Oh, he didn't deliver my message?" I asked, fluttering my lashes innocently.

He shook his head.

I let the mock innocence fall away and snarled, "That you could kiss my ass."

Then, I turned and stomped up the stairs before he could reply.

By the time I reached the apartment, I was almost hyperventilating. Where had that bravery come from? Kai hated me, and something told me he wasn't used to losing. If he wanted me gone, that meant he was going to do whatever it took to make it happen. He was not someone to fuck with. So why was I doing exactly that?

It was the tattoos.

They'd given me temporary insanity.

Kai was not someone to mess with. Or flirt with. Or daydream about. He was an asshole. And definitely not someone I wanted to get naked with.

He was someone to avoid.

A toxic jerk exactly like the kind I'd just run away from.

So, why did I find myself wanting to run toward him instead of away?

Oh yeah, because I was an idiot.

6

The conversation I'd overheard between Oscar and Kai raised a lot of questions. And even more red flags. One thing was clear, though. My time in Ridley Falls was going to be short-lived. Whether Kai kicked me out or I went willingly. Sometime between three and four in the morning, I'd decided to stay here only as long as it took me to save up for a car and a plan—and then I was out. My choice. My terms. Sure, "bad boy" Kai was the hottest thing on two legs, and he had a jawline and set of eyes that could melt ovaries on the spot. But he was a dick. And if there was one thing I wouldn't put up with ever again, it was an asshole who wanted to control me.

First, Dad. Then, Vorack. And now, Kai.

It wasn't okay.

In fact, I refused to let it happen.

So, Operation Temporary had begun. No getting attached. No divulging personal information. No making friends. It was all about making a new plan. Figuring out my next move.

And as if the Universe agreed, I showered and arrived downstairs the following morning only to find the place empty and the Closed sign still displayed.

"Where is everyone?" I asked.

"Off," Oscar said.

He sat on a barstool at the counter, sipping coffee and reading the paper. When I didn't answer, he looked up. My look of confusion must have clued him in, and he added, "It's Sunday. We're closed on Sundays."

"Oh."

Perfect. I had the entire day to work on my plan. And my bruises were finally able to be covered by makeup—which I still needed to buy. But, hey, the day was looking up.

I wasn't even put off when Oscar gave me a grocery list and asked me to pick up some things. That only made it easier to venture into town. At least, I didn't have to sneak out.

"Here's my card," he added, holding out his plastic debit card.

I looked up and met his gaze, noting the spark in his direct look.

"I'm not going to steal your money," I said, taking the card and slipping it into my back pocket.

"I know," he said, and I rolled my eyes at the forced nonchalance in his tone.

Right.

"I might have to make a couple of trips," I said.

"Why's that?"

"I don't have a car or a trunk, so I'll have to carry the bags on foot."

"That's ridiculous. Here." He pulled a set of keys off the hook behind him and held them out to me.

"What's this?" I asked, worried it belonged to a motorcycle, which would be a serious problem considering I'd never even touched one before.

"See that Honda parked at the curb?"

I looked over, scanning the cars through the window. When I didn't answer, Oscar sighed. "The blue one," he added.

"Oh. Yeah," I said, spotting the four-door sedan with relief.

He shook his head. "Take it."

"What? No, I can't just—"

"Trust me, it's worth having someone else grocery shop for me," he said, waving off my protests. "Just be back by noon."

"What happens at noon?" I asked.

"I have to be somewhere. And I need you home."

I frowned. This was about his conversation with Kai. About keeping me locked inside this place.

Whatever. I'd play along.

Wait until Oscar left. Then maybe follow him. I was sick of secrets. And if Kai wanted to play "town badass," I had no problem finding out what he was so intent on protecting about this place.

Then again, some alone time with Oscar's computer and the internet was more in line with "Operation Temporary." More than once, I'd entertained the idea of asking Oscar what he'd meant about my dad, but something held me back. If he wanted me to know, he would have told me about it. Besides, if I asked him, I'd have to admit to eavesdropping. And I couldn't afford to piss off the guy currently offering me food and shelter.

"Okay," I said. "See you by noon."

I took the keys and double-checked that I had my ID, and then headed out. Thanks to Oscar's directions—and the fact that this town was too small to get lost in—I found the grocery store easily. In fact, everything I could have possibly needed was right here on Main Street. Okay, it was actually called Southbend Turnpike or something like that, but it had that "main street" feeling. Right down to the open stares and outright whispers I noticed from the others around me in the store.

I pretended not to notice any of them until someone spoke directly to me.

"Ash, right? Fuckin A, the rumors left out that you're hot."

"Excuse me?" I looked up at the face of a handsome guy with messy brown waves and sparkly green eyes that seemed to lure me right in like some kind of pied piper. His words slowly dawned, and my eyes narrowed, but he only grinned bigger.

"Isaac, you can't open a conversation with something like that."

A girl stepped out from behind him. Bright red hair, obviously dyed considering the unnatural flame color, and braided down to her stomach. Her green eyes looked like they'd come from the same DNA pool as the guy.

"Sorry about my brother," she said as she strode up to me. "He has no social skills."

"I blame the Falls for being so socially stunted," he declared with a hair toss that had me smiling in spite of the weirdness the two exuded.

"It's okay," I said. "I mean, it's not like I couldn't tell people were talking about me."

"Exactly. At least we came and said it to your face," Isaac said.

The girl rolled her eyes. "That does not make it better," she insisted. "Ugh." She turned back to me. "I'm Idrissa, and this is my twin brother, Isaac."

"Twins, wow."

"Yeah, I know. I really should have eaten him in the womb or something."

My expression must have shown the insult because Isaac waved it off.

"Don't worry. Everyone always tells me I look like a snack." He winked.

I laughed.

"Pray for me," Idrissa said with mock suffering. Before I could formulate a response to any of this, she pointed at my cart and added, "So, can we help you get all this back to the Throttle?"

"Oh, you don't have to do that," I said.

"Yes, we do," Isaac insisted with a look I couldn't decipher but also couldn't figure out how to say no to.

"The sooner you're free to hang, the sooner we can kidnap you and hold you hostage until you agree to be our bestie," Idrissa explained.

"It's our master plan," Isaac said, his eyes lit with a hope I couldn't resist.

"I see," I said slowly. "And how many others have you tried this plan with?"

"You're the first," Isaac said.

My brows rose.

"More of an experiment than a plan," Idrissa added.

"Do you two always talk like two halves of one brain?" I asked.

Isaac grinned. "As a matter of fact, together, we sometimes equal one whole brain."

"Depends on who you ask," Idrissa said wryly.

I laughed. "Okay, a kidnapping sounds great. Especially if it involves a tour of the town."

They exchanged an uneasy look.

"Okay, maybe tour is the wrong word." I bit my lip. Something about these two felt a little risky but in a fun way. Maybe even in a friendship kind of way. It had been too long since I let myself make a friend. And even though it was in direct violation of Operation Temporary, I couldn't walk away from the chance now that I had it.

"Nah, it's perfect," Isaac said. "You should know what you're up against—"

Idrissa punched Isaac in the arm, silencing whatever else he'd been about to say.

I decided to leave it. For now. But... up against?

"Come on," Idrissa said, hooking her arm through mine and leading me away from my cart.

"Um, my groceries—"

"Isaac will get it. Won't you, brother?"

She didn't give him time to argue before leading me outside. Behind us, I could hear Isaac complaining, his voice rising steadily with each declaration.

"This is why we have toxic gender roles," was all I heard before the doors slid shut behind us.

Outside, Idrissa stopped in front of a white convertible mustang. Shiny, vintage though new looking, definitely running—unlike my own car.

"Wow, this is gorgeous," I said.

"I wanted red, but Isaac talked me into this instead," she said. "I'm warming up to it. White for purity and all that."

I almost snorted. I didn't know her well enough yet, but something told me no one would use the word "purity" in a sentence about Idrissa.

"Well, I'm in that blue one over there," I said, leading the way toward Oscar's Honda.

Isaac came walking out of the grocery store, arms laden with paper bags. I hurried to unlock the car and open the trunk for him.

"Thanks," I said when he'd set them all inside.

"Of course, gorgeous."

"We'll follow you back," Idrissa called, sliding into the driver's seat of the mustang and starting the engine.

"See you there," I said as Isaac blew me a kiss and jogged over to where his sister waited. The moment he hopped inside, she peeled out and disappeared onto the main road.

I stared in shock at the crazy way she'd driven off then finally turned to my own borrowed car and got inside. Much slower than the twins, I left the parking lot and headed back to Oscar's. If my kidnapping-slash-tour of the town meant riding with them, I wasn't sure I wanted it anymore.

By the time I walked inside the front office of Oscar's shop—or Throttle, as Idrissa had called it—the twins were already inside, talking to Oscar, who stood behind the counter with his mug in hand. His expression was strained and a little thoughtful at whatever they'd been discussing. When they saw me, they all fell silent.

I set the two bags of groceries on the counter and looked between them all, trying to read their faces.

"Everything okay?" I asked warily.

"Peachy," Isaac announced. "Oh, I'll get the rest of those." He slipped out before I could argue.

"I'll help," Idrissa said, heading for the door. "Gender roles and all that." She rolled her eyes and followed her brother out.

I turned to Oscar. "I met them at the store," I said by way of explanation.

"They want to take you for a drive," he said.

"Yeah, I think they want to interrogate me for gossip."

Oscar frowned.

"I don't have to go," I began.

"No, I think it's actually a good idea. The Close twins are good kids." He snorted. "Better than some others anyway. Just stay with them. No venturing off alone, especially today, all right?"

"Sure."

"And be back by dark."

"I thought it was noon."

"If you're with them, you can be out until dark. But only if you stay together and do what they say."

What the hell was with this guy? Did he really mean to treat me like a child?

I lifted an eyebrow. "Look, I know it's your house, your rules, but I am an adult."

"Just for tonight," he added in a clipped voice. "It's not safe."

I wanted to ask what the hell that meant, but the door opened and the twins returned with the rest of the groceries.

"I'll get these put away," Oscar said. "You go on."

"Thanks." I handed him back his debit card with a pointed look. "Feel free to check your account and the receipt."

His lips quirked. "I'm good. Oh, here. I found this." He held out a phone charger. And my very dead cell phone. "So I can reach you."

"I don't have a current plan," I began, my cheeks heating with embarrassment at having to disclose this in front of Idrissa.

"I took the liberty of connecting it to my plan," he said.

I blinked, stunned at the simple kindness.

"Thanks."

Still recovering, I gave him my number, and then Idrissa was practically pulling me out the door.

"Y'all kids be careful," Oscar called.

Idrissa just laughed, which only scared me a little. It should have scared me a lot.

7

Idrissa drove. A fact that didn't seem to actually upset Isaac so much as give him a reason to talk shit to his twin from the backseat. "I can sit in the back," I said, trying to make peace, but Isaac waved me off.

"Nah, I just like to give Idrissa a hard time."

"He's a better backseat driver than an actual driver," Idrissa said with a smirk as she revved the engine and slingshotted us into traffic.

I gripped the armrest, knuckles white, as she zipped around slower cars on our way through downtown.

Finally, Idrissa shot me a sideways look.

"You okay?" she asked.

"Is Isaac really a worse driver than you?" I asked.

Isaac snorted from the backseat.

Idrissa scowled. "I'm a fantastic driver," she said gravely.

This time, I snorted.

"Fast and fantastic are not the same," I told her, which only made Isaac openly cackle.

"I've never been in an accident," Idrissa said, her tone haughty though I could see the amusement in her eyes.

"But how many have you caused?" Isaac shot back.

"Bite me," she said, and we all cracked up.

Just ahead, I spotted a group of people my age crowded around a music store. Music blared from inside loud enough for those on the sidewalk to move to the beat. A blonde girl shouted something and grinned, lifting what looked like a beer high above her head as she danced up on some guy.

"So," I said, "What's the actual deal with this town, anyway? Oscar acts like I need an escort for my own safety." I almost mentioned Kai's warnings but decided against it. Those felt more...personal. Like he was trying to protect the town from me instead of the other way around.

Idrissa's eyes flicked to the rearview as she and Isaac exchanged a look.

"Is there a gang of pedophiles or serial killers nearby or something?" I asked, half-joking. But Idrissa didn't laugh, which only made the question sound super dark and kinda scary.

"What the hell, guys?" I said warily.

"Okay," Idrissa said as we came to a lurching stop at a red light. "Isaac and I have decided to make you a deal."

"What kind of deal?" I asked, instantly wary.

Deals were for gamblers and loan sharks and people like Vorack. I didn't want to do any deals.

"We'll show you around Ridley Falls. If you promise not to talk to anyone but us."

"Okay," I said, drawing out the word as confusion replaced suspicion.

"It's for your own safety," she added then frowned.

"Are you saying talking to people puts me in danger?" I

asked, my thoughts flitting to Kai. Talking to him certainly felt risky.

"Danger's a strong word. It's for your own good," she amended.

"You sound like Oscar." I frowned.

"Sis, you're digging yourself a hole," Isaac put in.

Idrissa looked over at me. "Those are the terms."

Frustration welled up. "Are you going to tell me *why* I can't talk to anyone?"

"We just did," she said with a shrug. "For your own good."

My eyes narrowed. "That's not an answer."

"Fine." She batted her lashes. "Because we want to horde you all to ourselves. We're people hoarders."

"Hot girl hoarders if you want to be specific," Isaac added.

"Yes, exactly." Idrissa's expression remained completely serious.

"You two are insane." I shook my head as the light changed and Idrissa took off fast enough that my body pressed into the seat from the momentum.

"Look, there are a lot of people in this town who don't like outsiders," Idrissa said as she drove.

Businesses and shops flew by on either side, and I wondered how she planned to give me a tour while speeding past all there was to see in this tiny town.

"So I've been told," I said wryly.

"Relax, there are no pedophiles," Isaac piped up.

It should have made me feel better, but I couldn't help noticing how he'd failed to mention the serial killer part.

"The good news is," Idrissa said, cutting a knowing look at Isaac in the rearview, "if Oscar said you can stay, that means you're here for as long as you want. And that means you need to know a few things about how it works in Ridley Falls."

"How it works," I repeated.

She nodded.

"For my own good," I said again.

"Exactly. Now you're getting it."

I shook my head.

I couldn't help but think Operation Temporary had just taken a turn into left field. Staying, learning how things worked here, hanging with the twins—all of it felt a lot like permanence rather than temporary. And I couldn't deny that it felt a hell of a lot better than living on the run did.

Dad might have told me to come here for safety, but he couldn't have meant for me to stay forever. Nowhere was safe, according to him. Not from whatever monsters supposedly hunted us.

Curiosity, I told myself.

That's all this was. I'd figure out what they were hiding. Maybe save some money in the process. And then I would get the hell out.

"Okay," I said finally, "Deal."

At my agreement, Isaac cheered.

"Where should we start?" he mused.

"I'm thinking we start at the hub," Idrissa said. "Work our way out."

"The…. Oh." Isaac whistled. "Damn, sis. You're starting off with a bang."

"Bad idea?" Idrissa shot him another look in the mirror.

He shrugged. "It's our funeral."

"Whoa. I don't want to cause trouble," I said, but Idrissa ignored me and shot Isaac a grin that showed way too much teeth.

"Good thing we both like to live on the edge," she said.

Before I could argue, she hit the gas and we flew through town and out the other side. But not before I caught two kids, who couldn't have been more than twelve, spray painting a van. Okay then. Crime in broad daylight. Constant partying. What the hell was with this place?

I was just about to ask when I realized we'd left anything resembling civilization in the rearview. With the shops behind us, along with everything that looked like Ridley Falls, I turned to look at Idrissa.

"Is this the part where you kidnap me?" I asked.

"This is the part where we show you the real Ridley Falls," she said.

I had no idea what that meant, but soon enough, it made sense. Sort of. After a couple of miles that went by way quicker than the actual speed limit allowed, Idrissa pulled into the parking lot of a large, squat building with peeling brown paint.

The sign above the door read Bo's. No indication as to Bo's "what." Dive bar, from the looks of it. On all sides was an open field that gave way to thick forest. Behind it, an aging barn stood framed along the backside by mountains.

I scanned the long line of bikes parked out front. Several of them were occupied by those either coming or going. A brunette covered in tattoos and piercings leaned over and planted a lingering kiss on a guy with a gray beard and a black bandanna wrapped around his head.

Someone else whistled at them.

The girl gave everyone the finger.

The guy laughed and motioned for her to hop on the back of his motorcycle. As soon as she did, he started it up and sped out onto the main road. His exhaust was loud enough to drown out everything else.

Well, almost everything.

I had a strange feeling now; a slow sort of tingle starting at the base of my spine and working its way up. Still scanning the row of bikes, I felt him before I saw him, which was kind of insane, but also undeniable considering my eyes weren't deceiving me. Standing beside the motorcycle on the end, short sleeves revealing arms covered in tattoos, was Kai.

8

Helpless to look away, I watched as Kai swung a leg over the side of his bike and started it up. Two girls walked over, blocking his exit. One of them leaned over and said something, a flirty smile on her mouth and enough cleavage spilling out of her top to choke a horse. The other girl had a hand on her hip and jean shorts that only covered the top half of her ass. Kai frowned at the girl who'd spoken. Then he shook his head. She jutted out her lip in a pout and backed away. From the group of others hanging out, one of the guys yelled something and motioned to the girl. Kai looked relieved when both of them retreated.

Revving the engine, he kicked it into gear and glided out of the lot onto the road. When he was out of sight, I looked over and realized both twins had fallen silent to watch me.

My face heated.

"What?" I demanded.

"Daaamn," Idrissa said.

Isaac whistled.

"What?" I said again, this time more defensive.

Idrissa got out of the car, and I did the same. Behind me, Isaac lifted himself out of the seat and swung his legs over the side, planting his feet on the gravel.

They both stood and looked at me in the warm sunlight.

"You've got it bad, girl," Idrissa said with a sad shake of her head.

"For Kai?" I snorted, but even I knew it wasn't convincing. I tried again, looking directly into Isaac's knowing eyes as I said, "He's an asshole."

"So, you two have met then," Idrissa said.

"He works at the shop," I said, hoping my tone sounded disgusted.

"Kai Stone is someone you want to steer clear of," Idrissa said, but the warning wasn't necessary. I'd already learned the hard way.

"Believe me, he's not someone I plan to befriend."

Then another thought dawned.

"You two haven't… I mean." I stopped, face heating as I felt the nosiness of my question.

But Idrissa's eyes widened. "Hell, no," she said with enough conviction that I knew she meant it. Isaac hooted with laughter.

"Idrissa and I used to be friends with Kai," Isaac explained when he saw my expression.

"Used to," Idrissa echoed.

"What happened?" I asked.

She looked away, her expression hard.

"Kai started running with Silas and Presley," Isaac said with a shrug. As if that explained everything.

"He parties, takes what he wants, and doesn't care what anyone thinks," Idrissa added.

"Sounds like everyone else in this town," I said.

She snorted. "He's angry as hell and doesn't care who he takes it out on."

"Doesn't mean he isn't delicious," Isaac said.

I shrugged, refusing to allow them to see just how much I was fighting off the drool when it came to Kai. "I like my men without all that toxic rage," I said.

Isaac responded by making the sign of the cross. "The ovaries want what the ovaries want, though. Am I right?"

I snorted. "You're so dramatic."

He chuckled and threw an arm around my shoulders, leading me toward Bo's. "Kai Stone makes us all dramatic," he declared. "Now, come on. We'll introduce you to the seedy underbelly that is Ridley Falls, North Carolina."

Before we could even make it to the door, the bikers sitting out front whistled. A few catcalled but the two girls from earlier only glared.

"Hey, new girl," called a male voice. "You want to stay in this town, you gotta earn it."

I averted my eyes, increasing my pace.

Maybe the twins were used to places like this, but it only reminded me of a world I wanted to leave in the past.

"Shut your cakehole, Devon," Idrissa snapped.

Out of the corner of my eye, I watched the guy grin. "Make me, Dris."

"You fucking wish," she muttered and then to me, "Come on."

Idrissa held the door.

The three of us walked inside, and I stopped, blinking to let my eyes adjust to the dim lighting. The smell of cigarettes and whiskey and stale bodies washed over me. It reminded me of my dad enough that I faltered.

Grief hit me like a wave, pulling me under. The scent of our trailer after a night of one of his benders. The dirty laundry I'd carry to the laundromat when our car broke down. His pillow. All of it blended together into a scent memory that hit me like a brick now. I couldn't breathe.

Idrissa appeared in front of me, frowning.

"Ash," she said sharply, and I realized she'd called my name more than once already.

"Yeah, I'm good," I said, shaking off the nightmare still clinging to the edges of my mind.

"You sure?" she said uncertainly.

Isaac crowded in beside her. "We can go if you want. There are other places we can show you—"

"I'm good," I said again, more firmly this time. "I promise."

Neither one looked convinced, but they let it go. Idrissa led the way and very quickly, I realized everyone inside had stopped talking and turned to stare. At me.

Several tables had been dragged together to accommodate a group of seven. Four guys and three girls. Every one of them had a drink in their hands, and something told me it wasn't their first of the day. Cards had been dealt, and in the center was a pile of miscellaneous items. Money. Jewelry. Lottery tickets. Condoms.

They all stopped their game to look at me.

I did my best to ignore them, but the stares weren't exactly friendly. It felt like being under a microscope. A very big, very hostile microscope.

Idrissa sailed past them, ignoring their greetings to her, and sauntered up to the bar. She leaned forward and snapped her fingers at the bartender. Behind me, Isaac had stopped to say hi to the group playing cards and a few others who called his name.

"Hey, Teddy," Idrissa called as the bartender looked up.

"Dris," he said, offering her a chin nod. He glanced past Isaac and looked straight at me. His dark brown eyes were intent and direct. "Who's your friend?"

The entire bar remained quiet, and something about the not-so-subtle nosiness made my patience thin.

"I'm Ash," I said, stepping up beside Idrissa. "Oscar's my uncle, and I'm staying with him for a while. Can we get something to drink?"

Teddy blinked like he hadn't been expecting me to just spill all my details like that. He recovered, nodding. "Sure. What'll you have?" he asked.

"You like margaritas?" Idrissa asked me.

"Um, I can't," I said. "I'm only nineteen—"

"Three margaritas," Idrissa told him, cutting me off. "On the rocks."

"Coming up." Teddy went to work, making the drinks.

"Come on," Idrissa said, and I fell into step behind her with Isaac bringing up the rear.

She wove a path around the tables to an empty booth at the back. A couple of dartboards were mounted to the wall beside us, and on the other side of those was a jukebox. An actual, honest-to-goodness jukebox.

What year was it in here, anyway?

Idrissa slid into the booth, her back to the wall, and I took the seat opposite her. Isaac sat next to me and immediately slouched down so he could prop his feet on the seat beside his sister.

The hairs on the back of my neck stood up, and I knew the stares hadn't abated even with only the back of my head for them to admire. Thankfully, the conversations had resumed, at least. And the card game was back in full swing. Someone bet their pet snake, and I tuned them out. Gambling was not something I wanted to be around ever again.

"Well, that went better than expected," Isaac said.

Better?

"What did you expect?" I asked.

The twins shared a look.

"Tell me," I hissed.

Before they could answer, Teddy appeared with our drinks. He set them in front of us and said, "Your tab's been paid. Compliments of a friend at the bar."

"Which friend?" Idrissa asked, eyes narrowing.

Teddy just winked and left.

Behind me, something must have caught her eye because Idrissa muttered some curse words that impressed me with their creativity. I heard the name "Vinny" mingled in amongst the worst of it and decided not to ask.

"Okay, I have questions," I said.

"Hit me," Isaac said.

"First, no one cards here?" I asked.

Isaac grinned. "We're sort of like VIPs around here. No carding for us."

"Why are you VIPs?" I asked.

"Our family was one of the founding members of the Falls," Isaac said. "And our dad is on city council. It makes us a big deal."

"Isaac, don't fill her head with your delusions," Idrissa said. She looked at me. "We are not VIP. Or not any more than the others. Teddy doesn't card us because he doesn't card anyone."

I shook my head. A town official whose perks included illegal drinking for his teens? A bartender who endorsed it? "Um, that only gives me more questions."

"I'm full of answers," Isaac said.

"More like full of yourself," Idrissa snorted.

Isaac shot her a glare, but she was too busy staring people down at the bar to notice.

"Why is everyone staring at me?" I asked.

"You're new and shiny," Isaac said.

"Is it really so strange to get visitors here?"

"Remember the whole 'outsiders' issue?" Isaac said in a tone that felt more like an answer than a question.

"This entire town has serious trust issues," I muttered, which, for some reason, made Isaac hoot with laughter.

The noise drew more stares, and Idrissa looked ready to spit nails at everyone in here.

"Why did you bring me here then?" I asked. "I mean, if they were going to treat me like a window display at a porn shop, why bother?"

Idrissa's mouth curved. "A porn shop, huh? Well, we don't have one of those, so I wouldn't know. But you wanted to see the Falls so here it is."

"This is the real Ridley Falls?" I asked, echoing her earlier words. "A dive bar in the middle of nowhere?"

"This is where the locals hang out," she said. "When we're not burning it down at a bonfire or house party, I mean. Besides, free drinks."

She motioned to my untouched margarita.

"I don't drink," I said quietly.

"Uh-oh. Something tells me we fucked up," Isaac said.

"No, it's fine. I just…my dad drank. So," I shrugged. "I just don't."

I expected them to look uncomfortable. Change the subject. Most people didn't pry once they realized they'd scraped a wound. But Idrissa looked right at me and nodded.

"Is that who gave you those bruises?" she asked.

"I…" I raised my fingers and pressed them gingerly to the bruise I thought I'd done a decent job of covering up. "No. My dad would never hurt me."

I stopped, unsure about telling them the rest.

But Isaac looked like he wasn't going to give it up. And

they weren't nosy like the rest of the town seemed to be. This felt like they actually gave a shit.

"My dad made some bad choices," I said carefully. "And one of those choices took it out on me."

Isaac's expression tightened, and he looked genuinely angry.

Idrissa's hands fisted on top of the table. "I hope they got what was coming to them for knocking you around like that."

I shrugged, unwilling to give more than that.

"I'm sorry about your dad," she said, and I was grateful she wasn't going to press it about the bruises. "It's hard losing people we love."

My eyes tingled with moisture as I remembered the funeral I'd been forced to attend via internet rather than in person.

"I didn't realize you knew," I said. "You know, about him..."

I couldn't bring myself to say the word "dying," so I just let it hang there. Idrissa held my gaze, and I swallowed hard at the emotion that rose in my throat. One thing, though. Idrissa was direct. I appreciated that. No one else here had been.

She had the grace to look sympathetic as she said, "Everyone here knows pretty much everything about everyone else."

"Everything?"

My expression must have conveyed my distaste because she added, "Unfortunately, there are no secrets in small towns. Look, if you don't want people in this town to know something, don't tell anyone."

"Except us," Isaac put in. He leaned closer. "We can keep a secret."

His grin was infectious, and despite my grief and uncertainty, I found myself believing him.

"The truth is my dad drank too much," I said. "It consumed his whole life, and watching him kind of turned me off the whole alcohol thing. It's also what led to the other stuff like the gambling and, you know, the assholes who did this." I pointed to my face.

"Shit," Isaac said. "And where did we bring you to? A bar. We suck, Ash. We suck fat donkey—"

"Okay, whoa," Idrissa said and made a disgusted face. "Don't finish that sentence."

"You don't suck," I assured him.

"Your secrets are safe with us," Isaac vowed. He held up two fingers like a peace sign. "Scout's honor."

"Isaac, that's not— You know what, never mind." Idrissa pinched the bridge of her nose before looking back at me with an exasperated expression.

I found myself smiling. "I'm not sure why you guys decided to be nice to me, but thanks. I needed it more than you know."

"Whoa, Dris, that's the first time you've ever been called nice." Isaac jerked his thumb at me. "We clearly have her fooled."

I laughed, but Idrissa only looked more serious. She leaned forward across the table and lowered her voice.

"Ash, you should know...people in the Falls are assholes," she said. Empathy mixed with concern as she watched me soak in her words. "They don't like outsiders, and they aren't nice about conveying that."

"Believe me, I've experienced that," I said.

"I know you think so," she said, which sent a ripple of unease down my spine. "But it only gets worse from here."

I opened my mouth to ask how she could possibly know that, but Isaac cut me off.

"Speaking of which, who do you think paid for these?" Isaac asked, nodding at our drinks.

His was already halfway empty, so I slid my full one toward him.

"It was either Vinny or Silas, and they're both pissing me off," Idrissa said, looking back toward the bar again.

Her warning had created a somber, weighted mood that had already shifted with the change in conversation. I couldn't stop thinking about her words: *it only gets worse from here*.

"Why does it matter?" I asked. "A free drink is a nice thing, right?"

"No one in this town is nice," she said. "Remember what I said, Ash. No one in this town is selfless. If they do a nice thing, it's because they want something from you."

Did she mean like carrying my groceries?

Before I could point out the hypocrisy, someone yelled from across the bar, and by the time I turned to look, two men at a small table in the corner had shoved their chairs aside and jumped up, rushing at one another. They each wore a leather vest with the image of a wolf stamped in white on the back. Before I could make out the words printed around it, the two men collided, chest, fists, even foreheads, all crashing together in an all-out brawl.

Chairs and tables were upended. Glass fell, shattering as their beers and pitchers hit the floor. The card game went flying, and the players all yelled as they jumped back.

I froze, watching it all unfold and feeling a little surreal.

The other customers jumped up too, crowding around them, yelling, cheering. Most of them also wore vests with the wolf printed on the back. I waited for them to wade in and pull apart the drunken brawlers, but no one did. Some cash was waved around, exchanging hands as bets were called out about the predicted winner and loser.

A couple of others even joined the fight, making it two on two. Then four on four. The rest of the patrons yelled their encouragement to whatever side they'd decided to root for.

Neither one of the twins moved a muscle.

If anything, they looked annoyed. Maybe even bored.

"Gordon's such a dumbass," Idrissa said between sips of her drink.

"Silas has been waiting for an excuse to shove his fist into Gordon's mouth," Isaac said. "It was only a matter of when and where."

"You mean when." Idrissa rolled her eyes. "The where is easy when it comes to Gordon."

Isaac snorted his agreement.

"Isn't anyone going to stop them?" I asked, my anxiety spiking as one of the men picked up a chair and smashed it over another's head. The man stumbled, careening toward us before he went sprawling across the dirty floor where his body stopped beside our table. I looked down and spotted the logo printed on the back of his leather vest.

A white wolf's head was tipped up in a howl. Underneath were the words "Lone Wolf MC." I stared at the image, feeling a slow sort of dread working its way into my skin. I'd seen it in one other place in my life, and finding it here, now, was not something I'd been prepared for.

I swallowed hard, heart hammering, and looked over to find Isaac giving me a strange look. "It's okay," he said. "We won't let anything happen to you."

I nodded, blinking the fear from my eyes and the

wolf's image from my mind. Later. This wasn't the place to lose my shit.

Forcing my attention back to the scene unfolding, I scanned the room.

Beyond where the unconscious man had fallen, Teddy was hopping around, scooping up glasses and trying to save what serving ware he could. It would have been comical if not for the actual blood flowing from the fighters' various busted noses and lips.

The guy with the chair walked over to where the unconscious biker lay. He looked from the guy on the floor to us, his expression a little glassy and a lot unhinged.

"Vinny, back off," Isaac warned.

"Make me," the guy slurred.

Isaac groaned. "Paper, rock, scissors?" he asked his twin.

Idrissa sighed, sliding toward the edge of the booth. "Nah, I got this one."

She stood up and walked over to the guy who held the chair by its leg. He straightened when he saw her coming, his eyes blazing with a fury that didn't dim at the sight of the gorgeous redhead stalking his way.

"Vinny, I swear to God, how many times do I have to explain the chairs are off-limits?" she said.

"Don't start with me, woman," he growled and barely had time to finish his words before Idrissa's fist slammed into his face, sending him to his knees.

My jaw fell open.

Idrissa waited until he swayed once and then planted her boot against his chest and shoved. Hard.

Vinny went flying backward, his head slamming into the bar with a crack that was probably his skull.

I gripped the table, shocked.

Vinny slid down a little farther and then stopped moving completely, his chin sagging as he passed out.

My shock turned to horror.

I hopped out of the booth and rushed over to where Vinny sat slouched on the floor. His back was to the bar, and his head had lolled forward. I grabbed his face, propping it up with my hand to find his eyes were closed. I fumbled for a pulse and found it, sagging in relief.

"Holy shit." I looked up at where Idrissa now stood behind me with her arms crossed. "You knocked him out."

She shrugged. "He was damaging Bo's property. And he's been warned."

"But you… What if he…" I trailed off, unable to form the words as worry took over. I felt gingerly against the back of his head, my fingers coming away with sticky blood. Panic spiked, and my breath caught.

I stared down at the blood on my hands.

"He's bleeding," I said, my voice cracking.

Looking past the blood, I caught sight of the wolf emblem printed on Vinny's jacket. The howl it was making in the illustration echoed inside my head. The room tilted, and everything drifted a little. Suddenly, the fighting felt far away. Or maybe it was me who'd drifted. I was no longer here. This wasn't really happening. No blood. No barfights. I was safe. Dad was alive.

I—

"Ash!"

I looked up and leaned away just in time to avoid a serving tray flying through the air. It crashed into the bar right where I'd just been crouched and clattered to the ground at my feet.

I looked down at it, chest heaving, then up again. At the far end of the bar, the fight had stopped. That meant the tray hadn't been an accident. There was no collateral damage. Someone had done it on purpose.

My eyes landed on an angry face glaring at me, and I pushed to my feet.

A guy around my age stood watching me, arms folded. I'd seen him earlier at the table with the poker game. His brown hair hung past his ears, and his muscular arms flexed as he pumped his fists open and closed, open and closed. His expression hardened, and just like with Vinny and Idrissa, he didn't back down at the sight of me.

As I faced him, my grief and fear and all of the turmoil of the last few days collided. Something inside me snapped, and I forgot to be afraid of what he could do to me or concerned that his muscles were bigger than my kneecaps. He'd tried to hurt me. On purpose. And I was done cowering to the assholes in this town. In any town.

"You threw that tray at me on purpose," I said, anger replacing the fear that had paralyzed me before.

"So what?" he challenged. "You shouldn't be here," he said, and the words were so repetitive and irritating by now that I rolled my eyes.

"You're right about that. This place seems to have one rule: only assholes allowed. You fit right in."

He snarled and took a step toward me. I planted my feet, ready for a fight. If he swung, I wasn't going to walk away. It took a special kind of asshole to hit a female, but this guy seemed special in all the wrong ways, so I wasn't expecting anything but the worst.

Apparently, his friends expected it too because the others who'd been at the table with him finally took notice and crowded in closer behind him. Fantastic. He had a full baseball team's worth of support in his bullying.

"Whoa." Isaac stepped between us, his palm hovering just above the guy's chest. "Silas. What the fuck."

It wasn't a question or a request. Isaac's voice held steel now, a tone I didn't even know he was capable of. But the happy-go-lucky Isaac was gone. This version of him wasn't one I recognized.

"Isaac, get the fuck out of my way," Silas growled.

"Not happening. Take a walk."

Idrissa stepped up beside me, her arms folded as she regarded Silas with a cool, murderous gaze. "Listen to my brother, Silas. Get some air. Before someone chokes it from your lungs."

"Try it," Silas said, shoving against Isaac a little as he lurched toward Idrissa.

Idrissa simply smiled.

But Isaac returned the shove, and Silas was forced to take a step backward. I noted the wolf emblazoned on his vest then glanced to his friends. Some of them had a vest to match. Shit. Fear spiked through me. Isaac and Idrissa couldn't take on an entire biker gang alone, no matter how well Idrissa's punches landed.

"Last warning," Isaac said.

Someone else walked up behind Silas and laid a hand on his shoulder. "Come on, man. Let's get out of here."

"She's not one of us," Silas said without taking his eyes off me.

"Damn straight she's not," called a girl standing behind Silas. She crossed her arms and glared back at me.

"Tiffany, eat shit," Idrissa said.

Tiffany gave her the finger.

My heart hammered against my chest. What the hell was so bad about being from out of town? These people were like a dog with a bone.

The newcomer stepped around Silas to look at me, and I finally saw his face for the first time. Short blonde hair done in a side-swept wave that reminded me of old, classic Hollywood. He wore a leather jacket that really cemented the whole James Dean vibe right down to his distressed jeans and scuffed ankle boots. His smile was the kind that melted hearts—or, at least, I suspected it would if he ever flashed it fully.

For now, I got a half-quirked lip and sparkling blue eyes that were so not in line with a biker guy persona. "So, this is Ashes, huh?"

Ashes. Who the hell had thought up that stupid nickname, anyway?

"It's just Ash," I told him icily. "As in kiss my ash."

The half-quirk turned to a full one. "You've got sass."

"Your friend here was trying to assault me. If he tries that again, I've got a lot more than sass for him."

I reached down and pulled my blade from my boot, making sure everyone saw it. Oscar's butcher block was now missing a small paring knife, but I couldn't feel bad about that now. Especially considering I'd been smart to swipe it. Never mind that I'd used duct tape to make an ankle holster.

Idrissa grinned proudly. "Pres, you need to take Silas out back and hose him off or some shit, okay? My girl is one of us now. And she's with me and Isaac."

"Is that right?" Pres—or James Dean—asked.

"Even if she were *like* us," Silas said in a hard voice, "She's not one of us until she fights. You both know that."

Isaac hadn't moved, but his shoulders sagged a little at that. Something about the way Silas said it made it seem more important than a bar brawl.

"The fights are barbaric, Silas. We're not animals," Idrissa said.

Silas gave her a weird smile. "Aren't we though? Besides, look at her face." He gestured at me. "It clearly wouldn't be her first."

I felt my cheeks burn at that, but Isaac saved me from answering.

"She's not fighting," he said in a voice that, though quiet, dared anyone to argue.

"Then she doesn't get to come in here," Silas said. "Or anywhere else in town. Those are the rules, and you know it."

I shot a look at Idrissa. Had she known it? Had she expected something like this to happen? Is that what Isaac had meant about their funeral?

My temper flared at that, and I stepped away from Idrissa, making it clear I was fine on my own. Without putting my knife away, I stalked back to the table and grabbed my bag then crossed back to where Isaac and Silas still faced off.

Meeting Silas' angry gaze head-on, I said, "Whatever kind of bull shit club forces you to fight for the right to day drink with losers like you, I'm not interested anyway."

He growled.

I ignored it and turned to Pres. "Someone should really check on that Vinny guy. He's bleeding and unconscious, and it's not a good look."

Before he could reply, I turned to Isaac. "You ready?"

"More than." He held Silas' stare for one more moment and then turned to lead me out the door. Idrissa didn't move, and I had the sense she was waiting for me to include her. Like she was giving me the chance to choose her as a friend the way she'd chosen me.

"Idrissa," I called.

"Coming," she said and hurried to follow us out.

Still clutching my knife, I walked right past the other patrons, not bothering to acknowledge a single one of them. By the time we made it out into the bright afternoon sunlight, my insides were shaking, and I was a little worried the toast I'd eaten for breakfast was going to make a reappearance.

"Holy shit, that was amazing," Isaac said when we reached the car.

"Was it? Because I actually thought we were going to die," I said, a little wobbly as I slid my knife back into my boot and reached for the car door.

"I got it." Isaac opened the door and practically shoved me into the backseat. I was fine with it. This way, I could stretch out and faint if I needed to.

Idrissa slid into the driver's seat and started the car without a word. Isaac climbed in beside her, and together, we drove away from Bo's in a weird Bonnie and Clyde sort of silence. I didn't even bother complaining about the batshit crazy speeds or erratic turns.

In fact, none of us spoke again until Idrissa pulled up and Isaac let me out of the car in front of Oscar's shop.

Finally, I couldn't hold it in anymore.

"You did that on purpose," I said, looking at Idrissa.

"What?" Isaac looked shocked or pretended to. "No way. We—"

"Yeah, I did," Idrissa said, looking up at me.

"Why?" I asked.

"For your own—"

"Good," I finished along with her. "Yeah, that's a running theme, and frankly, I'm sick of it."

I looked away, staring blankly at the road and the turn that would lead me out of town again if I chose it.

"I know this must be hard," Idrissa said.

I scowled.

She didn't know the half of it.

"Tell me why Oscar let me leave with you," I said. "And why I have to be home by dark. And why everyone in this town thinks I'm a disease. And don't lie to me," I added when Idrissa's expression turned innocent.

She sighed, looking resigned. "Oscar trusts us to protect you," she said finally. "That's why he let you hang with us."

I waited, but she didn't go on.

My temper flared. "That's it? You're not going to tell me the truth?"

"I'm not lying," she said.

"Refusing to explain is just as bad," I said.

Idrissa's hands tightened on the steering wheel. "I told you we'd show you around town. The real Ridley Falls. And we did."

"So, the real Ridley Falls is bar brawls and day drinking?"

Instead of answering, Idrissa got out of the car and stood before me. All of the anger and defensiveness were gone. Now, her expression was open and a little pleading.

"The real Ridley Falls is dangerous," she said. "I mean, what you saw today, that's a typical scene."

"I'm feeling a bit dangerous myself right now," I shot back.

"Damn right you are. Good call with the knife," Isaac called out.

I ignored him.

"What did Silas mean that I have to fight?" I asked.

Idrissa hesitated. I could see in her eyes that she didn't want to tell me. My hands fisted in frustration.

"If you don't tell me, I'm leaving right now—"

"The Falls has a code," she blurted. "To be initiated into town culture and accepted by everyone here, you have to fight. It's stupid. I know. Barbaric. Archaic. Ridiculous. But that's what he meant."

I opened my mouth to respond, but she stopped me. "I

know. That sounds crazy. Who would want to live in a town where people just beat the crap out of each other every day, right? We're all Neanderthals."

"I was thinking more along the lines of law enforcement," I said.

"The fights are all organized. They're held in a neutral space, and it's voluntary."

"And what happened at Bo's today?" I asked. "Is that organized and voluntary? Because I'm pretty sure physical assault will get you two to four."

Her brow lifted. She looked like she wanted to ask how I knew that. Instead, she hung her head, and I could see how much she hated what had happened earlier.

"The cops aren't interested in anything that happens at Bo's," she said.

"What about hospitals? Are *they* interested? Because Vinny looked like he needed a doctor."

"Vinny will be fine, I swear."

She sounded so damn sure.

Hell, maybe this wasn't the first time she'd knocked him out. Still…

"You shouldn't have done that."

"I know. I'm sorry. Look, Ash, if you're going to stay here—and I really hope you do, which is selfish but the truth—you need to know what it's like."

"So you decided to throw me to the wolves rather than just explain it?"

She gave me a strange look then blinked and slowly returned to normal. "Yeah, I guess so. Subtlety and softness aren't my style. I'm sorry. But you have to know I wouldn't have let anything happen to you. I swear it."

"Yeah, I noticed. Hell of a right hook you've got."

She grinned. "Thanks."

"That Vinny guy," I tried again.

"He'll be fine. Trust me," she said.

I cocked my head, wondering how she could be so sure. Actually, I was wondering a lot of things. And I was pretty sure I wouldn't like the answer to any of them.

The silence stretched, and Idrissa's smile slipped. I knew she was waiting for me to forgive her, but I couldn't quite bring myself to do it. Not when I wanted nothing more than to escape the violence and chaos that had made up so much of my life. And now I'd just walked right into more of it.

Isaac got out of the car and walked around to stand beside us.

"Are we having our first fight?" he asked, looking back and forth between us. "Because if so, I don't want to be left out."

"We're not fighting," Idrissa grumbled.

"Well, we should," he said.

I shot him a questioning look.

"Friendships are stronger after they survive conflict," he explained. "I read it on Buzzfeed."

I snorted. "You sound like you've never had a friend before."

"We haven't," they said in unison.

I blinked at them, surprised. "Seriously?"

"I know. It's lame," Isaac groaned.

I looked at Idrissa.

"You saw what it's like here," she said. "Friendships aren't really a thing in the Falls."

"Silas and Pres are friends," I pointed out.

"Presley and Silas are in an alliance," Idrissa clarified. "It's different."

"Yeah, they aren't exactly painting each other's nails," Isaac said.

"I see."

I studied the twins, trying to make sense of it all. The fighting. The animosity. Some of it seemed to be centered around me but not all of it. That barfight had broken out completely separate from us. Then there was Vinny—the way Idrissa had kicked his ass. Like she'd done it many times before. And Silas. He clearly despised me, but I got the feeling he despised everyone.

I'd been friendless all my life as a result of my dad's paranoia. They'd been friendless because no one in this town was capable of it.

Despite everything, my heart warmed as I realized, at the end of the day, we were the same. The idea of leaving town suddenly felt a lot lonelier.

"Maybe next time, we'll just stick to the grocery store and my place," I said.

Idrissa and Isaac grinned, the tension broken. "Deal," she said.

"But someone else carries the groceries," Isaac pouted.

9

The twins and I exchanged numbers, with Isaac insisting I program him into my contacts as "Main Dish" and Idrissa as "Side Piece," to which Idrissa threatened to punch him like she had Vinny. They were hilarious, and even though Idrissa had pulled a dick move by taking me into that bar completely clueless, I could see the reason for her strategy. And I could respect her no-fluff methods. Idrissa was someone I wanted on my side in a fight, that was for damn sure.

"I'll text you tomorrow, and maybe we can have dinner after work or something," she said as she and Isaac climbed back into the Mustang.

"Sure, I'll have to cook for Oscar first," I said. "Part of my deal for staying here rent-free. But after that, we can hang."

"You can cook for me," Isaac said, eyes gleaming. "I like anything marinated in alcohol or infused with cannabis."

Idrissa rolled her eyes. "I'll talk to you tomorrow, and listen, no opening the door for anyone tonight except Oscar, okay?"

"You sound just as paranoid as he did," I said.

"Yeah, well, now you know why."

"Good point." I shuddered at the idea of Silas showing up on my doorstep tonight. "Okay, see you later."

They waved as they drove off.

The office and garage were eerily quiet as I made my way through and up to the apartment. Oscar had already left for whatever mysterious—or nefarious—appointment he'd mentioned earlier. I remembered their warnings, though, and made sure to lock everything behind me as I made my way through the shop.

Upstairs, I turned music on to chase away the silence and took a shower as hot as I could possibly stand before changing into the same pair of comfy sweatpants Oscar had lent me that first night. A sports bra doubled as a shirt, and I made a mental note to ask Idrissa to take me to the thrift store as soon as possible.

The fridge was fully stocked, thanks to my grocery run, but I had zero energy left to cook, especially considering it was just me. After pulling out some steaks to marinate for tomorrow, I settled for a sandwich and a water and sank into Oscar's aged couch.

Part of me wanted to examine and dissect everything Idrissa had said. And especially everything she hadn't. There was a hell of a lot more going on between the lines of her explanation than what she'd actually explained—of that, I was damn sure. But I also had a feeling that the more I dug, the less I'd like it. *It will only get worse from here.* That's what she'd said. And it had proven true already.

I couldn't stop thinking about that wolf I'd seen emblazoned on the biker vests earlier. It meant something. I just didn't know what. And I wasn't sure I wanted to, honestly. Because if I looked too closely, I'd have to do something about it.

So, I did the thing I'd done with my Dad for years. I landed somewhere between coping with the truth and denying the inevitable fallout to come.

Avoiding anything that resembled reality, I let Netflix lull me. It didn't take long for the exhaustion to set in and sleep to claim me.

I woke later to find the sun had long since set and Netflix had shut itself off from inactivity. Through the window, I saw that the moon had risen high, and even without checking the microwave clock, I knew it was late.

I got up, carrying my dishes to the sink until a wolf howl froze me where I stood. The haunting, mournful sound sent shudders up and down my spine. It was loud too, which meant it was close.

I peered out the small window above the sink and into the trees that encroached along the edge of the back lot.

Something moved inside the forest, and my breath caught. Dark hair. Broad shoulders. Muscled arms. A flash of eyes that always looked angry.

It had to be my imagination. But I could have sworn I'd just seen Kai Stone standing at the woods' edge, staring directly up at me.

I gripped the counter and waited, watching to see if he'd reappear. But he'd vanished into the cover of trees as if he'd never been there at all.

It felt like the last straw. Secrets were one thing. Stalking me was another.

I hesitated another moment, weighing the sanity of what I was about to do.

"Screw it," I said and grabbed my jacket as I slipped out the door and down the stairs.

Outside, the howling had stopped, but a distant growl

sounded, pulling me toward it like a magnet rather than sending me running back inside to safety.

I started walking.

In less than five minutes, I was inside the trees, swallowed up by the forest itself. The lights of the road vanished until the town was only a distant idea. There was only me and the forest—and whatever apparition of Kai I'd conjured up.

This was stupid.

I knew it, and yet I continued forward, picking my way across fallen logs and around low-lying forest growth.

Not a single sound broke the silence, which probably should have made me turn back too. Even the night insects had gone quiet. I thought of the wolf I'd heard. If a predator was around, the silence of the other night animals was usually a good indication.

This was such a bad idea.

But the moon lit the trees in a bright glow that was more than enough to illuminate the shadows. If anything, it all seemed lighter here. Ethereal even. Like the light was drawn to this particular part of the forest more than anywhere else. It was so weird. And weirder still was the fact that my feet kept moving me forward.

I should have been terrified out here alone.

I should have hauled ass back to Oscar's. Hell, I hadn't even thought to bring my phone with me on this insane little jaunt. But I'd never been one to make the safe or wise decision in the face of danger. More than that, though, something pulled at me like a magnet. Insisting I keep moving. So here I was, still walking toward the growling and howling that seemed to pull me like some sort of magical lure.

Finally, the trees broke, and just ahead, I caught sight of a clearing. Except it wasn't clear. Or empty.

It was full of wolves. Large ones. Like, bigger than I'd ever seen—even on TV. Bigger than should have been possible.

They were monstrous, and even at a glance, I could tell they were deadly. The way they stood. Casual but ready. Alert.

I froze, unable to move away and damn sure not willing to go closer.

Wolves shouldn't have stood around so casually, right? Like they were waiting for something.

But that's how it felt.

I crouched behind the brush—entranced, horrified, afraid to move—until eventually, my legs began to cramp. I tried to gauge how long I'd been here. Or how long they'd all been standing around like they were just waiting for someone to tell them what to do next. But maybe I didn't want to know what came next. Maybe what came next was eating me. And by then, my cramped muscles would render me immobile and helpless to flee.

Forcing myself to get the hell to safety, I turned, finally willing to retreat.

But then I stopped when I saw a figure moving through the trees on my right. If it had been another wolf, I probably wouldn't have stopped to watch. Not when it only added to the danger of being so close to such a large pack. But it wasn't a wolf.

It was a human.

A male human whose broad shoulders and messy hair and chiseled jawline I knew way too well already. And this time, it was no apparition.

My belly leaped at the sight of Kai Stone striding

confidently through the forest—right toward the den of wolves who would surely devour him.

I didn't think. I just…reacted.

Ignoring my cramped muscles, I took off at a sprint for Kai. If I could get to him in time, I could pull him back, and we could run before they—

Right before my eyes, Kai peeled his shirt off, and it took me a full blink to realize the rest of his clothes were already gone. In the next second, he shuddered and transformed. Then he dropped to the ground on all fours. But not hands and feet. Four *paws. A snout that hung open revealing deadly sharp teeth. A body covered in thick, brown fur.*

Holy shit.

Kai Stone was a werewolf. And when his glowing eyes landed on me still approaching him at a run, he looked just as deadly as the rest of them.

But I didn't have time to stop myself now. I was too close. I—

A hard chest slammed into me, knocking me sideways. We both went tumbling, and the air was knocked from my lungs. A strangled scream got stuck in my throat.

When I rolled to a stop and managed to look over, I could only stare in complete surprise at the person who'd saved me.

"Oscar?" I whispered.

He jumped up, looking beyond pissed and a little desperate. "Ash! What the hell are you doing out here?"

"I—"

A wolf growled from somewhere way too close by.

I looked over and met a pair of eyes that should have belonged to Kai. If they hadn't been looking at me from the face of a giant black wolf.

This time, the scream unstuck itself, and I opened my mouth and let it rip.

The other wolves in the clearing growled and snarled as they began to make their way closer. I imagined teeth gnashing at my flesh any moment now.

Oscar jumped up and grabbed my arm, yanking me backward fast enough that I nearly tripped. Only his iron grip on my arm kept me on my feet.

"She's not to be touched," he yelled.

Was he talking to the wolves? Was he insane?

Before I could decipher what was happening, he was turning me around and urging me into a dead sprint.

We took a different path than the way I'd come in. I stumbled over brush and barely avoided running into trees.

Over and over again, I looked back, but there were no wild beasts on our tails. No wolves running us down so they could eat us for dinner. Still, I didn't slow, and by the time we reached the gravel road and Oscar's parked pickup truck, my lungs were burning, and my vision blurred.

Oscar hurried to the truck, yanking open the passenger door. "Get in," he ordered.

I didn't argue.

The moment I was inside, Oscar slammed the door and hurried around to the driver's side. He slid in and started the engine, gunning it so hard we kicked up gravel and spun out until the tires caught and we were propelled out of there.

I sucked in large gulps of air, struggling to get my thoughts under control. My heart slammed against my ribs in wild, erratic beats. My lungs burned, and my hand gripped the armrest of my door like it was the only thing anchoring me to my own sanity. Maybe it was. Because what had just happened…it was insane.

I was actually legitimately crazy.

That was the only explanation here.

Because the alternative was too unbelievable to fathom.

10

Ten minutes later, we pulled into the gravel lot behind the Throttle, and Oscar cut the engine. I started to get out, but Oscar stopped me with a hand on my arm. I met his eyes, still reeling.

"I need you to go inside, lock the doors, and don't come out again until I get back," he said firmly.

"You're leaving?" I asked, panicked, terrified, and more alone than I'd ever felt.

He winced but held his ground. "I need to make sure you're safe."

"I'm right here. With you," I said. "You can see that I'm safe."

"No, I mean—"

His phone rang.

"Yeah," he answered it.

He listened for a few seconds then said, "Okay. Yeah. Thanks."

Then he hung up.

"Never mind. Let's go inside."

Relieved, I let him pull me across the bench seat and

out his door. His arm remained around me as he led me across the gravel and inside the Throttle. I waited while he re-bolted the back door then followed him farther into the garage.

He didn't bother turning the overhead lights on, and that only made me more scared of whatever might be chasing us. Instead, he clicked the switch on a small lamp over his workspace.

"You're safe here," he said like he'd read my mind. "Have a seat."

He gestured to a stool I'd seen him use while working on bikes.

But I couldn't sit.

And I damn sure couldn't go another second without an explanation. Because whatever the hell those wolves were doing in the woods just now, Oscar clearly knew all about it.

"What the hell was that?" I demanded, my voice only shaking a little.

Oscar winced.

I could tell, even after everything, he really didn't want to explain any of this. For some reason, that hurt. I thought of my dad, never actually explaining his paranoia or what he was afraid of. No answers. Just running. Constant running. From ghosts. From monsters. From me. And now Oscar, the only family I had left, was doing the same.

"This town isn't like other towns," he began.

I bit back the sarcasm that wanted to slip out, waiting for more. But he remained quiet.

"That's it?" I asked. "The big reveal is that your town is different?"

"It's the truth."

"You know what, forget it."

I turned for the door, and frustration flashed in his eyes.

"We don't allow outsiders for this exact reason," he grumbled. "Explanations get complicated."

My eyes widened. "You're making this my fault?"

"No, I'm not— I don't know where to start. What to say." His expression softened, and for just a moment, I could see he was trying.

I swallowed some of my panic and said, "How about you start by telling me how it's possible that Kai Stone just turned into a werewolf."

"First, we prefer the term shifter," he said. "Werewolves are a product of Hollywood, but we were born this way so—"

"Wait. *We*?" I echoed.

He nodded; his expression wary now. "I'm the same as Kai. And so are the other wolves you saw."

My heart thudded, but it wasn't anything I hadn't already guessed. Oscar being there earlier could have only meant one thing. He'd known the wolves would be there.

Except that now he was saying he *was* one of the wolves there.

"You're saying all of you turn into wolves," I said. "Shifters."

Oscar nodded.

I frowned, my thoughts careening in a direction I knew I couldn't return from. Oscar seemed to understand and simply waited while I put the pieces together.

"But if you were born that way, does that mean your entire family line was too?" I asked, not sure I wanted to know the answer.

Oscar nodded, slowly, deliberately. His eyes never left mine, and I knew he was gauging my reaction as the truth sank in. What he'd said about my dad being one of them…

It finally made sense. And I wasn't sure how I felt about that.

"My dad was a shifter," I said.

He nodded again.

For some reason, it was a relief. Having an explanation for the monster he'd become. It looked nothing like the wolves I'd seen tonight. It had been much grislier. Less formed. More stunted. And definitely angrier.

But somehow, they were the same creature.

At least, I could dismiss the idea he'd been possessed by a demon.

That left only one question.

"And me?" I asked quietly.

He nodded again.

I blew out a breath and slowly sank onto the stool he'd offered.

"You don't look nearly as surprised as I expected."

Oscar's words shook something loose. The words bubbled up and out of me, probably more from holding them in than wanting to trust Oscar in any way.

"The night my dad died," I began, "before they shot him, he…he changed. Became something else."

I didn't look at Oscar as I spoke. If I had, I would have given in to the tears that burned my eyes as I spoke of those last moments. Instead, I stared blankly at the red toolbox against the far wall and did my best not to feel anything about what I was describing.

"He didn't look like the wolves tonight. His change was different. And it seemed to cause him a lot of pain. The monster that came through was deformed or something. Not quite wolf and not human either. Bones sticking out. Snout half-formed. It was like something out of a horror movie."

Oscar muttered a curse.

I swallowed hard and forced my gaze to Oscar's. "What happened to him?"

"It sounds like your dad probably stopped shifting when he left," he said. "It happens. If wolves aren't around their own kind, the ability to shift recedes. Becomes suppressed. If he hadn't shifted in a long time, he was probably unable to complete the process."

"Like, he got stuck or something?"

He nodded, a pain flashing in his eyes. "I've seen it a few times. It isn't pretty. And the beast becomes more monster than animal."

"So, he did it to himself?" I asked.

"More than likely."

I didn't know what to say to that. My dad had always made it sound like someone else was after him. Some threat hunting him down who wanted to harm him. To know he'd denied his nature—as unbelievable as this all seemed—and done this to himself, was a hard blow.

We both fell silent.

But all too soon, more questions bubbled to the surface.

"How have I never…? I mean, I've never changed into —into that."

"If your dad's wolf was suppressed, it probably kept yours from rising in the first place. It happens."

"Does that mean I'll never…you know, shift or whatever?"

Oscar frowned. "If you hadn't come here, I probably would have said yes."

My temper flashed. Once again, he made it sound like this was all my fault.

"I didn't ask to come here," I snapped.

I huffed. He had a point, but that didn't help my mood.

"You could have told me," I said.

"From the moment you walked in, I tried scenting your wolf, but it's not there, kid."

"So?"

"So, I am not going to just spill all my secrets to an outsider. And a human one at that. You might be family, but so are those wolves back there. And I won't put my people at risk, not even for you."

I looked away, fighting tears again. Everyone had someone—except me.

Instead of the piercing loneliness, I embraced anger. It was safer. Less vulnerable.

"I get that you think I'm a risk," I snapped. "But you're at fault for this too. Especially after deserting my father and leaving him alone all those years."

It was a dick move, blaming Oscar, but my emotions weren't exactly playing nice right now.

Rather than act offended, Oscar shook his head sadly. "Your dad left when he was twenty-six and never came back. I searched for him for years but never could find a trace. I didn't know you existed until the moment you walked into this shop two days ago."

"So, that's your excuse for not telling me you're a ..."

"You can say it."

For some reason, his calm, steady demeanor pissed me off. I spoke through clenched teeth. "A fucking wolf."

"That's ridiculous," said a familiar voice from the doorway. "I don't fuck anyone when I'm in wolf form."

Kai's sarcasm, or maybe it was him showing up here at all, only spiked my temper more. Not to mention the hurt. Which I refused to acknowledge. Why in the hell Kai's secrets were hurting my feelings was not baggage I wanted to unpack. I hardly knew the guy. He sure as shit didn't know me. Why did it matter?

"What the hell do you want?" I demanded.

Instead of answering me, he looked over at Oscar, their eyes meeting across the space and conveying much more than I could understand. "I can take it from here."

"You sure?" Oscar asked.

Something like worry flashed in Oscar's eyes. Worry for Kai. It would have made me laugh if I wasn't such a mess. Hadn't Oscar just saved me *from* Kai? And now he wanted to save Kai from me?

"Yeah, I think we need to get some things out in the open," Kai said, his gaze hard and glittering as he stared at me. "For her own good."

"If I hear that phrase one more time—" I said, my fists clenching as I pictured how satisfying it would be to knock Kai for a loop Idrissa-style.

Oscar nodded slowly. "All right. I'll be upstairs if you need me."

I had no idea if he meant me or Kai. Maybe both. He gave me a concerned look as he left.

When we were alone, I stood up and walked over to the counter, leaning against it. Something about that stool, and being lower than Kai, didn't feel right.

He smirked knowingly, which only made it worse.

I glared at him, enough anger left in me to keep me from giving in to the nerves that trickled down my spine now that we were alone. And underneath it all was that same visceral lure that always seemed to pull me toward him. Why did I always want what wasn't good for me?

"You okay?" he asked.

His words almost surprised me into being nice, but this was Kai. I knew better.

"Yes, no thanks to you."

"You have no idea what kind of thanks you owe me."

"What the hell is that even supposed to mean?" I

demanded. "You want me to thank you for scaring the hell out of me and almost eating me?"

He blinked slowly as my words registered.

My cheeks heated at the innuendo I'd just accidentally made. The air between us seemed to thicken with tension, and I wondered if he was seeing the same mental images as me. Isaac hadn't been wrong about the deliciousness that was Kai. Just the idea of him eating...

Ugh. Stop it, Ash!

"I was never a threat to you," he said, forcing me to refocus.

I crossed my arms. Mostly to hide the fact that my nipples were hard now.

"Then why did Oscar have to tackle me and get me out of there? I saw you growl at me. Seems like you were the threat in that scenario."

"I would never hurt you, Ash."

His expression, the way he said it—I had no doubt in my mind he meant it. And more, I'd never felt threatened by Kai's wolf. Only surprise. And awe. He was huge. And beautiful, although, I didn't plan on telling him so.

"I growled in response to the others picking up your presence. And what I knew they would do if they got to you. I told Oscar to grab you, and I stayed behind to make sure you weren't followed."

It was incredibly terrifying to think he was telling the truth. I'd nearly been torn to shreds back there, and my brain couldn't let me go there. If I did, I'd lose my mind. Or maybe my bladder. Covering my fear with sarcasm was so much easier.

"So, you what? Fought an entire pack of wolves for me? Right."

At my words, whatever softness had come over him vanished, and the scowl returned. "In fact," he went on, "you're lucky I was there. Otherwise, the others would have—" He broke off and ran a hand through his already mussed hair.

"Would have what?" I demanded. "And who *are* the others?"

When he didn't answer, my anger spiked again. More secrets. It never ended.

"I already know Oscar is part of your little pack. Who else?"

"I'm not betraying my pack," he said in a low voice. "I'll tell you anything else, but not their names."

"Fine. What were they all waiting for then? Other than for my legs to cramp so I couldn't flee?"

He looked at me like I was crazy. "What are you talking about?"

"I don't know. When I got there, they were all just standing around like they were waiting on something. It was weird."

He gave me a strange look.

"What?" I demanded.

"Nothing." He shook his head. "You're a lot more perceptive than I gave you credit for."

My brows rose. "Is that supposed to be a compliment?"

He sighed. "They were waiting on me."

"You?" I frowned. "Why?"

"Because I'm sort of like their leader. Well, me and Oscar, though for him, it's more of a formality, I guess."

"What are you, like, the alpha or something?"

If so, would that make Oscar the beta? Man, I was pulling from every werewolf movie I'd ever seen. Mostly Twilight and Teen Wolf, but I wasn't about to tell him that.

"No. I'm not the alpha. Our pack is different."

"Different how?"

"We're— Ugh. Fuck, you ask a lot of questions." He ran a hand through his hair. Again. "The bottom line is you shouldn't have been out there."

I crossed my arms. "If you're about to tell me all the ways I'm the one in the wrong, you can save your breath. Oscar already did that."

His dark eyes flashed, and he strode over to where I leaned against the counter.

I straightened, refusing to be intimidated by the way he towered over me. This close, I could smell the woods on him. That pine scent of his reminded me of those handfuls of seconds I'd seen him as a wolf. Those dark eyes trained on me. The way he'd transformed. And the fact that I'd seen him naked just before he'd shifted. An image I would never, ever forget.

"Oz is trying to protect you, Ash. We both are."

"Please," I snorted, shoving away the mental image of a naked Kai before I did something super embarrassing. Like mount him. "At least have the decency to stop piling on more lies. You're here to protect your secrets. And your little werewolf family. Not me."

I'd used "werewolf" on purpose, just to piss him off.

Bull's eye. His expression hardened. "Fine. Believe what you want about me. I'm here to tell you that leaving is no longer an option."

"What is that supposed to mean?"

"It means you know too much, Ashes. And the only way I can keep you safe is to keep you here."

Ugh. That stupid nickname was really starting to piss me off.

"You can't *keep me* anywhere," I said. "You don't control me—"

His mouth landed on mine, cutting off my words. I made a sound—shock, maybe protest—but Kai didn't let up. His mouth was hot and harsh, and everything about the kiss should have been insulting. Instead, I found myself wrapping my arms around his neck and pulling him closer.

His chest pressed against mine, the heat between us threatening to ignite me as I became aware of all the places our skin touched. His hand wrapped around my neck, making it impossible for me to pull away. Not that I had any intention of that.

Kai Stone was kissing me, and all I wanted was for him to keep doing it forever.

But abruptly, he pulled away, ending the kiss and glaring down at me like I'd somehow just offended him.

He dropped his hand from my hip and stepped away, forcing me to let him go. His chest heaved, and for a moment, we just stared at each other as we struggled to catch our breath.

His expression was an accusation.

I hated it.

Even as I wished he'd kiss me again.

"You don't smell like a wolf," he said roughly.

Of all the things he could have said...

"But you don't smell human either."

"Um."

"None of this makes any fucking sense," he ground out.

Before I could say something—or throw something—or do anything, he turned and walked out.

11

I woke feeling numb. Like maybe last night had been a dream. Between witnessing Kai Stone turn into a wolf—there, I said it—and him kissing me like I was his dying breath, I wasn't even sure what was real anymore. Up until that moment in the woods, Kai had seemed just like all the other guys in this town. Partier. Womanizer. Asshole. Then again, the way he'd stormed out after our kiss hadn't done much to redeem him in the end.

Basically, he was the most confusing person I'd ever met. Person. Wolf. Ugh. I didn't even know what noun to assign him. A fact made all the more complicated by how much I wanted him to see me naked.

The only thing I knew for sure was that Ridley Falls had definitely lived up to the mysterious reputation everyone had given it. Danger. Violence. And hot as hell alpha holes. Someone should put that on a bumper sticker.

I'd only barely wrapped my head around the fact that Kai and Oscar were wolf shifters when I'd remembered that made me a wolf shifter too. Technically speaking. That was a whole different denial train to ride. My father —his secrets, the town he'd left behind, everything he'd never told me about what we really were—had been one big lie.

I had no idea why he'd spent his entire life keeping me from the truth only to send me running straight into the wolf's den when he'd died. But I was going to find out.

Operation Temporary had become Operation Get Fucking Answers, and I wasn't going to stop until I knew the truth. About him. Me. My family. And maybe even what sort of threat my father had been running from. I couldn't believe he'd fled Ridley Falls just because they liked to day drink and bar brawl. It wasn't enough of a reason to move cities every time the wind changed direction.

He'd obviously been running from something. His fear and paranoia were real even on his drunkest days. I wanted to ask Oscar about it all, but I wasn't sure how pissed he still might be at me for stumbling into his little shifter rendezvous last night. Not to mention the white wolf I'd seen printed on those biker vests. I needed to find out its significance. But Oscar had made it clear his loyalties lay with the people of this town. And until I knew who to trust, I needed to protect my secret at all costs.

I'd have to uncover that particular mystery on my own.

When I finished my shower and peeked into his room, his bed was empty. I found a note on the counter, reminding me of the shop hours today. A clear message that work came first.

Work.

Such a mundane, normal, human thing to do.

Maybe that's exactly what I needed in order to get my head on straight again.

Right. Like the shock of finding out wolf shifters existed could be smoothed over by surrounding myself with the overpowering scent of brake fluid and testosterone.

Ugh.

With a few minutes to kill before heading down, I picked up my phone and scrolled through a couple of texts from Idrissa I'd apparently missed.

Uh-ohhh. Word on the street is the cat—or dog—is out of the bag.

I stared, wide-eyed, at her words. Idrissa knew about Kai and Oscar?

Then I read the next text.

Shit. Now you know that I know.

I couldn't help but snort at that.

Isaac made me keep the secret. Be mad at him.

I shook my head and clicked on a text from Isaac.

Drissa is full of shit. It was all part of her "tough love" plan to keep you in the dark. Let's do each other's hair and talk shit about her. Call me.

Being friends with the twins would never be boring, at least.

I was just about to head downstairs when my phone rang. I grabbed my phone, answering it without even looking.

"You're both in trouble," I said, not even caring whether it was Idrissa or Isaac.

But the voice on the other end was definitely not a twin. Or anyone else I ever wanted to hear from in this lifetime.

"I'd say it's you who's in trouble, Miss Langford."

My stomach dropped, and I gripped the phone tightly against my ear.

"Vorack," I managed.

"You didn't think I'd forget about you, did you?"

Rage coated my fear, heating my skin, and I gritted my teeth.

"Right back at ya, asshole. I'm not going to forget what you did to my father."

"Good. Let that serve as a lesson," he said, his voice dropping into something much more sinister. "You owe me, and if you don't pay, that same fate awaits you too."

"Your debt was with my father. Not me."

"A debt unpaid gets passed to the next able body," he said. "That's how my business works."

"Your business, huh? Wonder what the authorities would think of that business? Maybe I should let them know."

"You have fire in you," he said, his voice deadly now. Hungry. Like any moment he was going to reach through the phone and wrap his hands around my throat. "I'm going to enjoy breaking you of that before I extract what you owe me."

"Fuck you," I whispered, my confidence waning.

"Precisely."

I shuddered. "I left town," I said. "You won't find me."

"Challenge accepted, little bird. I'll hunt you down. And when I do, I'll enjoy this payment much more than my others."

The call ended.

I stood, shaking with a mixture of rage and fear, for a long time before I finally made my way down to the office.

Downstairs, the shop was already open, and Oscar gave me a few grunts of disapproval for being late, but that was it. I didn't tell him about the call or ask him any of the million questions I had about my dad and his paranoia. Instead, I avoided him and tried to reassure myself that Vorack would never find me here.

Maybe I could find a way to change my name. Oscar had said my father's legal last name was Lawson. If I could find a way to change it, Vorack wouldn't be able to track me that way. But every time I tried to ask Oscar about it, he was busy with a customer or gone on a break.

Even Kai steered clear of me most of the day, coming and going through the garage as he did repairs and test drives and customer deliveries.

My nerves recovered slowly from Vorack's call, but even so, I barely had time to think about things like wolf shifters and panty-melting kisses, so that was something.

"Can you put this invoice in?"

I looked up to see Kai holding out a sheet of paper full of handwritten scribbles. He was staring at my mouth. I found myself equally turned on and pissed off. I decided to acknowledge the pissed part.

"I would if I could read your chicken scratch," I said.

He rolled his eyes, tossed the invoice on the counter, and walked out, which only made my irritation worse.

Fine.

Two could play this bull shit game.

For the rest of the day, I avoided him, stepping out of the office when I saw him coming and waiting to hand out job orders until he was busy.

Late in the afternoon, a customer walked in, and I tensed. His face was familiar, and then I remembered. He'd been at Bo's, playing poker with Silas.

"Hey," he said, a cocky smile spreading as he walked up to the counter. Behind him, two friends hovered, and I had the distinct feeling they were here to watch the show.

"Can I help you?" I asked.

"Actually, I'd love to help *you*."

I rolled my eyes. He didn't notice.

"I'm Devon. This is Cade and Luke."

"Do you need work done?" I asked, not bothering to glance their way.

"Oh, shit," Devon said. "Hell yeah, I do." He leaned forward across the counter. "What's your going rate for bodywork, Ashes?"

He winked, and I bit back the surge of temper that tempted me to take out one of the beers Oscar kept in the mini-fridge at my feet and shatter it over his dumbass skull.

"You couldn't afford me," I said.

His friends hooted at that.

Devon's eyes narrowed. "Tell you what. You give me a freebie, and I'll put in a good word with Kai to let you stay awhile."

Yep, fuck it. He was getting a beer bottle to the dome.

"Sure, let me just get my purse." I batted my lashes at him and then reached into the fridge and grabbed a cold, brown bottle. The sound of a familiar voice stopped me from swinging it.

"I'm not sure when you were promoted to pack advisor, Devon."

I looked over sharply at Kai, who stood at the end of the counter glaring at Devon.

"Hey, man," Devon said, unconcerned with being caught. "I was just hanging out with my special friend Ashes here."

"We are not friends," I said.

Devon chuckled. "Right. Strictly professional." He winked, and I considered using the bottle despite Kai's presence.

"You're late for work, Dev." Kai's expression was tight. It gave away nothing. Although, the rage rolling off him was unmistakable.

"Relax, dude. I'm just—"

"You only have one more strike with Joey before you're fired," Kai said. "I suggest you get the hell over there."

"Such a fucking buzzkill, man." Devon sauntered for the door. His friends followed. "Poker at Bo's tonight," he added over his shoulder.

"See you there," Kai said flatly.

He didn't move until Devon and his friends had gotten on their bikes and rode off. Even then, he returned to the garage without so much as a glance at me.

"Thanks," I said sarcastically into the silence when he was gone.

An hour later, Idrissa texted again, asking about dinner plans. I held off, unsure about how much I could trust her. Between Kai and Vorack, there was no way she wouldn't notice something was up. And I just wasn't used to sharing my secrets with people. Besides, she and Isaac had kept a lot from me too.

Trust was hard-earned and easily lost, in my experience.

Still, getting out of here for a few hours sounded way too tempting. And Oscar had made it clear the only way I could do that was with the twins as my babysitters.

Unless I left town, of course. And maybe that was the smartest move, given what I knew about this town. Better the danger I didn't know than the threat I did.

It wasn't until closing time that I remembered Kai's little declaration from last night. Suddenly, Vorack was forgotten, and I found myself marching over to where Oscar stood cleaning up his tools.

"Is it true?" I asked.

"Is what true?"

"I can't leave town because of what I know?"

He shot a glance toward where Kai was cleaning up at the other end of the garage, too busy to notice us. I rolled my eyes. Oscar was on his own for this one.

"It's what's best," Oscar said, looking back down at his tools. "For now."

"What's best *for you*," I said. He started to respond, and I cut him off. "Who do I talk to about this?"

"What?"

"Who do I talk to? Who's in charge of your pack or whatever? The alpha, I guess."

He frowned. "No alpha. Just… talk to Kai."

"Kai's in charge of the pack?"

His words from last night returned. About how the wolves had been waiting on him and Oscar to show up.

"Not exactly. But—"

"Then, I'll pass."

He shut his toolbox and shrugged. "Suit yourself. I'm going to finish up some paperwork, and then I'll head upstairs and give you a hand with dinner."

I scowled as he walked off.

Across the garage, Kai looked over briefly then headed for the exit. I watched him go, my heart hammering in my chest. Was I being a chickenshit about facing him after that blazing kiss last night? Yes. Was I going to stubbornly outlast him in this game of silent treatment we were both apparently playing? Also, yes.

Maybe I could get Idrissa to spill some things to me now that I knew about the wolves. I dialed her but got her voice mail. Same with Isaac. Dammit.

I blew out a breath and flicked off the lights. With

nothing else left to do, I headed for the apartment, finally admitting my defeat, if only silently.

"Hey."

I looked up, startled by the voice. Drake stepped out from behind a bike sitting up on a lift. "Oh. Hey." I blew out the breath I'd been holding as my heart rate returned to something normal. "I didn't see you there."

"Sorry. Didn't mean to scare you."

"I thought everyone else had gone home."

"Forgot my phone." He held it up, and I nodded.

Something about the guy gave me the creeps. That probably wasn't fair. Everything about today had given me the creeps, especially after that call from Vorack.

"Listen, the alpha thing… it's a sore spot, so no one likes to talk about it. Don't take it personally."

I stopped short, surprised he'd brought up the whole wolf thing so casually.

"Your dad left a lot of people upset when he split. Even without the current state of things, losing our alpha was a hard blow."

"Wait. Do you mean… was my dad the alpha?"

"You look a little shocked." He chuckled.

"I guess I just didn't expect that. Or you to put all that out into the open. I mean, everyone else has been so secretive."

"Yeah. The CIA's got nothing on the secrets this town holds."

"Why is that?" I couldn't help but ask.

Shit. My dad, the alpha…

"Our pack has trust issues."

"Our pack," I repeated. "So, you're…."

"A wolf shifter." He shrugged. "Yeah. Everyone in this town is."

"Oh."

Wait. Everyone?

As in… literally everyone??

"They don't trust anyone from out of town because we can't risk letting humans know our secret."

"So, this is about the outsider thing again."

"It's about a lot of things."

I wanted to ask what that meant, but I didn't want to push him past what he wanted to share. Already, he was being more open than anyone else.

His eyes flicked to something below my chin.

"Where did you get that?" he asked sharply.

My hand came up, fluttering over the crystal moon pendant my dad had given me.

"My dad gave it to me."

"Hmm."

I could tell he wanted to ask more, but I couldn't bring myself to continue. It felt too personal to talk about just yet.

"Is there someone I can talk to?" I asked, changing the subject. "About my being stuck here, I mean?"

"You want to leave?"

"Is that so hard to believe?"

"I don't know. I figured you came here for a reason."

I hesitated. Drake was being a lot nicer than Kai or Oscar had been, but that didn't mean I was going to spill my guts to the guy. I knew a thing or two about secrets as well.

"I needed a change of scenery," I said, shrugging lightly. "But I can do that anywhere, and it seems like Oscar's got his hands full, so…"

"Gotcha. If you don't want to deal with Kai, I'd say talk to Silas," he said, and I groaned.

"Of course it would be him."

Drake's brows went up. "I take it you've met him?"

"In a manner of speaking, yes."

He laughed. "Uh-oh. That doesn't sound good."

"Let's just say we won't be BFFs anytime soon."

"Trust me, no one's calling Silas their BFF." He chuckled.

"There isn't anyone else I can talk to, is there?"

"There's Oscar and the rest of the council," he said. "It's made up of some of the older pack members. But honestly, their authority isn't really holding water these days. Silas, Kai, Presley, the Close twins—they all kind of do what they want."

The Close twins?

"You mean Isaac and Idrissa?"

"Yeah. Their dad's a council member, but like I said, they kind of just do their own thing. We all do."

The twins were wolves. Of course.

I shook my head. The secrets were just pouring out now. I thought of the bar brawl and what Idrissa had said about how they were treated around here. Like there was no law or order. Just chaos.

"Aren't wolf packs supposed to be more, I don't know, united?"

He lifted a brow. "I think it's obvious we're not a normal pack."

"Point taken." I sighed. "Okay. Silas it is."

Drake's brows drew together. "Can I give you a piece of advice?"

"Sure."

"Don't lie to them."

"Why would I—"

"We've had spies try to infiltrate before."

"Um, I'm not a spy." I tried to laugh off his words because, hello, insane, but one look at his expression, and I knew laughing would not go over well. His gaze turned sharp, and I knew he was trying to detect something specific about me. But what?

"That's what they all said too."

"Look, I don't know who you think I am. But—"

"Not who. What."

"Excuse me?"

"We all want to know *what* you are."

"I guess I'm like you," I said uncertainly.

He shook his head. "Walks like a human. Smells like a human. Except…not quite."

He cocked his head, the friendly expression suddenly wiped clean from his face. Instead, he looked calculating. Suspicious.

"What are you, Ash Lawson? My guess is the rumors were true about your old man and you're working for the hexerei. And that makes you the enemy. Or didn't Cohen explain all this?"

Frustration bubbled to the surface, and I glared at him. My patience was sitting at a negative number right now. After the last twenty-four hours, being accused of…whatever this was…definitely wouldn't end well for him. What the hell was a hexerei anyway? And why did people keep accusing me of working with this Cohen person? And now there were rumors about my dad? That was the last straw.

"Listen, Drake. I've had a fucking day, so why don't you just take this fake friend, fishing for gossip bull shit act of yours and shove it up your—"

His expression twisted, and his eyes flashed as he stepped close enough that I drew back out of reflex. "If you have magic, they'll know," he hissed. "And if you lie about it, they'll kill you. And not even Kai fucking Stone will be able to stop them."

He turned on his heel and slipped into the shadows.

Rattled, I didn't wait to hear the door shut behind him before I hurried from the garage and up to the apartment. I had no idea what half of his accusations even meant. Cohen. Magic. Rumors about my father. It was all foreign to me. But the look in his eyes and the threat in his body language was clear. And it felt different from Kai or the others. Crueler. With a sharper edge to it.

I found myself actually scared of whatever he was alluding to. Maybe being confined to these walls for the foreseeable future wasn't such a terrible plan after all. Ridley Falls just kept getting weirder and weirder.

12

By Friday, my bruises were completely healed. Or, at least, the ones anyone could see. I'd spent the last three days playing the role of obedient niece and avoiding anything remotely real with Kai Stone—who honestly just kept getting sexier the longer he pretended I didn't exist.

What was it with me and assholes?

Why couldn't I have gone for the Momma's boy who loved holding doors for me and reciting turn-of-the-century poetry?

Oh, because those kinds of guys didn't exist in this town. Literally, every male resident, and honestly the females too, were all pretty short on patience and kindness.

It was weird.

Oscar was surprisingly attentive, though. Every night after the shop closed, he'd head upstairs and help me with dinner. Then, we'd do the dishes and watch TV together until bedtime.

He never asked or pushed me for information about

Dad or what I thought about the wolves. Or Kai. Especially Kai, actually.

If anything, he seemed content to avoid conversation beyond small talk and chores. But he was present. And it was nice to have someone there who didn't spend their waking hours watching for ghosts or drinking until they didn't feel watched all the time.

Oscar was sane, and he was nice to me.

It was the best living arrangement I'd ever had, which only made me feel more like shit about what had happened to Dad in the end. And it kept me from mentioning my run-in with Drake. The last thing I wanted to do was admit one of his employees had it out for me. Or worse, force him to choose a side. I couldn't be sure he'd pick me, and why should he?

Drake had been here for years. I'd shown up mere days ago with a sob story and a broken face. I was a burden with baggage that dragged on the floor behind me. And everyone had a line on what they could handle. I didn't want to find Oscar's.

I did wonder about the rumors Drake mentioned. And about my dad being alpha. What had made him leave? And did it have something to do with whatever we'd been running from all of those years?

Was someone in this town the reason my dad had pulled up stakes and ghosted his own family? If so, Oscar didn't seem aware of it. He seemed just as mystified as me about what had driven my father away.

On Friday, just after closing, a familiar Mustang pulled up out front, and judging from the way the tires screeched to a stop, I knew it had to be Idrissa behind the wheel. Sure enough, I watched her climb out and march inside to where I waited behind the counter.

"Bish, are you trying to ghost me or what?" she demanded.

"No, I'm not ghosting you," I said. "I texted you back."

We'd texted a lot, in fact. About shifters and about how she and Isaac hadn't been at that wolf meeting but they damn sure had known it was happening. And about my dad. Apparently, Idrissa didn't know why he'd left either. Only stories. And rumors. None of which she'd share with me even when I'd begged.

"I know that," she said, her pouting lip reminding me of a similar expression Isaac had given me once. "But your texts are vague, and we haven't hung out, and it's giving me a complex."

My brows rose.

"Besides," she added, "Isaac is busy with some guy he met on Hinge, and I'm bored."

I'd already learned Isaac was a serial dater. Never more than once with the same person, though.

"Well, I'm on house arrest, so I can't help you," I told her.

"Yeah, about that…I talked to some people, and I'm here to spring you."

"What people?" I asked, suddenly wary. She made it sound way too easy.

She sighed. "Silas. My dad. Oscar. Kai." Her gaze flicked to the garage, but I waved her off.

"He already left," I said, referencing the latter.

"Right. Well, anyway, they all agreed that as long as you're with me, you can leave the shop."

"Why?" I asked.

"Why what?"

"Why are they letting me leave, just like that?"

"Because it's me," she said with way too much smug confidence.

My eyes narrowed. "You didn't punch anyone, did you?"

"Of course not," she protested then pouted. "I'm insulted you would think so."

I snorted. "Apologies, gentle maiden. Of course, you would never stoop to violence."

She flashed a scary sort of smile. "Unless they deserved it."

"Speaking of which, how's that Vinny guy?" I asked.

"He's fine," she assured me. "Actually, your concern for him was noted by Presley and a few of the other guys. I think it's what helped change their minds."

"About what?" I asked.

She shrugged. "Hating you so much."

"Gee, thanks," I said wryly.

"You wanted full disclosure," she reminded me.

I had made her promise, no more secrets.

"I thought he was dead," I admit, remembering how Idrissa had knocked Vinny clean out that day.

"Yeah, we need to chat about your little fugue state that day," she said, and I tensed at the memory of how Vinny's blood had freaked me out. "Later," she added. "For now, we need drinks."

Apparently, my aversion to alcohol had not dimmed Idrissa's enthusiasm about consuming it herself.

"Actually," I said, "I could really use some new clothes."

Her eyes lit up. "Oh, thank baby Jesus," she said. "I was trying to be polite and not mention the whole redneck receptionist vibe you have going, but it's seriously not okay with me."

I looked down at the shop shirt I'd borrowed from Oscar and leggings with brake fluid stains so faint that, hopefully, no one could see them. Girl had a point.

"Let me talk to Oscar," I said.

"We'll talk to him together." She followed me upstairs without waiting for a reply.

Ten minutes later, Oscar had given the green light, and I'd insisted Idrissa not subject me to her driving. Instead, we were walking the three blocks to the thrift store. I debated spilling everything to Idrissa about Drake's accusations and what it all meant about my dad, but the moment wasn't quite right. Or maybe I was still holding back my trust in friendship. Either way, I kept my mouth shut about all of the crazy shit that had been happening.

"I can't believe you have me hoofing it," Idrissa complained.

"You drive like a bat out of hell. I don't need the heart attack today," I said.

Before she could answer, a familiar figure waved and hurried toward us from the other end of the block.

"Hey, boo!" Isaac closed the distance and pulled me into a hug that completely lifted me off my feet. "Finally. I missed your face."

"I thought you were on a date," I said as he set me down.

"He wasn't a dog person," he said simply and Idrissa muffled a laugh. "What are you two bitchachos doing?"

"Clothes," Idrissa said, pointing to me.

"Say no more." Isaac grabbed my wrist and pulled me into the thrift store. "I got here just in time."

For the next hour, the three of us pulled clothes off the rack, made choices, tried things on, and laughed until I was sure we'd get kicked out. It was the most fun I'd ever had shopping. Watching the twins poke at each other while they waited for me to check out made my chest ache with a happiness that also felt a little sad.

I was nineteen years old and just now experiencing some of life's most simple joys for the first time. I was also being hunted by a cold-blooded killer and living under the watchful eyes of a town full of wolf shifters who thought I was the enemy. Oh, and then there was the biker gang I'd pissed off.

Life was complicated.

Outside, the twins helped me carry bags, and we visited a few more stores that left my stash of cash much smaller than when we'd started. But I had clothes. And after a week of owning literally only the clothes on my back, having possessions again—even just a few bags full—made me feel steadier somehow. Like I really did have a place in this world.

Isaac sensed my mood change and put his arm around my shoulders.

"Tell me his name, and I'll run over his dog," he said.

"Who's name?" I asked.

"Whoever made you look so damn sad. I'll kill him for you. No questions asked."

The look on his face made it clear he meant it too. That should have disturbed me, but after the week I'd had, at least the murderer was on my side this time. Shit, where was a friend like Isaac all my life? I could have used him back at those shitty diners I'd worked at where the customers were constantly trying to get me to go with them at three am.

Okay, wow, and on that note, I was losing it.

"Actually, I was wondering when we were going to talk about the fact that the two of you are wolf shifters and you didn't bother telling me."

Isaac dropped his arm. "Damn. Busted."

"We talked about it through text," Idrissa protested.

"Not the same," I said, pinning them both with a look.

Idrissa elbowed Isaac. "Guess you're running over your own damn dog."

Isaac looked stricken. "Not Galileo."

"Your dog's name is Galileo?" I asked. "Wait. You have a dog?" I looked back and forth between them. "Isn't that a little ironic?"

"Are you about to make some weird joke about how we *are* house pets?" Isaac asked, eyes narrowed. "Because you should know I'll only allow it if you make it kinky. And Idrissa won't allow it at all. She usually punches people right about now."

I eyed Idrissa who didn't contradict Isaac. "Noted," I said. "And I didn't mean to insult you, but maybe if you explained some shit, I wouldn't accidentally say the wrong thing."

"She has a point," Isaac said to his sister.

Idrissa sighed and glanced up and down the street. "Fine. But not here. Come on."

She turned and led the way through a narrow alley, and I followed, fully expecting some secret hideout—or den—hidden behind the dry cleaners and crystal shop we'd cut between. Instead, I found myself in a garden. Stone borders held up raised beds that overflowed with lush, green plants.

Large shade trees rose up at each end, plunging the whole space into shadows. It was cooler here too. And getting cooler the further we went.

I rubbed absently at my arms to ward off the chill.

From other directions, stone pathways all led to a common space in the very center of things. Somewhere nearby, water trickled. A fountain maybe? Or a pond? It smelled like algae.

"What is this place?" I asked, turning a full circle as Idrissa stopped at a small table and chairs set in the very center where all the paths converged. It felt . . . magical. If magic were actually real. And according to Drake and his rude accusations, it was.

"It's called a garden," Idrissa said, brow arched.

"Hilarious," I said.

"I couldn't resist."

She gestured to one of the chairs. The iron back was cold underneath my hands, but I pulled it out and sat, dropping my bags to the stone ground.

Isaac took one of the other chairs, and we both looked expectantly at Idrissa.

"The crystal shop owner is a friend of mine," Idrissa explained.

"I thought you didn't have any friends," I said.

She smirked. "Okay, well, we *were* friends until she slept with my boyfriend senior year, but then I slept with her brother. We've decided to call it even."

I stared at her. "You're serious."

"What? You never slept with someone's brother?" she challenged.

"I slept with someone who had a sister," I said slowly, frowning at the memory. "I didn't know who she was and use it against her."

Nicholas Andre. He'd been a terrible kisser, but I'd needed to feel something, anything that wasn't the constant stress of dealing with my Dad. Turns out I didn't need to feel it bad enough to go back for seconds. In fact, every guy I'd slept with—three, which wasn't many—had been a one-and-done. And not just because of Dad. There was just never anything to them that made me want to go back for more.

Kai, on the other hand, made me wonder if I'd ever stop once we started.

I blinked, forcing my thoughts back to the conversation, and found Idrissa grinning back at me in a way that made the hairs on my neck stand up. "Too bad," she declared as if pitying me. "It was a fucking rush."

I shook my head. "You're crazy."

"Blame our wild wolves," she said with a shrug. "Tori's cool now though. Or cooler than some of the others. Isaac and I helped her put all this together a couple of years ago."

"It's beautiful," I said.

"Our wolves like the outdoors," she told me, and I nodded.

Even without the ability to shift, I'd always appreciated nature too. The smell of the earth. The wind. Being underneath an open sky. It felt like … freedom. And looking around, I could appreciate how someone had brought little hints of all that freedom into such a small, tight space.

Making do with what you had.

I could appreciate that too.

"Listen, we just want to start by saying we're really sorry for keeping this from you," Isaac said.

Idrissa nodded.

"We didn't want to. But Oscar and Kai insisted."

I scowled.

"I forgive you," I said. "As long as our promise holds true about being honest from now on."

They both made the motion of a cross over their heart.

"We swear it," Isaac said.

"Good. Can I ask you guys something then?"

"Anything," Idrissa said.

"Was my dad really the alpha before he left?"

"Yeah." Idrissa looked thoughtful. "It was before our time, obviously, but our parents have told us the pack history."

"Do they know why he left?" I asked. "What drove him away?"

She shook her head. "No. I mean, no one knows for sure. There are theories. Rumors." She shrugged. "But nothing concrete."

"What does Oscar say?" Isaac asked.

"As little as possible about pretty much everything," I said. "I just feel like I keep making mistake after mistake, and if someone would just explain it all to me, maybe it would keep me from making it worse."

"You really had no idea about any of this," Isaac said sadly. "About what you are or anything."

"No."

"Damn, girlie." He grabbed my hand. "No one should have to find out like this. I'm sorry."

"Thanks." I offered him a small smile. "I'm so glad to have you both."

Isaac sniffled and wiped a tear. "Me too. We're going to tell you everything you need to know, okay?"

I nodded.

"Okay, here's the facts," Idrissa said, getting down to business like only Idrissa could. "Isaac and I are werewolves."

"Wait. Oscar said you don't like that term," I said.

She rolled her eyes. "The older shifters think it's offensive and stupid, but I think it sounds badass." She grinned. "If Jacob can be a werewolf, so can I."

I laughed. "Got it."

"Anyway, like I said, Isaac and I are both wolves. In fact, basically, everyone in this town is a werewolf. And now that you know, they don't want you to leave because they're afraid you're going to blab about it and the Men in Black will show up to run experiments on us or make us learn to fetch or whatever."

I blinked, a little surprised at her candor. But also appreciative. Idrissa didn't beat around the bush, and I loved her for that.

"Okay, that's fair," I said.

"It is?" Isaac asked.

"Yeah." I shrugged. "I've been thinking a lot about this, and I get it. I wouldn't want to risk being found out either. But how do I convince them I'm not going to tell anyone?"

"So you can leave?" Isaac asked.

"I don't know."

"We know about your plan to cut out," Idrissa said.

My jaw dropped. "How could you possibly know that?"

"Oscar called me yesterday," she said. "He checked your browsing history and found internet searches for job postings in three different towns a couple of hours from here."

"What the hell, Ash." Isaac clearly hadn't known, judging from the scandalized look he gave me. "I thought we were soul sisters."

My chest panged with a regret that didn't even exist yet. "Listen, I don't know what I'm going to do, but even if I do leave, I want you both to know your friendship means a lot to me."

Isaac huffed.

Idrissa simply lifted her brow. "Funny way of showing it," she said. "Leaving us without a goodbye."

"We all have things we needed to say but didn't," I pointed out.

"Touché." Her expression grew serious. "But look. I'm telling you now. The Falls is full of werewolves that will hunt you down if you so much as cross the county line. As your friend, I need to advise you against that idea for now. Okay?"

I swallowed hard as her words hit me. "You realize you just casually mentioned I might get murdered, right?"

Isaac grabbed my hand. "I will casually fuck someone up if they even try."

I offered him a tentative smile. "Thanks. But I think it would be best if I made peace instead." I looked from him to Idrissa. "Which brings me back to my earlier question. How do I convince them I won't spill their secrets?"

She shrugged. "You prove you're one of us."

"But...I'm not."

Isaac bit his lip, hesitating. "Ash, you're Oz's niece. Your dad was pack alpha before—" Idrissa punched him, and he winced. "Before he left," he finished hastily. "That makes you one of us."

I shook my head. "I've never shifted. Oscar said he can't smell my wolf at all." I glanced at Idrissa. "What's wrong with me?"

She frowned. "I don't know, but the pack thinks you're a wolf," she admitted. "Like Isaac said, it's in your blood. And even more so considering your dad was the alpha. They see you as a threat or at least an equal competitor."

"But I've never even shifted," I said.

"They don't believe you've never shifted. Or that you can't."

"How do I convince them? Will they leave me alone then?"

She shook her head. "I know it's a Catch-22, but the only way to get them off your back about that *is* to shift."

"And to fight," Isaac added.

Idrissa shot him a look.

"What?" he demanded. "She should know everything."

"Whatever it is, just tell me," I pleaded. "I'm sick of not knowing stuff I'm clearly supposed to know."

Idrissa glared at Isaac then swung her gaze to me.

"Remember Silas and his comment about having you fight?" she asked.

"Yeah. So?"

"So, it's how we do things here. Newcomers fight, and it solidifies their place in the pack. Once you're one of us, you also get things like pack protection."

"Protection from what?" I asked, suddenly interested.

She shrugged. "Each other. Outside threats. Whatever. It means you have support."

"Can I report douchebags like Devon harassing me at work?" I asked.

"Devon being a douchebag is nothing new," she said. "But yes. Fighting for your place here would offer that kind of protection. As well as prove to them what you are. That you can be trusted. If you refuse to fight, you can't stay."

"Hmm. They do know this isn't the Dark Ages, right?"

"I know it sounds barbaric from a human perspective, but wolves do things differently. It's part of our animal nature to use our beasts to understand where we fall in the pecking order."

"They want me to fight…as a wolf?"

"That's the only way to survive," she said wryly. "Considering your opponent will be a wolf too."

Isaac grabbed my hand. "But you don't have to do it. We're going to protect you. They won't fuck with us."

"Can't I just opt out and take the bottom place or whatever it's called? Part of the pack but not a threat?"

Idrissa shook her head. "It's more than hierarchy," she said. "It's like a rite of passage."

"Can't your alpha or council or whoever make an exception?" I asked.

"We don't have an alpha," Isaac said, and I swore he sounded almost sad.

"That's what everyone keeps saying. I don't understand. Don't all wolf packs have alphas?"

"We're a little different than other packs," Isaac said.

"But you used to have an alpha," I reminded them. "So, what happened after my dad left? Why was he never replaced or whatever?"

He and Idrissa shared a quick look.

"Great, more secrets," I said.

Idrissa slid closer in her chair and lowered her voice. "It's not…I can't…" She squeezed her eyes shut, and when she opened them again, they were lit with a painful determination. "There's a curse," she finally said.

"A curse," I said.

She nodded.

Isaac leaned toward me. "Magic binds us," he whispered. "We can't…say much…"

"Magic," I repeated, stunned.

He nodded.

"And you can't tell me," I realized. "Like, literally can't."

"We want to," Isaac assured me.

Whoa.

"Okay. So, magic is real. And your pack is spelled or something?" I said slowly, trying to put the pieces together.

"Sort of."

"Cursed," Isaac said, looking strained as he pushed the word out.

"Okay, your pack is cursed by magic," I said.

"Yes, exactly." Isaac smiled like I'd just figured out some complicated math problem.

"We call ourselves the Lone Wolf Pack because that's what we are. A bunch of lone wolves banded together."

"Wait. Lone Wolf… That's the symbol I saw on that biker's vest. The name of the motorcycle club." I looked from her to Isaac. "That's the name of your pack?"

"Original, I know," she said with an eye roll.

Uh, originality was not my concern.

"Are you telling me you're all part of that biker gang?"

Isaac took one look at my expression and cackled. "Is that more disturbing than knowing we're all wolf shifters?"

"Well, yeah. Kinda," I admitted. "Bikers are notoriously dangerous."

Idrissa lifted a brow.

I sighed. "Touché," I muttered.

Isaac hooted, clearly enjoying this. I thought back to the brawling men I'd seen at the bar, Bo's. So, everyone in Ridley Falls was a wolf. And everyone was also in a biker gang. I'd never underestimate the weirdness of my life again.

"Also, I can't really picture you in a leather vest," I told Isaac.

"So true," Isaac agreed. "Leather chaps, sure, but the vest is way too cliché for me."

Idrissa folded her arms. "You two done yet?"

"Yeah." I shook my head. "Sorry, you were saying. You're all in a pack, but you're lone wolves because you don't have an alpha. What does that have to do with magic? Or a curse?"

"For starters, I'm sure you've noticed that without an alpha, our wolves are a bit unsettled."

"Unsettled?" My brows rose. "Is that what we're calling the violence and the mayhem I saw at that bar the other day?"

"We don't exactly have control—"

Her words were cut off by the revving of a loud engine from the direction of the main road followed by a chorus of yells that sounded urgent.

"Shit," Idrissa hissed, jerking her gaze to Isaac's. They shared a nervous look.

"Who is that?" I asked as the yelling grew louder. Closer.

The engine cut off.

I stood as the twins shoved to their feet, grabbing bags and pulling me toward the exit.

"What the hell," Idrissa snarled, stopping short.

Peering past her shoulder, I saw a figure blocking the alleyway we'd used to come in. Broad shoulders. Longish hair.

Silas.

My stomach clenched.

"What does he want?" I asked, knowing whatever it was, it couldn't be good. Not from the serial killer look he wore.

"You," Idrissa said simply, which still didn't really answer my question.

People wanted me for a lot of things these days. None of them sounded like fun for me, though.

"Take her through the back," Isaac said. "I'll hold him off."

Idrissa didn't argue. She grabbed me, tugging me to follow her in the opposite direction.

"Wait, we can't leave Isaac," I said, but Idrissa was strong, and I had to nearly run to keep up with her or risk faceplanting.

"He'll be fine," she assured me. "We need to get you out of here."

Behind us, Isaac said something to Silas in a growly voice. Silas responded, a lot closer than he'd been before. I couldn't make out the words, but judging from the animalistic sounds, they were either already shifting or were about to.

I picked up the pace, ready to be out of here. Suddenly, the garden wasn't so much secluded as isolated. If Silas did something to me back here, who would know? How long would it take Oscar to find me?

I hurried ahead with Idrissa, but at the mouth of the alley, she stopped short.

I peeked around her shoulder and spotted Presley, the James Dean look-alike. He was just as pretty as the other day. But he looked a hell of a lot meaner and intent on violence now.

"Pres, you don't want to involve yourself," she said in warning.

"She needs to fight, Dris. You know that."

Shit.

"She can't shift," Idrissa told him.

Her voice held no trace of the panic I felt. She shoved me behind her as Presley took a step forward.

"She should have thought about that before she decided to crash our hunting party the other night."

Hunting party? Is that what their gathering had been about? And why Kai had said I was lucky he'd been there to protect me from them?

I shuddered.

"If Cohen sent her, we'd know by now," Idrissa said.

I blinked. There was that name again. I really needed to find out who this Cohen person was. So far, he'd only made things complicated for me, which was bullshit considering I'd never heard of him.

"She has to prove it," Presley said. "You know that."

"She didn't grow up as a wolf," Idrissa told him. "She doesn't understand how it works."

"I'm just following the rules," he said.

"What rules?" Idrissa demanded. "Lone Wolves do what the hell they want." But I could hear it in her voice. Presley was going to win this argument. Maybe not today but eventually. It was some sort of code they had.

"Not when Silas is involved," he said.

"Fuck Silas," Idrissa hissed.

Pres smiled in a beautiful-yet-deadly show of teeth. "I think Isaac's doing his best."

Idrissa started to turn back to check on her brother, and Presley's eyes glittered in anticipation. I realized too late he'd only said the words to distract her. The moment Idrissa looked away, he dropped into a crouch, and before I could even blink, he'd shifted. His clothes exploded off his body, the shredded fabric flying in all directions.

This was nothing like Kai's shift. When he'd shifted, it had been graceful. Fluid. And maybe I should have been terrified then, but Kai didn't scare me. Not even as a giant wolf. Not like Presley did.

I screamed, and Idrissa whirled

An enormous wolf with a coat the color of vanilla crème stood staring back at us. It bared its teeth, first at Idrissa, then at me.

Idrissa cursed and then shoved me, whispering, "When I attack him, run. Get back to the Throttle, and lock the doors."

I didn't even have time to nod before she shifted too.

Idrissa's wolf was a dark, dark chestnut, so brown it was almost black. Her tail brushed my hand, a silent signal, and then she jumped at Presley.

I didn't wait to see who would win the battle before I fled for my life.

13

Heart racing, I rounded the corner, slipping past Presley while Idrissa distracted him. A hand closed over my arm, yanking me sideways. I screamed, the sound muffled as another hand clamped over my mouth.

A body pressed in close.

I inhaled the scent of pine and broody male.

Kai.

He loomed over me, wrapped in shadow from where he'd pinned me against the side of the building.

"Don't scream," he mouthed.

I nodded, eyes wide, and he dropped his hand. Despite his intimidating posture, relief flooded me. Kai was an asshole who spoke his mind without thought to other people's feelings. But he wasn't a killer. Or, at least, not when it came to me. I wasn't even sure how I knew that. Especially since Silas and Presley probably wouldn't hesitate to do just that. But Kai Stone was safe for me.

I didn't know how I knew it; I just did.

"Follow me," he said, his voice barely a whisper.

He grabbed my hand and led me through an opening barely large enough for me to squeeze through sideways.

On the other side was a motorcycle parked facing the street.

Kai hurried to it and handed me the helmet hanging off the handlebar.

I shoved it onto my head, and Kai reached over and snapped it underneath my chin, his fingers practiced and agile. His knuckles grazed my chin, making me shudder, but he didn't seem to notice as he turned and swung a leg over his bike, motioning for me to climb onto the back. I slid a leg over the side, pressing my body to Kai's.

My hands fumbled a bit as I tried to figure out how to hold on.

Kai reached back and grabbed my wrists, wrapping my arms around his chest in silent instruction. I grabbed fistfuls of his shirt, heart pounding in both fear and excitement. Kai started the bike, the engine rumbling to life around us.

My body hummed with the vibration of the engine. It was thrilling, the feel of the powerful machine. And Kai's body pressed hard to mine. Adrenaline coursed through me but not from fear. My arms squeezed his torso as Kai kicked us into gear and shot out of the alley. He didn't even slow or stop to check for traffic before zipping onto the main road. A car honked, and I held my breath, braced for impact, but none came.

When I let myself look up again, we were speeding through town, weaving in and out of cars with an ease that took my breath away—this time out of pleasure.

The wind whipped my hair until it stung where it hit my cheek and collarbone. A chill snaked up the back of my shirt, but I didn't mind it. The sensation of being on the back of Kai's bike felt like flying. Here, I was safe. Here, I was free.

Kai drove us out of town and down a series of windy back roads until I had absolutely no idea where we were.

As the chill on my skin worked its way toward cold, I thought briefly about the bags of clothes I'd dropped in the garden in my haste to get away. That sucked. Then again, losing a few clothes seemed like a small price to pay for keeping my life.

Finally, Kai pulled off the road and cut the engine.

The sudden silence echoed around me, and I reluctantly peeled my hands off Kai's chest so I could climb off. Kai did the same, and for a long moment, he just looked at me, his eyes searching mine. Then, he reached up and unhooked my helmet.

I shivered, and his eyes darkened knowingly. Whatever wall he'd put up between us, it was crumbling now. I could see some of the emotion he'd been hiding. And the attraction. It made my skin tingle.

He released the clasp and dropped his hands. I slid the helmet off, shaking out my hair now hopelessly tangled from the wind.

"Thank you," I said finally, mostly because the silence was killing me.

"For what?" he asked.

"Saving me," I said.

His brow lifted in challenge. "How do you know I didn't bring you out here to kill you?"

"Because you would never hurt me."

"You shouldn't trust me, Ashes."

"Why not?"

He sighed. "I'm a Lone Wolf," he said as if that explained everything.

Instead, all it did was make me go completely still.

"What did you say?" I asked slowly.

"I said I'm a Lone Wolf." He sighed. "It's the name of our pack."

"Your… and the symbol is a white wolf's head tipped back in a howl?"

He shrugged. "Yeah. So?"

I swallowed hard, heart racing. My head was a jumble of panic and fear and sudden understanding. If I'd been standing before anyone else on the planet, I would have fled. But this was Kai. And I knew one thing for absolute certain.

"You won't hurt me," I repeated, more firmly this time. Mostly for my own benefit. "I can see it in your eyes when you look at me."

He held my gaze until my racing heart had nothing to do with my fear from a moment ago and everything to do with the way he always seemed to draw me in and make me want to jump his bones.

"And what else do you see when I look at you?"

His voice was quiet and just rough enough to rake me over with its sharp edges.

"You want to be friends with me."

He smirked. "Is that right?"

"But I think you don't know how to be friends. Or don't want to let yourself be happy. Why is that?"

He winced at that. "Ash, there's a lot you don't know."

"You mean the curse?"

The smirk fell away. "I'm going to kill those twins," he muttered.

"They're just trying to be honest," I said. "Something friends do."

He grimaced. "Look, we might not have an alpha, but there are a few things the pack agrees on, and this is one of them. We don't talk about the curse."

"Don't or can't?" I cocked my head. "It seemed like they were literally unable to say the words."

"Both."

I crossed my arms. "How are you able to say the words?"

He rolled his eyes. "I can say the word 'curse,' Ash. It's the specifics that get complicated."

I hated the way his tone made it sound like I was somehow slow for not understanding it all.

"And Silas and Presley trying to kill me just now," I snapped. "Is that complicated too?"

His expression tightened. "Their wolves see outsiders as a threat. It's instinct to protect the pack."

"Then why are you protecting me?" I asked.

"I don't know," he growled.

It wasn't an answer, really, but it felt closer to honesty than we'd been before. Something told me he was holding back. And not just about the curse or the pack. This was something between us.

"Does it piss you off that I trust you?" I asked, trying to understand.

"It pisses me off that you're here at all."

My chest panged at that, and I wondered why it hurt me so much to hear a rejection like that from him. Kai had never been nice to me. Had never given me reason to think he would want me around. So why did it bother me to hear him say it?

"Well, don't trouble yourself anymore," I said, refusing to push it. If he wasn't going to talk to me willingly, I refused to beg. "Just take me back to Oscar's, and I'll be out of your hair."

I started for the bike, but Kai grabbed my wrist, pulling me toward him. He stepped forward, closing the distance until our bodies collided. Chest, hips—and mouths.

Just like the first time, I felt my body go still in utter surprise. Kai had a way of doing that, apparently. But then his mouth moved against mine, and I felt myself responding instantly. My hands came up, wrapping around his neck as I clung to him, pressing in close before he could push me away again.

Except, this time, he didn't do that.

His hands gripped my hips, sliding up my body and around my back. Tangling in my hair. His lips parted, coaxing mine to do the same, and his tongue explored my mouth in that same confident, pushy way he'd had since day one.

I couldn't get enough.

A small sound escaped my throat, and Kai groaned, lifting me off my feet and backing me against a tree, kissing me harder. His hands roamed my body, and when they reached the hem of my shirt, I lifted my arms so he could pull it over my head.

Our kiss broke then, and he stared back at me, his dark eyes stormy and unsettled. His expression was intense, like he was just about to walk away. Or just about to strip both our clothes off right here and take this all the way.

My need for the latter was a liquid fire in my veins.

I reached for him, and he started to lean close again, but then his eyes dropped to my bared hip and he stopped, leaning away to look closer at the black mark on my skin.

"What is that?" he asked, looking back at me with eyes quickly turning cold in the wake of what we'd just done.

"A tattoo," I lied in a strangled whisper.

Shit.

How could I be so stupid?

I'd completely forgotten. But then, Kai had a way of doing that to me.

"Where did you get it?" he demanded.

He'd stepped back, putting distance between us. A foot of space that felt like a chasm. His expression shuttered. Cold. Detached.

I swallowed hard, trying to think of something that wouldn't make me sound like the enemy they thought I was.

"I've had it for a long time," I said finally.

His eyes narrowed. "You lied."

His voice was hard, but underneath the stone-like quality, I heard a trace of hurt.

"I didn't lie," I said firmly. "You didn't exactly volunteer your secrets, so neither did I."

"Ash…" He trailed off, and his eyes flashed with something I couldn't read. It felt like distance, and the idea that this could end, whatever we were heading toward wasn't something I could handle.

Quickly, I reached down and pulled the waistline of my pants back into place, covering the image of the wolf on my skin that was very clearly an exact match to the Lone Wolf pack symbol.

"Fine, I've had it my whole life," I said, the truth tumbling out. "My dad says I was born with it. I don't know how that's possible, but he refused to explain. In fact, there wasn't much he would say except that I should never stay in one place too long or people would hunt us down and hurt us. I have no idea who or what he meant. Maybe he meant shifters. Maybe I've just walked right into the den of monsters he spent his whole life running from. I don't know. But it's just a birthmark. And I'm just a girl."

Kai looked at me with an expression that stirred me in places I'd never known I could feel. "Ash, you are never going to be just a girl. Not for me."

But just as quickly as the heat had come, it vanished. He looked sad. And that terrified me most of all.

"Why do you sound like I just ran over your dog?" I tried to joke.

His hand cupped my cheek, and my skin tingled from the contact. It was everything I could do not to lean into his touch.

"You have no idea what you are," he said, his nose brushing my jawline as he inhaled deeply against my throat.

"Tell me," I whispered, willing to plead and beg if it meant Kai admitting what he really felt.

But he pulled away and dropped his hand, the longing in his expression freezing into something colder. More aloof.

"I believe you," he said.

"About what?"

"That you have no idea what the mark means. Your dad was clearly protecting you." He took a breath and said, "Twenty years ago, a witch cursed our pack. No alpha can ascend and no wolf can mate. Without either of those to ground us, our wolves are restless. Untethered. Wild. It's why we're so full of violence and chaos."

"Hence the name Lone Wolf Pack," I realized, stunned by the story until confusion took over. "But what does that have to do with me?"

"I can't—" He started to shake his head, but then his eyes cleared and stared at me in shock.

"What is it?" I asked.

"I think … I can say the words."

"What words?" I asked, but then I remembered the

way Isaac and Idrissa had been bound somehow to keep them from explaining things to me. "The magic isn't stopping you?"

"I don't know." He ran a hand through his hair and started to pace. "My throat usually closes up if I so much as think about uttering the story." He stopped and pinned me with a look. "What did you do?"

"Me? Nothing. Why the hell would you think it was me?"

"Because." He jutted his chin toward my hip. "That wolf is the mark of the curse breaker. The one who'll come to free the pack from the magic that binds us."

"You think I unbound you or whatever?"

"No idea, but I couldn't even say that much ten minutes ago. All I know is the symbol of our wolf is on your skin, and now I can tell you whatever you want to know about it, apparently."

"Okay," I said, "Let's just say there is a curse breaker—whether that's me or not—what's the rest of it? How is the curse supposed to be broken?"

He shrugged. "There are only legends and rumors. Stories. Tall tales. No one knows for sure. But the marked one will come, or so they say. And free us."

The marked one.

I took a step toward him, caught up in the story now. "But if it's true, and I can break the curse, that's good, right? I mean, wouldn't the pack want that?"

But even as I asked the question, I knew there was no way this could be good. If it were, my dad wouldn't have hidden me away my entire life.

Kai shook his head. "Legend says the curse breaker will be the next alpha. You've met Silas and the others. They aren't the type to let that role go to an outsider."

"But…I don't want to be an alpha. Even if I did manage

to break the curse, I'd just give up the role," I said, stepping forward. Reaching for him.

But he backed away. "They would never let you live long enough for it to get that far. You're not safe here. You need to go. Now."

Panic clawed at me. I was so stupid. Walking right into the danger I was supposed to be running *from*.

"You just told me I couldn't leave or the pack would hunt me down." My voice rose as frustration built. "This whole thing is insane. A cursed pack. Killer wolves. What the hell, Kai? What am I supposed to do now?"

"Dammit, Ash, I don't know," he yelled. "I don't have the answers. I just need you to live."

"Why the hell do you even care?" I demanded.

We were yelling now. Taking our anger out on one another. It was toxic as hell, but I was past caring.

"You don't even like me," I pointed out.

"Fuck, Ash. Of course I like you. Don't you get it? That's the problem." He was in my face now. His breath hot on my lips. I backed away until my shoulders hit the tree again.

"And now we're back to this being all my fault somehow," I said. "Well, I'm so sorry I'm here ruining your life," I ranted. "Maybe you're the one who should leave."

He blinked. "Maybe I should," he said softly, and the words were so heartfelt I immediately wanted to erase them.

"What?"

"But I can't." He hung his head, closing his eyes for a moment. Then he opened them again and looked right at me. "You're all I see, Ash Lawson. You have been from the moment I laid eyes on you." He laughed humorlessly. "It's insane how far gone I am, considering the curse prevents the mating call from ever happening, but here we are. I can't leave you, and I can't let them kill you."

"Mating call?" I squeaked, confusion and disbelief coating my words. "I thought that wasn't possible."

He shook his head. "It shouldn't be," he agreed. "I mean, it's not. Fuck, I can't figure it out, and it's been driving me half crazy ever since you arrived."

"What has?"

"This…thing between us. I know you feel it too. The pull."

I bit my lip but then nodded. "I do," I admitted.

He ran a hand through his hair. "Our pack can't recognize a mate, so it doesn't make sense, but from the moment you showed up, nothing has been the same for me."

"You've felt this way since I got here?" I asked.

Anger, surprise, pleasure, and desire all slammed into me at once. For someone who claimed to be interested, he had a damn funny way of showing it.

"I wanted you the minute you walked into the Throttle," he said. "Of course, I chalked it up to lust, but then the next day, I caught your scent, and well, let's just say my wolf agrees with me."

My thoughts drifted back to that moment when he'd backed me against the wall in the front office. I'd watched, no, *felt* his whole energy change. He'd gone from irritated at my very presence to interested to completely confused before he'd slammed out the door. Now I knew why.

"What does this mean?" I asked.

"I wish I knew. My wolf feels strange. Like it doesn't know what to do with you. It can't recognize you as a mate, but it can't let you go either."

I didn't understand any of the mate-talk, but I knew

how he felt about not wanting to let go. Even if it did mark me as insane. Who fell for a guy they'd just met?

"And what about you?" I asked quietly. "Your human side or whatever?"

His eyes darkened, a storm of unspoken emotions swirling in their depths. "I'm yours, Ashes. Even if you don't want me."

He was a walking contradiction. Hot and cold. And he wasn't denying the fact or even apologizing for it. But all I could hear were those three words playing on repeat over and over again in my lust-filled brain. *I'm yours, Ash.*

I cleared my throat, hating the way my cheeks were already flooding with heat as I made myself say the words I was thinking.

"What if I do too?" I asked quietly. "Want you, I mean?"

His dark look shifted into pleasure, and he leaned close. "That makes things easier," he said quietly. "Especially considering there's nothing you can do to get rid of me now."

"I know," I said, a smile forming on my lips. "I've already tried."

He laughed, a dark, mysterious sort of sound, and kissed me again.

14

I wanted that kiss to go on and on. Forever, like he'd said. But too soon, Kai was pulling away and looking down at his phone. It took me a minute to realize he'd stopped because the stupid thing had dinged.

"What's wrong?" I asked, noting the slant of his mouth as he read the text.

"Something happened."

"Silas?" I asked.

"No. Worse." He grabbed my helmet and held it out to me.

I hesitated. Considering everything I'd learned, was going back to town smart? Or was I walking right into the very danger I was supposed to be running from?

Kai met my eyes steadily, and the fear receded. He wouldn't let anything happen to me.

I took the helmet and shoved it on my head.

"What's worse than Silas?" I asked as Kai hurriedly reached over to secure the strap underneath my chin.

"Witches," he said and then swung a leg over onto the bike.

He didn't wait for me to climb on before starting her up, and by then, my questions were lost underneath the sound of the revving motor. Just as well. Where the hell did I even begin? I'd just wrapped my head around wolf shifters, and now they were talking about witches?

Was anything make-believe anymore?

My lips still tingled from the kiss as I climbed on behind Kai and wrapped my arms around his torso. This time, there was no hesitation as I pressed my palms against his chest, and I secretly hoped we never made it back to town. Not just because I dreaded another crisis—and Kai's reaction certainly seemed to suggest that's what waited for us—but because riding on the back of his motorcycle gave me a valid excuse to touch him.

My body thrummed with the vibration of the motorcycle. It didn't hurt that I'd pressed myself tightly against the guy who'd proclaimed to hate me then kissed me like I was his oxygen.

I still wasn't completely clear whether we'd resolved the hating part, though. Kai was hard to read. One minute, he wanted to strip me down to my barest parts, and the next, he wanted to be rid of me forever.

He'd told me he was mine.

That meant something. Even if he'd also wanted me to leave town and never come back.

The guy was confusing as hell.

The moment we hit the main street cutting through downtown, I knew something was wrong. No traffic clogged the streets, and I didn't spot a single pedestrian strolling from shop to shop as we sped past cafes, shops, and offices.

We pulled up in front of Oscar's, and Kai cut the engine, pulling me along with him so that I barely had time to shed the helmet before we were hurrying around back to the gravel lot.

A crowd had gathered inside the chain-link fence that made up the back lot where Oscar stored his customer's bikes. The moment we rounded the corner and into view of them all, Kai dropped my hand and increased his pace, putting some distance between us.

I tried to ignore the pang of hurt at his actions. Maybe he'd been bullshitting me about how he felt. Maybe he'd just wanted information. That thought hurt worse than anything Silas or Presley had tried to do to me. But I shoved it aside.

It didn't matter. None of it did.

Kai had his pack to think about, and I had myself—and this damned mark. Whatever the hell that meant.

At the end of the day, we were enemies.

I needed to remember that. Especially here.

Up ahead, I spotted Idrissa and Isaac. When they saw me, they broke away from the crowd and rushed toward me. Both of them grabbed me in a tight group hug.

"You're okay." Idrissa breathed in relief against my windblown hair.

She drew back.

Isaac grabbed my cheeks in his hands and brushed his nose against mine. "You scared the doggy biscuits off us, girl."

"Sorry," I said.

"You smell like the road," Idrissa added, her expression framing it like a question.

"Kai gave me a ride," I explained.

She gave me a look that I knew meant there'd be an inquisition later.

"Oh, did he now?" Isaac said with a sly grin.

Rather than answer that innuendo, I pulled his hands

from my face, craning my neck toward the gathered crowd behind him.

"What happened with Silas?" I asked.

"Not enough," Idrissa muttered, but before I could ask more, someone screamed.

I jerked toward the sound, but whoever had made it was obscured by the bodies pressing in around one another. They were all focused on something in the center of it all.

The scream came again.

I shoved past the twins, who both tried calling me back, and into the crowd, moving shoulders and arms out of my way until I broke through into the middle.

I stopped short, taking in the scene before me.

Silas stood across the circle, his hands fisted and bruised as he loomed over a man crouched on his knees. Blood leaked from the stranger's nose and a nasty cut below his eye. His lip was puffy and swollen, and his entire body was covered in sweat and gravel.

Beside Silas, Drake and Presley stood like sentinels. Behind them, Devon and Cade crowded in. I even recognized that girl Tiffany from the bar inching over so she could stink-eye me. They all wore matching expressions of absolute hate, and my memory flashed to Vorack; to the night he and his men had come for my father. Ganging up in this way so we never stood a chance.

Something inside me broke.

I had no idea who the man on his knees was, and I didn't care. It only mattered that he was outnumbered and being attacked by a mob.

I wasn't going to let that happen a second time.

With a cry of my own, I launched myself at Silas. The force—okay, probably the surprise—sent him sprawling, and I managed to knock him to the ground.

He took the brunt of the fall for us both, and the moment he was down, I rolled away, knowing better than to let him get his hands around me. With a violent jab to his ribs, I managed to twist away before he could grab me.

I came up and met the eyes of the man they'd detained.

"Run," I screamed at him and then twisted again, slipping out of the hands that grabbed for me.

I broke into a run.

The crowd parted but not before someone sturdy and unmoving slammed into me from behind. Arms came around me and lifted me clear off the ground. I kicked wildly, but my feet met only empty air as my captor dodged every defensive maneuver I made.

The others moved aside, and I was carried away from it all—straight through the back door of the Throttle and into the empty garage.

"Let me go," I screamed, but if anything, the grip around my arms and middle only tightened until suddenly, they released me. I fell in a tangle of limbs onto the hard concrete floor.

Pain radiated up from where I'd landed on my arm, and I hissed through closed teeth. Turning quickly, I looked up into the eyes of my attacker.

"Oscar, let me out of here," I demanded.

"Not a fucking chance, kid. Are you trying to get killed?"

I glared at him. "I'm trying to stop a mob from killing an innocent person."

"Innocent, huh?" He rubbed his salt and pepper goatee. "Do you know something about that damned spook that we don't?"

"Spook?" I echoed, confused.

Movement caught my eye, and I felt a fresh wave of fury at the sight of Kai striding up behind Oscar. With him were Silas, Drake, Presley, and the twins. Fear coiled in my gut as I took in their faces one at a time. No one looked okay about seeing me here. Or what I'd just done.

I stood up, hating the feeling of having to look up at them all. My arm twinged, but I ignored it. No way would I show any of them a weakness now.

"I told you she was a threat," Silas said.

His eyes were trained on me as if his stare alone could extract whatever punishment he had in mind.

"She's not one of them," Oscar said in a hard voice that sounded almost like a warning. Almost.

Except that he was still looking at me like he wanted to whoop my ass too. They all did.

"One of who?" I asked, mostly because it seemed like whoever that guy was, aligning with him was about to get me in way more trouble than I could get out of.

"Like she doesn't know," Silas scoffed. He glared at me. "Stop playing stupid."

"She's not playing," Oscar said and then winced when he realized he'd accidentally just insulted me.

"Look, I don't know what that guy did, but it doesn't make right what you were doing to him," I told Silas.

"That *guy* was trying to climb in your window," Silas said, and I blinked, suddenly at a loss for words.

"Oh, now he deserves what he gets huh?" Silas shook his head.

I looked over at Kai, but his expression was too intense for this moment. He wasn't moving to defend me, which only made my heart hurt.

I looked at Idrissa. "Is that true?"

She nodded. "It's why we were so worried about you after..."

She shot a look at Presley, who looked completely

unharmed by their little battle earlier. In fact, they both did, which only made me more wary of them all.

"Why would some stranger want to get into my room?" I asked, but even as I said the words, I knew.

Vorack.

He'd found me.

"Good question," Silas said. He crossed his arms over his chest, and I knew he'd seen the answer written in my eyes. "Why don't you tell us."

I hesitated. But keeping my secrets wasn't an option anymore. Not after this. My shoulders sagged.

"My dad owed some people money," I said quietly. "Bad people. They came to collect, and when we didn't have it, they killed him for it."

My eyes burned with tears, but I refused to let them fall. Not in front of these people.

"Ash," Oscar began, but I ignored him, forcing out the rest of the story before I lost control of my emotions.

"Yesterday, the guy, Vorack, called me and said I still owed the debt and that he'd find me so I could pay him—one way or another."

Kai cursed under his breath, but I didn't dare look over. I couldn't take any more shit about keeping secrets or one more lecture about how I shouldn't be here.

"You should have told me about the call," Oscar said.

"I didn't take it seriously," I said. Not entirely true, but I'd had other things on my mind that felt way more of a threat. "How would he ever know to look for me here?"

Idrissa whispered something to Isaac, and I looked down at the floor. This was it. The moment they all chased me out of town for being too big of a burden to deal with.

"What a heartbreaking little story," Silas said into the silence.

I met his glare with one of my own. "Go to hell."

"Oh, trust me," he said with a snort, "I'm already there."

Presley snickered.

"If you don't believe me, that's your problem," I said. "I'm telling the truth."

"Oh, we believe you, Ashes," Silas assured me, his gaze condescending and hard. "The problem is that it has nothing to do with that guy out there."

"What are you talking about?" I shook my head, confusion warping my logic. "You just said he was trying to break into my room—"

"That guy is a spook," Presley said. "A spy for the hexerei."

I frowned, remembering Drake's use of the word. I still had no idea what it meant. "What are the hexerei?"

"Witches," Drake said with a pointed look.

And one by one, the pieces began clicking into place.

Witches. The pack's enemy number one. The people who'd cursed the wolves all those years ago and made them into what they were now: Violent. Unsettled. Wild. And above all, mateless.

No wonder they'd been beating the shit out of the guy. He'd come here to spy on them and probably use whatever information he uncovered to make their lives even worse.

Maybe innocent had been a strong word.

"I still don't understand. Why was he trying to get into my room?" I asked.

"Didn't we already try this line of questioning?" Presley looked at Silas in mock confusion. "Because I feel like we already tried this once."

"She clearly doesn't know," Idrissa said. "Just give it a damned rest."

"We'll give it a rest when we know the truth," Silas snapped at her. "Kai?"

Everyone turned to him, and I let myself pretend, just for a moment, that he'd be on my side.

But he didn't even meet my eyes.

"She's been through some human drama that's got her all jammed up," he said flatly.

"We could bring her in," Drake said. "Make her talk."

My insides twisted with fear at that. I didn't need to ask to know whatever he planned wouldn't make the interrogation pleasant.

Kai shook his head. "I don't think she knows a damned thing about any of it. Her pop lied to her about everything. This shit isn't our problem. We should be out there dealing with the spook."

Silas looked reluctant to agree.

Presley was neutral as always, but Drake stood his ground.

"I think we need to rule it out one way or another before we can let her stay," Drake said.

"She's nobody," Kai said, and I felt his words like a punch in the gut.

"Then let her prove it," Drake said.

"How the hell do I prove I'm not a witch?" I demanded. "You going to toss me into a lake and see if I sink or float? Because—fake news."

Isaac snickered.

Silas shot him a dirty look.

Isaac gave him the finger.

"You wish," Silas muttered.

"Nah. I don't want your mother's leftovers," Isaac said in an acidic voice.

Silas growled and took a step, but Idrissa slid between them.

"Easy, boy," she whispered.

"She fights or she leaves," Drake said, drawing everyone's attention back. "Those are the rules, right?"

For a long moment, no one spoke.

Silas and Presley were the first to nod their agreement.

"Guy has a point," Silas said, looking way too smug as he glanced over at Kai.

"Idrissa?" I asked quietly.

She gave me a pained look. "Those are the rules," she said.

I looked at Isaac.

"I'll shit on every one of their pillows tonight, I swear it," he said solemnly. And then, after a pause, "But those are the rules."

Silas grinned, and I wanted to claw the smile right off his violently handsome face.

"Kai?" Oscar said, and one by one, they all turned to him.

They might not have an official alpha, but Kai Stone was apparently as close as it got. And now, my fate rested in his hands.

He glared back at me, and I could practically hear the words being projected from his brain: you shouldn't be here.

It was a tired refrain.

And for once, one I agreed with.

But there was no going back now.

"I'll fight," I said, condemning myself before Kai could do it for me.

Everyone looked at me.

Idrissa's eyes were wide. "Ash, no," she hissed.

It was stupid; even I knew that. But if I was going to die, I'd do it on my own terms. Not theirs. And if, by some miracle, I survived, at least, I'd have some shred of protection against them doing shit like this to me in the future. Not to mention Vorack—should he ever find me.

"Just tell me when and where," I said, exhaustion creeping in to take over the adrenaline that had kept me going before.

"We'll let you know," Silas said.

He looked satisfied. For now.

Turning, he sauntered back toward the exit.

"Come on, let's go string ourselves up a spook," he called over his shoulder.

With one last look at me, Drake and Presley fell into step behind him.

Kai stood staring at me, his expression hardened into something completely unreadable.

"That was a mistake," he said simply.

And then he turned and followed his asshole friends out.

15

After Kai was gone, Idrissa and Isaac rushed at me, pulling me into a hug that I was quickly beginning to consider my lifeline to normal human experience.

"Ash, you're insane," Idrissa said, squeezing me tight.

"You're going to get yourself killed," Isaac added.

"No, she's not." Idrissa drew back and looked at me then Isaac. "We'll help. And we'll figure it out."

Isaac nodded. "We won't let anything happen to you," he said to me.

"Thanks," I said, my voice cracking now that the assholes were all gone. "Both of you. I can't—I mean, I should have told you about my dad, but—"

"Don't worry about it," Idrissa said firmly.

"Yeah, please." Isaac rolled his eyes. "I mean, we all have daddy issues."

"Okay, I'll take it from here."

The sound of Oscar's voice snapped me back to reality, and I stepped away from the twins, my heart thundering. Part of me wondered if Oscar would kick me out for good now. After all of that, maybe he agreed with Silas. Maybe he thought I was some kind of spy or infiltrator.

Idrissa and Isaac squeezed my hand and then left with a promise to talk soon. Oscar waited until they were gone and then simply said, "Let's talk upstairs."

I followed him up in resigned silence. If this was it, I wasn't going to beg. Oscar might be my only family left, but if he was going to toss me out when I needed him most, that would break the ties that bound us in a way that would never be repaired.

I braced myself for just that.

In the small apartment, Oscar closed the door behind us and gestured to the kitchen table.

"You want to sit?" he asked.

"No thanks."

He'd yet to meet my eyes, and rather than lose it, I crossed my arms and let my temper cover my fear. Leaning against the counter, I stared across the space at him.

When he still didn't speak, I decided ripping off the Band-Aid was probably best.

"If you're going to throw me out, just do it, and spare me all this build-up."

Finally, he looked up at me and met my eyes. Confusion shone back at me as his brows dipped and he shook his head. "I'm not throwing you out."

"You're not?"

"No, why would you think that?"

I dropped my arms and blew out a breath. "I don't know. Because I'm a spy or an outsider or whatever else."

"You're family," he said firmly. "I'm not turning my back on you."

For some reason, the simplicity of it all tugged at my

heart, and I felt a pang in the same place I felt my dad's loss every second of every day.

"Thanks," I said quietly.

He continued to frown.

"But something's on your mind," I added. "What's wrong?"

"You're brave for volunteering to fight," he said. "But you can't win unless you can shift." He ran a hand through his short, graying hair. "We need to figure out a way to get you out of this."

"I appreciate your concern, Oscar, but I can't continue to live in this town with a target on my back."

"If you show up to that fight, unable to access your wolf, that target will become a bull's eye, and those guys don't miss."

"What else am I supposed to do? I'm not allowed to leave. So, I either walk right up to them or let them hunt me down."

He hesitated. "We'll ask the twins to train you. If anyone can draw out your wolf, it's one of them."

Hope rose in me. Training with Idrissa sounded terrifying, but Oscar was right; it was my best chance. "Okay." I nodded. "How long do you think they'll give me before the fight?"

"Not long, knowing those jackasses." He glanced me up and down. "You'll need to put in some serious conditioning. Take a few days off. I can pay you vacation pay or something."

"No way. I'm not skipping out on my responsibilities."

"You're stubborn." He shook his head. "Just like your old man. Fine. Half days, and I'll dock your pay."

"Fine."

"You shouldn't go anywhere alone."

"Agreed." For the first time since arriving, I wasn't going to argue about the whole house arrest situation.

He grunted, apparently satisfied. When he turned to walk away, I made a decision.

"Oscar," I said.

"Yeah?"

"I think I need to show you something."

He looked instantly wary. I couldn't blame him. "What is it?"

I peeled the waistline of my pants down just enough to reveal the mark on my hip. Oscar stared at it for a long moment then looked up at me, eyes wide.

"That's the mark of the curse breaker," he said. Then his eyes widened. "Holy shit, I just said that. How in the hell… Do you know what this means?"

"I'm starting to think it's important."

He shook his head insistently. "Look, Ash, that mark is as sacred as it is dangerous."

"So I've heard."

His eyes narrowed, and he marched up to me. "From who? Who else knows about this, Ash?" His voice was urgent now.

"Kai saw it," I admitted. "Accidentally."

My face heated at the memory of that particular "accident."

"Shit," Oscar muttered. "Okay, Kai. That's not a problem. I'll speak to him. Anyone else?"

"No."

"Good. Keep it that way."

"But the twins—"

"No one else can know, Ash. I mean it. Not a single person in this town can be trusted with knowing about that mark on your body."

"This is so insane," I said. "I don't know where it came

from or why I have it, but suddenly it means I'm public enemy number one."

"You're already public enemy number one," he said, which was true, but still made me cringe. "If anyone sees that mark, you're dead."

I blinked, a little taken aback he'd just said it so casually. Okay, maybe not casually but still. My death shouldn't even be on the table, and here Oscar was, pointing out the serious likelihood.

"I won't tell anyone," I said quietly. "But I would like to know more about this so-called curse and how I'm supposed to break it using only a birthmark."

"The curse is very real," he said.

"No mates, no alpha, I've heard all that, but I don't understand why."

Oscar blew out a breath and motioned to the chair again. "Might as well sit. It's not a simple story. And to be honest, I've never been able to tell it until now."

He still looked dazed by that fact, and I was starting to develop a theory I definitely didn't want to face just yet.

This time, I took the chair.

"Twenty years ago, our pack was moving toward peace talks with the hexerei. A channel had been opened—which, by the way, took about fifty years, to begin with—and it seemed like we were headed in the right direction. Finally. After centuries of war and conflict."

"That sounds like a good thing," I said.

"It was," he said. "In some ways." He stared out the window over my head, his gaze far away as he recounted it all. "But there were many pack members who didn't want that peace. Didn't trust it. We'd lived through lifetimes of distrust and prejudice, and it's hard to let that go for some."

"So, what happened?"

"A summit was scheduled. We would meet the hexerei leaders at the border where our lands met and sign a peace treaty in blood."

"In blood? Seriously?"

"It probably sounds strange to human customs, but for wolves and supernaturals, it's a common practice. An agreement like that would be unbreakable, and the punishment for violation would have been severe. The pack was divided about it. There were protests. Riots. On both sides, so I've been told.

"Anyway, the night before the summit, there was talk of a secret affair. One of ours sneaking off to be with one of theirs."

"A wolf and a hexerei were in love?" I asked.

"Rumors," he said. "No one knew for sure. Then, the next morning, we all met at the border." His expression changed then. His faraway gaze became haunted. "We should never have gone to that meeting."

"What happened?" I asked.

"A spell had been cast on that spot. One that only affected our pack. The hexerei leaders claimed it wasn't them. That it had been cast the night before."

"Like a trap?"

He nodded. "And we all walked right into it."

"What did the spell do?"

"Untethered us from our alpha. One by one, until every wolf in our pack was removed from the bond. At first, that's all we knew. It took time to understand the full ramifications of that untethering."

"Kai said the curse makes it impossible to find your mate," I said.

"That's one of the little surprises, yes. Took us years to figure it out too." His expression darkened. "Whoever cast that curse wanted to prevent us from forming a mate-bond, which is sacred to wolves. It also makes us stronger as a pack, but more importantly, finding our mate settles our wolves in a way nothing else can."

"Not even an alpha?" I asked.

"Being tethered to an alpha is different. An alpha would, at least, have the strength to focus our beasts. Without either of those, our pack is wild. Basically, we're at the mercy of our baser instincts. If our wolf gets angry, we don't have control over the way that anger shows itself."

"You mean like bar fights and hunting me down in the middle of Main Street in broad daylight?"

"Silas will be dealt with for his aggression," he said, his expression flashing with a dark rage. For some reason, that made me feel better.

"So, what does all this have to do with my tattoo?"

"From what we know of the hexerei's abilities, every spell has a counterbalance. If you use magic to create something, somewhere at the same time, magic is created with the ability to uncreate it. Nature's balance, I guess. And it's absolute. Like universal law. We never knew what that counterbalance would look like, but we knew it had to be out there."

"And now you think I'm it?"

"That mark you wear on your skin is the symbol of our pack. The mark of the alpha who was torn from us."

Okay, that did seem a little concrete. Damn.

"And the alpha in question was my father."

He nodded.

I had to ask the question out loud or it would always hang between us. "Do you think my dad had something to do with it? The curse, I mean? If he ran right after..."

"I don't know," Oscar answered, and the look in his eye told me he'd asked himself that question many times.

We stood in silence for a moment.

"Why curse you this way?" I asked finally. "I mean, why unsettle or untether you at all? Why not attack you outright for whatever hate they had against the pack?"

"Apparently, destroying us wasn't good enough," he said grimly. "They wanted to make sure we destroyed ourselves."

16

Oscar's story answered so many questions for me. It also raised several more. A lifetime of living on the run, and here it was: My dad had been an alpha—right up until the day he'd fled his own pack. Had he seen them as the threat, or was he running from something else? The hexerei, maybe? I gritted my teeth in frustration. For every answer I got, another question rose in its place.

"So, wait, if my dad was the alpha, he knew about the curse and the hexerei. Why would he keep it a secret from me? Why not come back here and let me help the pack like I'm clearly meant to do?"

"That's what I'd like to ask him myself."

Memories of my father washed over me in grief-filled waves. All of the lies, the running—and he'd been running from his own people. The ones who needed him most.

I didn't want to hate him, but it was becoming harder and harder.

Shoving aside my feelings, I focused on Oscar again.

"Okay, so what about another of the pack from that

time? Doesn't anyone know more about how this whole counterbalance or curse breaking thing works?"

"There aren't many of us left," he said. "Me, Teddy, and Warner—the twins' father—are about the only ones left from the inner circle. The ones who attended the meeting that day," he explained. "And now you know everything we know."

"What happened to everyone else?"

"Moved away mostly. When the alpha bond couldn't be remade, most left to find another pack they could tether to. Didn't want their kids and wives left exposed to the more baser instincts of our nature."

"Why doesn't everyone leave?" I asked. "Do the same thing?"

He shrugged. "For me, this is home. And I've managed to tame my beast enough to keep it controlled. Some of the younger ones come here, looking for a pack like ours. They've been kicked out of their own clans or abandoned—everyone has their reasons."

"So this became a sort of pack of misfits then." I couldn't help relating a bit to that.

"That doesn't make us all the same, Ash." He gave me a warning look. "Don't forget that a lot of them, Silas included, came here because there was no one to make them fall in line. They like that."

"You're saying some of them don't want the curse to be broken."

"I'm saying you need to watch your back, especially until we can figure out more about this. And about how to call your wolf up."

"That's fair." I sighed. "What I don't understand is why the hexerei haven't offered to reverse the spell. I thought you said you were in peace talks back when this all happened."

"The hexerei claim not to understand the magic used."

"You look unconvinced."

"All I know is the hexerei leaders ran off that day and have only caused problems since. They send spies to watch us. Spooks to infiltrate. But they refuse to communicate directly."

"What about the guy they found today? Can't they try talking to him?"

"They'll try," he said wryly, "Believe me. But it's never worked before, and I doubt it will now. Every one of them is either trained to withstand our methods, or they're magically bound to keep from talking. They're keeping something from us; we just don't know what."

"No wonder you see them as the enemy," I said.

"Look, Ash, you've stepped into the middle of a giant shitstorm. I need you to know I've got your back, no matter what happens, but we have to play this very carefully."

My heart warmed at his words. Danger aside, I felt a rush of gratitude for Oscar. It had been a very long time since I felt like it wasn't me against the world. At least, now it was me and Oscar. And the twins.

"Should I worry about Kai?" I asked. "Will he tell anyone about my mark?"

His expression clouded with something I couldn't read. But he shook his head. "Nah. He won't say anything."

"How do you know?"

"Kai's wolf likes you," he said simply.

I looked at him in surprise. And even though Kai had been an ass earlier, my heart fluttered at that.

"How do you know that?"

"I've known Kai his whole life, kid. Besides, I smelled it on him that night you saw him shift. Trust me, my beast is never wrong when it comes to scent." His lips quirked toward something like a smile.

"Well, maybe Kai's wolf and Kai should have a chat. Because Kai, the human, hates me."

Oscar snorted. "If he hated you, you'd already be gone."

I wasn't sure Oscar knew what he was talking about, but I was too worn out to argue it.

"Oh, almost forgot. Idrissa brought your bags of purchases over."

I followed where he'd pointed and spotted my shopping bags in the corner near my room.

"Thanks," I said in relief and gratitude. At least, now I wouldn't have to venture downtown again and risk Silas and Presley hunting me down for it.

Oscar pushed to his feet. "Look, get cleaned up, and call the twins. You can start training whenever they're available. I've got to get back downstairs. You good?"

I nodded. "Yeah, I'm good."

He headed for the door.

"Oscar?" I called.

"Yeah, kid."

I waited until he turned back and then flashed a grateful smile. "Thank you."

He grunted something unintelligible and then walked out. I smiled. The grunts were starting to become endearing.

~

The following morning, Isaac picked me up for our first training day. We rode with the top down, and I closed my eyes, letting the wind whip at my hair as I imagined myself on the back of a motorcycle.

"Did you get laid?"

Isaac's question had my eyes snapping open again.

"No," I said. "Why the hell are you asking me that?"

"You had this weird look on your face just now. Like you were thinking of an orgasm."

"I was not thinking of an orgasm," I said.

"Riiight." He shot me a wicked grin. "Does the orgasm have a name?"

"Isaac," I warned.

"Your orgasm is named Isaac?" he shrieked.

"No." I growled in frustration. "It's way too early for this."

"I think our friendship has progressed more than enough for you to discuss your crush."

"I mean early in the morning," I said pointedly.

"Right. Not a morning person. Here." He picked up a coffee from the cup holder and handed it to me.

"You're giving me your coffee?" I asked.

"Sure." He shrugged. "I'll get another when we get home."

I stopped mid-sip. "Okay, first, thank you. Our friendship is officially solidified by this selfless gesture. Second, home?"

"First, our friendship will be solidified when you tell me what happened between you and the delicious Kai Stone after he whisked you away on his sexy steed yesterday. And second, yes."

Sexy steed. That didn't deserve a response.

"Nothing happened. And whose home?"

"Don't believe you. And mine."

"Okay, can we have just one conversation at a time?" I asked.

At the same time, he said, "Kai," while I said, "I get to see your house?"

He shot me a look. "Baby girl."

I bit my lip.

"I've never been to a friend's house before," I explained.

His eyes widened. "What kind of sheltered, toxically conservative life did you lead?"

"The kind where I refused to bring people home to my alcoholic-paranoid father and was too afraid to leave him to go anywhere else."

I waited for some snarky-yet-endearing comment like maybe how my lack of social skills finally made sense. But Isaac didn't say a word as he pulled into a roughly paved driveway that led up to a gray, two-story house masked by shade trees.

In fact, there were trees everywhere. Woods encroached along the back and sides, offering direct access to secluded forest. Perfect for a family of wolf shifters. To the right of the house, a detached garage sat open with a partly disassembled motorcycle set up inside. Idrissa sat bent over in front of the bike, a white bandanna covering her fiery red hair.

Isaac parked and got out, coming around to meet me as I climbed out of the Mustang. He grabbed me and pulled me into a hug.

"What's this for?" I asked against his broad shoulder.

"For being my friend," he said, pulling away and planting a kiss directly on my mouth.

"Whoa, this isn't that kind of training session," Idrissa said, and Isaac turned his grin on her as she walked over from the garage, a dirty rag in hand.

"You're just jealous that I kissed her first," Isaac teased.

Idrissa shot him a look then me. "So, you two huh?"

"What? No, Isaac was just… It was a friendship kiss," I said firmly with a pointed look at Isaac. The way his eyes danced in amusement said he knew it had been nothing more, but he clearly wanted to rile Idrissa.

"Ugh. Don't piss her off right before she has to teach me to fight," I told him.

"Ohh, whoops, good point," he said, wincing.

Idrissa rolled her eyes. "Come on, you two. Let's go get some water and towels." She eyed me. "You're going to need it."

I had no idea what that meant and was pretty sure I didn't want to find out either. But I followed her and Isaac into the house and was greeted by the smell of bacon lingering in the air and the yapping shriek of what looked like a possible rodent.

"What the hell." I jumped back as a blur of tan fur ran at me.

Yapping barks nearly drowned out Isaac's voice as he exclaimed, "Galileo!"

Before the animal could attack my ankle, Isaac scooped the rodent into his arms and snuggled it close.

I blinked, relieved to realize he was not, in fact, snuggling a rat.

"Is that a dog?" I asked.

Isaac looked offended as he said, "Of course it's a dog. This is Galileo. Galileo, meet Ash." He held the dog high so they were eye to eye and said with authority, "She's a friend, not food."

Idrissa didn't even laugh, which made the whole thing even weirder.

"Should I be worried?" I asked.

Isaac held the dog out so I could pet it, which I only did from a place of good manners. The dog tried to bite my hand, so I jerked it back.

"No," Isaac said. "I mean, don't come over without one of us here, though. He's kind of protective of his space."

"I don't understand," I said, glancing between the twins then back to the dog that looked like it belonged on a Taco Bell commercial. "You guys are more than enough to protect this place…right?"

"Galileo is a chihuahua," Idrissa explained. "He's very territorial."

Isaac set the dog down, and it nipped at my pant leg then stood there, growling at me.

Idrissa rolled her eyes. "I'll put him up." She grabbed the dog and put him inside a small crate against the wall.

"Okay, not trying to insult your wolf side, but…I have questions," I said.

Isaac grinned. "You're learning."

"Isaac begged for a dog for years," Idrissa explained. "But every breed we tried was terrified of our beast. They could smell it on us and quickly became overwhelmed and traumatized by living with what they perceived as constant danger."

"But not Galileo," I said.

"Nope. That dog has BDE," Isaac said proudly.

"BDE?" I repeated, confused.

"Big dick energy," he explained. "He thinks he's ten feet tall. Hell, he thinks he could take all of us put together." He shrugged. "So, he's not scared."

"He's too stupid to be scared," Idrissa corrected. She elbowed me. "Don't be like Galileo, okay?"

"Got it," I said.

"Good. Come on."

Ignoring Galileo's barking, Idrissa led the way through the house. We passed a living room full of large, cozy furniture and cluttered with an array of items—socks, shoes, a remote tossed against a soft blanket. It wasn't messy, just lived in. All of the markers that made a house a home.

My eyes stung at the sight of it, and I tried to remember if my house—any of the dozens I'd had with Dad—had ever looked so lived in. Probably not unless empty beer cans counted.

"Isaac, is that you?" an older female's voice called out. "Your sister needs to get that pan of oil off my porch before I kick her ass for staining the paint."

I tensed as Idrissa stepped into the kitchen first and I followed.

"Message received, Mom," Idrissa said.

A blonde woman stood at the counter of the kitchen island, a knife poised against an onion. She looked up as we entered. Her eyes fell on me, and she smiled, lowering the blade.

"Oh. You must be Ash," she said.

"Hi," I said tentatively.

She dropped the knife as she came around the counter and grabbed me, pulling me into a hug before I knew what was happening.

"It's so nice to meet you," she said, drawing back again before I could fumble with hugging her back. "Isaac and Idrissa speak highly of you."

"Oh. Thanks. I… They're great."

Behind me, Isaac snorted.

"They're something, all right," she said with amusement and affection shining in her friendly brown eyes. "I'm Amberly, mother of these two heathens."

"Hey," Isaac protested.

Idrissa just snickered.

Amberly ignored them both as she said to me, "You're welcome here anytime, Ash."

Her words held just enough meaning that I knew she meant them. I also knew she was aware that I probably wasn't welcome anywhere else in this town. My shoulders relaxed.

"Thanks," I told her. "I really appreciate it."

"You just tell Oscar to stop wasting his time with those losers over at the Throttle and to hire my daughter already." Amberly glanced at Idrissa and the rag clutched in her greasy hands. "Get her mess out of my garage and into his."

I smiled. "I'll tell him."

"Good, and make sure to use those words too," she said. "Drake wouldn't know a brake cable from an internet cable anyway."

Isaac hooted. "You tell 'em, Ma."

"Don't start with me," she said, her eyes narrowing as she looked at him. "You still haven't replaced my blender, and don't think I'm going to forget."

"What happened to the blender?" I asked.

"Uh, you know what? Let's grab those waters and head out," Isaac said, steering me out and through the house toward the back. "We'll meet you out there, Dris," he called and then barreled through the back door with me in tow.

Idrissa called out something I couldn't hear as we hurried across the back deck and down the steps to the yard.

"Your mom is cool," I said.

Isaac snorted. "Sure, as long as you don't break her kitchen stuff."

"What's the deal with the blender?"

"It's classified."

We both turned as Idrissa walked out. She tossed us each a bottle of water and dropped a couple of towels on the bottom step before crossing to where we waited.

"Mom's ranting about that damned blender," she told Isaac.

He snorted, looking not a bit remorseful. "She'll get over it."

"I still can't believe you tried mixing your clay mold in that thing," Idrissa said. "If you hadn't broken it, I would have, because no way was I using it ever again after that."

"What clay mold?" I asked.

Isaac pretended not to hear me.

"He made a clay mold of his dick and then put it on the mantle in the living room," Idrissa said.

"Seriously?" I turned to stare at Isaac, who winked at me.

"Mom said she wished she'd kept more of our old artwork from school, so I decided to give her something to display."

"You just wanted to see Dad's face when he realized what it was," Idrissa said.

He shrugged. "And there's that."

"What happened?" I asked, unsure whether to laugh or be afraid for Isaac's life.

"Nothing," Idrissa said. "I moved it before the fallout could take place."

"Where did you move it?" I asked, but Idrissa only smirked.

"She won't tell me," Isaac said.

"And that's what's called sweet irony," she said.

I laughed. "So, your parents have no idea what you used the blender for?"

"Not a clue," Isaac said, grinning. "Yet."

"You're an idiot," Idrissa said.

"Why?" he protested. "I think Dad would be proud of me."

Idrissa shook her head and then turned to me. "Okay, you ready to do this?"

"Depends on what *this* is," I said, still laughing about Isaac's dick mold.

"For starters, we need to trigger your wolf," she said, and my smile vanished instantly.

"How?" I asked.

"Well, for most of us, shifting happens naturally around the age of puberty," she explained.

"Yeah, that didn't exactly happen for me," I said.

"I know, and I'm so sorry you had to grow up without a pack to support you, Ash. I can't imagine how hard this must be. Our wolves emerge because we're surrounded by our pack. And the first changes can be rough, which is why having another wolf or your pack with you through those first few shifts is so crucial."

"So, we need to call up my wolf or whatever?"

She nodded. "For starters."

"Okay." I blew out a breath. "Well, I can't exactly get a redo on puberty, so how exactly do you propose we call it?"

She hesitated. "The other option is to force it out due to a threat."

"A threat," I repeated. She nodded, and her words sank in. "You mean against me?"

She smirked. "Show me your hands."

"No way." I took a step back. "I saw what you did to Vinny. I'm not trying to get knocked out."

Idrissa rolled her eyes. "I'm not going to hurt you, Ash."

"Really? Because you just said you need to threaten me."

"Yes, but I can do that without knocking you out."

I scowled.

"Do you trust me?" she asked.

"Yes."

"Okay. Then show me your hands."

Reluctantly, I lifted my fists in front of my chest. "Like this?"

"Dear God," Idrissa muttered. "Isaac? If you would?"

He stepped up and crouched low, hands open, palms out. His eyes were sharp on hers. "Bring it, bitch."

Idrissa didn't say a word before she flew at him.

The next few seconds passed in a blur of punches, kicks, twists, and turns that left me dizzy by the end of it all. When they finally stopped, neither one had gotten a single hit in on the other, but I was positive I'd never seen two people more deadly.

Idrissa looked at me expectantly. "Got it?"

"Are you fucking kidding me?" I looked back and forth between them, realizing, for the first time since I'd volunteered myself, that I was inevitably going to get killed in that fight.

"Just put your hands up," Idrissa said impatiently.

I did as she asked and then was promptly tossed onto my ass.

Rubbing my hip, I glared up at her from the ground. "What the hell?" I demanded. "You said you weren't going to hurt me."

"You have to plant your feet," she said.

"This is going to take a while," Isaac said and wandered off to drag over a lawn chair.

I took a deep breath and climbed to my feet for round two.

~

Two hours later, my ass whooping was complete, but my wolf hadn't so much as stirred. Isaac had switched with Idrissa halfway through, and I now knew better than to think he would be easier on me than his badass sister. He was not.

If anything, he was harder because he "believed in me" as he put it. Between punches and kicks, he shouted inspirational quotes like "you only get out what you put in."

I wanted to punch him but damn if I landed a single swing on that encouraging mouth of his.

Sweaty, exhausted, and pretty convinced I was going to die in that fight, I sprawled on the grass and waited for my lungs to either fail me or recover. I'd surrendered to either option at this point.

Isaac stood over me, drizzling water into my open mouth. Idrissa tossed a towel at my feet and paced.

"You need some serious conditioning," she said.

"How does conditioning help trigger my wolf?" I asked, mostly because the thought of hard exercise kind of made me want to eat donuts and yell curse words.

"Our wolves need the freedom of running, especially on the full moon. If you offer that up, maybe she'll take the bait and want to join you," Isaac explained.

Idrissa nodded her agreement. "We'll start with running every morning."

I groaned.

"Push-ups, Sit-ups," she went on as if I hadn't spoken.

"The bag at the gym would help with the sense of threat," Isaac said.

She stopped and gave him a look. "Yes, except the gym is full of Silas and his crew."

"Assholes," Isaac muttered.

Idrissa went back to pacing. "You also need to work on your—"

"What's that?" Isaac asked.

I looked up at where he stood over me, bottle of water poised to pour into my mouth. He was staring at something on my stomach. I followed his gaze and realized with horror that my leggings had tugged down on my hips.

Shit.

The mark.

"Nothing," I said, pulling the waistline up as Idrissa marched closer.

"It looked like ink," Isaac said.

"It's my zodiac sign," I said.

Isaac gave me a weird look. Idrissa huffed.

"We need to focus," she said.

"I'm focused," I told her.

"Okay, but can we just take this break to go back to the elephant in the room?" Isaac asked, taking a seat beside me in the grass.

I braced myself for the question he was about to ask. I didn't want to lie to either of them. But Oscar had made it clear no one could know about the tattoo.

"What elephant?" Idrissa asked.

"Kai Stone took our girl here for a bike ride yesterday, and there's a serious gap in time from when they rode into the sunset and when he brought her home." Isaac wiggled his brows at me. "You said we're friends now, so spill."

Idrissa stopped pacing and looked over at me. "For once, I'm siding with my brother on this one."

"Traitor," I muttered.

She smirked.

"We're not getting any younger," Isaac declared pointedly.

"We're not aging either," Idrissa said with an eye roll.

"Wait, what?" I asked.

Isaac rolled his eyes. "Drissa is referring to the fact that wolves age differently than humans, which I will fully explain right after you tell me what went down. Was it Kai? Did Kai go down…on you?" He made a licking motion with his tongue, and I groaned.

"No," I said, but despite my protest, my cheeks heated. The very thought of Kai's mouth on my—

"She wants him to, though," Idrissa said with a smug smile.

My eyes widened. "No way," I protested, but it was a weak lie.

Idrissa's smile widened.

"Is he a good kisser?" Isaac asked.

"Isn't this conversation more middle school speed?" I asked. "Dishing about who kisses better?"

Isaac shrugged. "You said you never had friends. We're giving you the full tour. So… is he?"

"You've lived in town with him all your life, and you don't know?" I shot back. "I thought small-town gossip would have treated you better."

"Kai's never kissed anyone in town," Idrissa said.

I blinked. "Seriously?"

The twins shared a look with enough unspoken words I wondered if they had telepathic powers.

Idrissa answered aloud. "Kai's dad was one of the original pack members. He was the pack beta, actually," she said. "The rumors say he suffered when the alpha bond broke and it changed him."

"Changed him how?" I asked.

"Not for the better," Isaac said. His expression darkened.

"Kai's mom died in childbirth," Idrissa said. "And Kai's dad blamed him for her death."

"That's terrible. It wasn't his fault," I said.

"No shit, but Victor Stone wasn't someone you could explain things to." Isaac shook his head. "That guy was scary as hell."

"Was?" I echoed.

"He died a couple of years ago."

"Kai doesn't have family?" My heart hurt for Kai just thinking about it. I knew what it was like to grow up without a mom. And to have a dad who wasn't exactly Father of the Year.

"It's better this way," Isaac said. Idrissa shot him a look. "What? Kai's old man was fucking terrible to him. Everyone saw the bruises."

"That's horrible," I whispered.

"Kai's always kept to himself a little more than the rest of us," Idrissa said. "And he's always been tough as hell. He's undefeated among the other pack members, which has sort of made him our unofficial alpha."

"What about Oscar?" I asked. "He seems sort of important too."

"He's the leader of the elders," Idrissa explained. "Our council of original pack members is a sort of acting governing body for the pack, but they don't hold much sway these days, compared to the younger members."

"Like Kai," I said.

They both nodded. "Our wolves care about who's strongest," Idrissa explained.

"And that's our boy, Kai," Isaac added.

"That's why everyone acts like everything has to go

through him," I said. And why Silas and Drake deferred to him during my interrogation.

"They defer as much as their instinct will allow," she explained. "But it's not enough to settle our wolves completely."

"Or break the damn curse." Isaac tossed a piece of grass away, scowling.

"Kai told me about it," I said, and both of them looked up sharply.

"He did?" Idrissa asked.

A slow smile spread across Isaac's face. "He likes you."

"I don't know about that. He basically yells at me every time he sees me."

"For what?" Isaac asked.

"He says I shouldn't be here, that it's not safe, that I'm going to get killed, that I'm stupid. You know, friendly stuff like that."

Isaac snorted. "He's worried for your safety. It's hot."

Idrissa shook her head. "I hate to admit it, but I think Isaac's right. Kai's never shown interest in another female."

"We were beginning to think maybe he played for the other team," Isaac said, wiggling his brows.

"You hoped it," Idrissa corrected. "I never actually thought it."

Isaac sighed. "A girl can dream."

I laughed.

Idrissa's expression sobered. "But you should know there are other pack members who would love to take that alpha role out from under Kai."

"Silas?"

"For one," she said. "Just be careful. If they find out he's interested in you, it could make you a target."

I snorted. "I'm already a target."

Neither one bothered to argue that.

"So, does Kai want to be alpha?" I asked.

"He's never refused the recognition," Idrissa said. "Why?"

I didn't answer.

My thoughts were taking me into territory I wasn't sure I liked. For one, Kai knew about my mark. And according to him, whoever broke the curse would also become alpha of the pack. If he was in line to become alpha already, didn't that make me a threat to him?

The twins claimed he'd never shown interest in anyone before, which was a nice sort of flattery for me. Except what if he was only showing interest now in order to get close to the one person who threatened to take away the one thing he wanted? What if he was only manipulating me so he could get me to break the curse and then get me out of the way so he could claim his alpha role?

I needed to play this carefully. Idrissa was right. I was even more of a target than I'd thought. And I was done playing the victim in my life. It was time to take control.

17

For the next several days, I bounced between working at the Throttle and training with the twins. Idrissa and Isaac tag-teamed it so that I was constantly with one of them, sparring, conditioning, or doing some weird wolf-triggering exercise that Isaac dreamed up. None of it stirred my wolf to make an appearance, but it did exhaust me as a human, that was for damn sure. Every night, I fell into bed, too tired to panic about any of the terrifying things going on in my life.

Oscar and I maintained our routine. Work during the day. Dinner at night. He grilled me about my training, but he also spent time telling me stories about growing up in the Falls. He even told me a few about my father as a kid.

Silas and Presley left me alone. I didn't see them at all, which was both a relief and terrifying. They'd gotten what they wanted. I was going to fight. Even Drake left me alone, ignoring me or keeping our conversations strictly about work. Invoices. Customers. Not a single accusation that I was a witch or a spy for witches. Twice, I caught him studying my necklace, but I refused to break the silence between us to ask why. Instead, I made sure to always have it tucked away underneath my shirt after that.

Drake wasn't a good person.

I wasn't sure how I knew or why I knew, but the feeling only seemed to grow more certain with each passing day. Besides, he'd thrown me under the bus during my interrogation, and I wanted nothing to do with him.

I saw Kai mostly in passing, and even when I was forced to interact with him, it was brief and clipped. Just like before our kiss, he was distant and completely uninterested in me. The fact that he'd gone from hot to cold so thoroughly only fed my suspicions. He'd gotten close to me and tried to gain my trust so he could find my weakness, and now that the fight was looming, he'd left me to face it on my own. Hell, maybe he didn't even care about breaking the curse so long as I was out of the picture.

That hurt way more than I wanted to admit, and despite his betrayal, I felt the constant tug to be near him. When he was in the shop, I knew exactly where he was. Like a hot-guy GPS, except I was pretty sure it was my lady parts pointing the way.

At least, Devon and the other guys had stopped coming around to flirt with me. I did wonder if Kai had something to do with that, but I wasn't about to ask him either.

At night, when my eyes were drooping closed from exhaustion, Oscar talked to me about wolf culture and proper etiquette for when the fight came. I tried not to let it terrify me more when he talked about deferring to a stronger beast by showing my belly. Or never turning my back on a threat.

I was definitely going to die.

There was no way around it.

I could either run and risk them hunting me down—not to mention Vorack—or march myself right into the executioner's arena.

Sometimes, I wondered what my dad would think if he could see me now. He'd said, "Don't let them put you in a cage," and in some ways, that's exactly what he'd done when he'd died and sent me here.

But I couldn't hate him.

He was my dad, and he'd loved me the best way he'd known how.

That would have to be enough.

To escape the constant stress of my own thoughts, I poured myself into learning the client invoicing system and motorcycles in general. Oscar had trained me on the basics, and I was using my free time between customers to go back and audit any unpaid invoices he had. And Google motorcycle parts I didn't understand.

My phone rang while I was knee-deep in line items and part names I had never heard of.

"Hey," I said when I saw Idrissa's name pop up on my screen.

"Hey, I need to bail on our training session tonight," she said. "My dad's taking me to an auction in Grandville to see about this DRZ."

"I don't know what those letters mean, but okay. Have fun?" I said uncertainly.

She laughed. "It's a dirt bike I've been drooling over forever, so yes, it'll be fun."

"Okay, cool. What about Isaac?"

There was a pause and muffled voices talking in the background. I recognized Amberly, the twins' mom, and then Idrissa came back on the line. "He said he's giving you the night off. Take a bath in some Icy Hot or something." She snickered. "You probably need it."

My muscles twitched in excitement over the idea of having a rest day, but I shook my head. "I can't afford a night off," I said. "Who knows when this thing will happen."

"Relax, Ash. You need to give your body a chance to recover."

"Tell Isaac I'll come by after work and run some laps. He doesn't need to do anything."

"Can't. He's going out with some chick he met online with a foot fetish." Idrissa shrieked as Isaac apparently responded to that by trying to inflict violence on her.

The next minute was filled with curses and screams and shrieks—from both of them. It would have been funny if I hadn't been so caught up in the lost training.

"I have to go," Idrissa said, breathless.

"Okay, call me tomorrow," I said.

"Bye!" The call ended before she'd finished yelling the word.

I sighed and set my phone aside, returning to the invoice I'd been deciphering with much less enthusiasm.

An hour later, Kai walked in from the garage. He tossed a job order onto the counter.

"This one's ready," he said.

"Got it."

I didn't even look up from the invoice I'd been studying for the last ten minutes. Kai's presence was something I felt on a subconscious level, and no matter how many times he went in and out, my physical reaction hadn't dimmed. Heart racing, palms sweating, stomach full of butterflies. But that didn't mean I had to acknowledge it. Or him.

This time, he didn't immediately walk out again. Instead, he inched closer to where I sat leaning toward the computer screen.

Finally, I looked over and found him watching me.

"What?" I asked.

"Drive shaft," he said.

"Excuse me?"

"That code you're staring at on that invoice means we replaced the drive shaft."

I blinked. "Oh."

Awkward silence fell between us.

I did not want to talk about drive shafts. Not unless it was code for exactly what I wanted Kai to do to me. My cheeks heated just thinking about it, and I looked away, determined not to let Kai see that I still wanted him even after his shitty treatment of me this past week.

"You're welcome," he said flatly then turned and walked out.

"Ugh."

I didn't see him again for the rest of the day. The only reason I knew he'd left was because I watched him ride by on his motorcycle as he exited the back lot and turned onto the main road.

Whatever.

I didn't care.

Hot, broody wolf shifters could go to hell.

Muttering curses, I flipped the "Open" sign off and locked up, heading upstairs. A night off from training meant sticking to my normal dinner routine with Oscar. I'd prep and cook, and by the time he came upstairs from closing up shop, it was ready to eat. Not a terribly equal system, but I didn't mind. It beat living on the street. Or worse. With Vorack.

"I bet your dad loved your cooking," Oscar said around a mouthful of baked potato.

"Maybe." I gave a small smile, but instead of holding it back like I would have with other people, I told him the truth. Dad was his brother, after all. And I'd already laid my cards out on the table, so to speak. There were no more secrets between us. "Dad stopped showing for family meals a long time ago."

"I'm sorry, kid."

"It's fine. Honestly, I preferred it that way. Other times, he did show up and then passed out in his plate or fell out of his chair."

"Shit, Ash. That's not… You shouldn't have had to deal with that."

I shrugged. "I'd rather that than—"

I fell silent.

"Can I ask you something?" I said after another bite.

"Shoot."

"Was my dad happy here? Before he left, I mean."

"I thought so," he said, his forehead wrinkling in thought. "Then again, I thought we were close too. Turns out I was wrong since he didn't bother telling me he was leaving in the first place. Or about you. Hell, I wouldn't have minded a niece to hang out with from time to time."

My heart cracked wide open at that. Grief. Love. So many emotions overwhelmed me as I pictured what life would have been like if we'd stayed.

"Once, when he was really drunk, he told me I was his greatest pride," I admitted. "And his worst mistake."

Oscar shook his head, looking pissed now.

"Your dad clearly became a different person than the brother I knew. Hell, Ash. If I'd known—" Oscar's voice was gruff as he stared down at his plate.

I reached out and grabbed his hand.

When he looked up, I shook my head. "It's not yours to apologize for. Besides, eating my dinners is enough."

He nodded.

I released his hand.

The urge to cry welled in my throat, and I swallowed it back, along with another bite of green beans. I had a feeling Oscar's warm-fuzzy quota had just been met. Hell, so had mine. I wasn't about to add to it with waterworks. But, for the first time in a lot of years, I was looking forward to future family dinners, and that brought a strange sort of grief-gratitude that I didn't know how to process.

Oscar did the dishes, which also nearly brought me to tears.

"Seriously, if you're going for Uncle of the Year, it's a lock," I told him.

"Funny," he deadpanned. "Don't you have training to get to?"

"Right. I..." I almost told him training had been canceled. But at the last minute, I changed my mind. "I better get going," I finished.

Grabbing my shoes and a sweatshirt, I slipped out and down the stairs before Oscar could somehow sense my lie.

It was stupid.

Completely reckless, actually. There were way too many wolves in this town who had it out for me. Going out alone was insane.

But I also couldn't afford to lose a night of training. Not with the fight coming. Besides, if I slipped into the woods out back, no one would notice. I could be home before anyone knew I was really alone.

It wasn't combat training. But a quick run was better

than nothing. And for the first time in, well, ever, I actually had the urge to stretch my legs this way. Hopefully, that was a good sign.

Downstairs, I stopped to slide into my shoes and then unlocked the door and slipped outside. It wasn't quite dark yet, and the setting sun cast long shadows across the sidewalk. The chilled mountain air was perfect.

I paused at the corner to stretch. With my arms dangling and fingers brushing my toes, I jumped at the sound of a voice behind me.

"I'm not sure stretching will help your odds much. Considering."

I straightened and whirled to see Drake slouched against the brick, eyeing me with a mixture of amusement and appreciation. It was a good bet he'd just been staring at my ass.

He hadn't spoken to me much since the night they'd captured the hexerei and interrogated me as a possible accomplice. And I wasn't sure I wanted to talk now. But I needed all the advice I could get.

"What *will* help?" I asked.

He gave me a once over. "Calling up your wolf wouldn't hurt."

I sighed. "Anything else?"

"Yeah, don't let them past your elbows."

My expression must have given away my confusion because he added, "If they get that close—wolf or human—you're dead."

"Thanks," I said dryly.

Super helpful.

"You could still leave, you know."

My eyes narrowed. "Nice try. You're not getting rid of me that easily."

It was an idea I'd considered more than once, but the

thought of leaving Oscar made me strangely upset. He was my family. And the closest thing to a safety net I'd ever had. I couldn't bring myself to give that up—no matter how risky it was to stay.

I pulled my ankle up behind me, stretching my quads. Out of the corner of my eye, I watched Drake. He didn't move to leave, and I couldn't help but wonder what his end game was. When we were alone, he talked to me like I might actually be someone he wanted to help. But when the others came around, he shut down and went right along with Silas and the rest.

I didn't trust him.

When I'd stretched both legs, I turned and looked back pointedly at where Drake still watched me with unabashed interest. Ugh. Asshole.

"Thanks for the help," I said, not bothering to leave the sarcasm out of my voice.

He pushed off the wall and walked over to where I stood. "Look, leaving is the only way to survive this, okay?"

"Noted and rejected," I said, refusing to back down or look away. He held my gaze so long that I felt like a kindergartener in a staring contest. Still, I didn't look away. Drake was a prick. But I'd hold my ground and just pray this wasn't some distraction to keep me here until Silas and the gang could show up and kick my ass.

Finally, Drake sighed. "If I were you, I'd check out exactly what it is I'm up against."

I frowned. "What do you mean?"

"You want to know what the fights are like?"

I nodded.

"There's a large barn in the field behind Bo's. Don't let anyone see you."

He shook his head like I'd brought this on myself then

turned and sauntered off. I watched him go, wanting to ask all sorts of questions about what he'd just said. Like what the hell would be in that barn, for starters. But I let him go. He clearly wanted me to find out for myself, and that's exactly what I planned to do.

18

It was probably a trap. I mean, I wasn't stupid. Okay, maybe a little stupid. I had taken the bait, after all. Up ahead, a large building loomed in the darkness. Light spilled out from around the closed doors, and the low hum of voices reached me where I crouched at the edge of the woods.

I'd taken a roundabout way here.

After Drake had left, I'd gone for that run after all. Jogging a good portion of the way up the road—my stamina only made possible by Idrissa's training—and then cutting through the trees before anyone from the pack could recognize me.

Drake hadn't been lying about the barn. There were definitely wolves here. I'd watched and waited until cars began to drive up. Not many. Most of the people I'd seen arrive had also come from the woods. Cade. Devon. Tiffany. I recognized quite a few of the faces.

Luckily, none of them had passed close enough by where I'd hidden for me to be discovered. Some had loped along as wolves until they'd reached the edge of the trees. I'd watched several of them shift back to their human form before heading to the back of a pickup where someone had apparently stashed extra clothes for them. No one seemed concerned with nudity, which was a whole new level of weirdness in itself. Still, watching the wolves was fascinating. I would have been lying if I'd said it wasn't cool as hell, watching the change come over their bodies.

Like magic.

Life was wild.

I still wished Dad had told me instead of keeping his secrets and then drowning them inside a bottle. But I also wasn't entirely sure I would have believed him. Not without seeing it like this.

My fascination turned to nerves as a familiar white car drove off the main road and bypassed the bar. I watched as the Mustang parked in the grass and Isaac and Idrissa got out and hurried toward the barn doors.

My heart twisted at the sight of them disappearing inside. They'd lied. Both of them. And they'd ditched me for…whatever this was.

More secrets.

It never ended with these people.

I waited as a few others arrived and the moon rose high overhead. The night air was chilled but not cold. My goosebumps were more from nerves. I had to get inside, and that meant sneaking past a hell of a lot of wolves in the process. If it was a trap, it was a terrible one. I mean, it was obvious I was walking into the den of my enemies.

From inside the barn, voices rose to a yell, and my curiosity won out. I had to know what it was Drake wanted me to see.

I crept closer, keeping low and hurrying across the open field toward the back of the barn. When I reached the back wall, I dropped to the ground and waited, sucking in deep breaths of air to calm my racing heart. My ears strained for any sound that meant I'd been discovered, but so far, so good. When I was fairly certain I wouldn't hyperventilate, I lifted up slowly onto my knees. The barn wall was made of wood that was probably newly constructed at least half a century ago. Time and age had left gaps between the boards, and I scooted closer and peered through the largest one.

Inside, I saw a small crowd gathered. Several were faces I recognized. Idrissa and Isaac. Silas. Drake. Presley. And Oscar.

I felt the sting of betrayal all over again as the sight of him registered. More secrets. More people keeping things from me.

Why had I ever expected any different?

The crowd stood assembled and facing me. For a panicked moment, I wondered if they'd all spotted me through the gap. But then a pair of legs moved into view just inside, and I realized they were looking at whoever stood facing them now.

There was a grunt and a shove and then another figure stumbled forward. The legs strode ahead, and I recognized the back of Silas' head as he grabbed at the shirt of his prisoner before the man could stumble and fall on his face.

When he turned his head to the side, I recognized the prisoner too. Even through the dried blood coating his face and clothes.

The hexerei.

"This asshole says he wants to defect," Silas called to the crowd.

The crowd booed, and even from out here, I could feel their energy building toward something dangerous. The hexerei seemed to know it too. His eyes were wide with fear through the swollen bruising around them.

"But hey, rules are rules," Silas said with a devious smile playing on his lips. "Anyone's welcome to join us so long as they fight for their place among our pack. Am I right?"

Cheers sounded, and my stomach clenched at what was to come. They were going to make the hexerei fight? In his condition? As a human? It wasn't fair. Which was obviously the point.

Shifting my position, I searched the faces for someone who might actually be sane enough to put a stop to this. But Idrissa and Isaac were no longer visible at the front of the crowd. Neither was Oscar.

Figured.

They all claimed to be against this cruel idea of forcing people to fight, but when it mattered, they disappeared.

"As you all know, new challengers are paired with who we deem their equal. Gotta keep the fights fair," he added, and people snickered.

Silas turned to the hexerei and put his hand on the guy's shoulder. "Don't worry, man. We've paired you with someone your speed. Gordon, come on up, man."

The name was familiar, and the moment I spotted him, I remembered why. He'd been the drunk who'd started the brawl at Bo's that first day I'd met the twins. He clearly hadn't been sober then. And he looked even more wasted tonight.

The crowd cheered again and then parted as a very drunk-looking Gordon was brought forward by Presley. I watched with disgust as Presley shoved Gordon into the center. Gordon stumbled and righted himself again, looking up with bleary eyes at Silas and then the hexerei.

"What's this?" Gordon grumbled.

"This asshole wants to join the pack," Silas told him.

Gordon sniffed, his lip curling up in distaste. "He ain't even a wolf."

"Doesn't matter. Rules are rules."

Gordon muttered something that sounded like "lupin hater."

A few people in the crowd laughed.

"You're up, old man," Silas said, clapping Gordon on the back.

"This is bullshit," Gordon muttered, and the crowd responded by yelling encouragements.

Silas spread his arms wide. "You want a place here with us," he said to the hexerei. "Fight for it."

From somewhere in the back, a bell rang. Silas stepped back, and the hexerei crouched, eyeing Gordon with a look of expectancy. Gordon stood, knees half-bent, swaying a little.

The hexerei must have sensed the advantage because he darted in and swung out. Gordon grunted as the hexerei's fist landed against his jaw. The blow drove him sideways, but he still managed to remain standing, and when he swung his head around again, he was glaring, and his eyes were suddenly glowing with animalistic instinct.

Gordon let out a roar and charged the hexerei, tackling him to the dirt floor. They rolled, each of them grunting and landing kicks and punches against the other. Clumsy, half-ass punches that didn't seem to faze either one.

It was ridiculous.

Drake wanted me to watch a drunk and an already beaten man fight it out? What the hell good would that do me?

It hit me then.

Drake was making fun of me.

He thought this was the recon I needed. Because this was the level of fighting he expected from me.

Asshole.

A snarl snapped me out of my internal raging, and I looked through the gap again just in time to leap aside as the two fighters tossed one another against the wall where I'd hidden.

Something crashed as I landed against the cold grass, and when I rolled over and looked up, I saw they'd broken clean through. They were outside now, still fighting but mostly just breathing heavily and swinging at nothing but air.

Neither one of them noticed me, but before I could get out of sight, Silas ducked through the hole they'd torn in the barn wall. His eyes landed on me instantly, and he smiled.

I froze.

Behind him, a few others trickled out. Drake. Presley. The rest of the faces were familiar by now too, and that wasn't a good thing. Every one of them wore a matching expression. Just like Silas, their smiles made every muscle in my body coil in readiness.

"Well, well, if it isn't Ashes. Huh. It looks like we're adding another fight to the roster tonight." Silas grinned.

"Hell yeah," one of the others echoed.

I looked right at Drake. "You're an asshole for this," I said.

"And you're naïve for expecting anything less."

I huffed.

He was right.

I only had myself to blame.

Slowly, I got to my feet. A few yards away, the hexerei had Gordon pinned. He was oblivious to us—or maybe knew better than to let up while he had the advantage—and pummeled Gordon with blow after blow.

Blood covered Gordon's face, and I winced at the damage being done to him. At least, he was probably too far gone to feel the pain.

"Hey," Presley said, finally tearing his hungry gaze off me long enough to notice Gordon's predicament. He went over and yanked the hexerei off Gordon by the back of the man's collar.

The man swung wildly, landing a sucker punch against Presley's chin. It was nothing more than a graze, but Presley's eyes narrowed, and he released the hexerei, his breaths coming in short bursts. His hands fisted, and he glared at the male witch, eyes practically glowing orange now.

"You shouldn't have done that, spook," Presley said in a low voice.

The air between them rippled.

Silas backed up, and the others followed.

I didn't need a crash course in Shifter 101 to know what was about to happen. And if Presley shifted on the hexerei, that guy had zero chance of surviving this night.

"Am I fighting or what?" I said loudly, stepping forward and drawing everyone's attention back to me.

Presley looked over and blinked, some of the rage in his eyes cooling as he refocused.

"Shit, when you put it like that," Silas said. "What are we waiting for?"

The guys around him whooped, eyes locked on me like I'd just become their midnight snack.

"You'll need to be paired, of course," Silas went on.

His eyes never left mine though.

"Of course," I said, refusing to back down.

My mind raced with possibilities. That Tiffany girl looked like someone I could take. She probably fought dirty though. Hair pulling. Clawing. I could make that work.

Except for the whole wolf part.

Shifting was still out of reach—a fact my opponent was about to find out.

I knew they could smell my fear. Probably even sense my slick palms. But I couldn't back down now. Out of the corner of my eye, I saw the hexerei watching me with interest.

"Silas!"

Idrissa shoved her way through the hole in the wall. The others moved aside. The ones who didn't move fast enough got shoved. Behind her was Isaac. He took one look at the scene unfolding and then reached over and grabbed one of the fallen scraps of wood. The others backed away from him, and he slid toward me.

"What the hell?" Idrissa demanded, looking first at me and then at Silas. "We had a deal. You promised me she'd have more time."

I blinked. "What?"

"She showed up on her own," Silas protested. "And then volunteered to fight."

Idrissa looked at me in disbelief. "Tell me this isn't true."

"You made a deal?" I asked her.

She didn't answer.

Oscar stepped through the opening, and his eyes landed on me. "Ash, what the hell are you doing here?"

"What do you think?" Silas answered for me.

Oscar rushed forward, stepping between me and Silas.

"She's not fighting tonight," Oscar said. "In fact, I thought she was with the twins until they showed up," he muttered, shooting Idrissa a dark look.

"She volunteered," Drake said.

I glared at him.

"This is bullshit," Idrissa said.

"Let her go," Oscar said, his voice a low growl. "She doesn't belong here, and you know it."

My hands fisted at that. I knew Oscar was just trying to protect me, but if one more person told me I didn't belong, I was going to scream.

"Well, someone ought to explain that to her then," Silas bit out. "She's the one who crashed our party."

Drake shot me a smug look, and I gritted my teeth. New goal. Get strong enough to kick Drake's ass.

"Besides, she's seen too much to remain an outsider," Silas went on. He gestured to the hexerei. "She can't be allowed to keep walking around with our secrets. Not until she proves herself."

"She will," Oscar said. "But not tonight. You already went too far, putting Gordon through this. Look at him. He's—"

Oscar stopped, and I followed his gaze to where Gordon had been lying in his own blood.

Now he was gone.

The hexerei held up his hands. "It wasn't me," he said.

"Like hell." Presley started for him, and the hexerei backed away.

A blur of movement startled me, and I watched as a

huge gray wolf leaped from the trees, its claws aimed straight for the hexerei.

Someone screamed.

It might have been me.

Everyone moved at once.

Oscar shoved me back toward the corner of the barn that remained intact. Most of the others backed off to give the wolf space. Presley and Silas rushed forward, straight at the oncoming wolf. Presley grabbed the wolf, using his arms to take it down in a sort of hug-tackle that pinned the wolf's claws to its body. Halfway to the ground, Presley shifted and knocked the wolf back again, this time with four paws. Silas went for the hexerei.

My breath caught as I watched, terrified Silas was going to end the guy's life right here and now. But instead, he pulled the hexerei back into the barn and away from Gordon-the-drunk-and-murdery-werewolf.

"Relax, spook, tonight's not your night," Silas said as they ducked back inside. "We aren't done with you quite yet."

The way he said the words sent a shiver down my spine.

Then Oscar was in my face, forcing my attention on him. "Listen to me You're going to take these keys." He pressed his truck keys into my palm so hard that it hurt. "You're going to drive home and lock yourself inside and not open the door for anyone. Do you hear me?"

He sounded pissed.

And honestly, so was I.

But I also wanted to live.

"Yes," I said.

"Good. Now—"

"Ahh!" Someone yelled, and we looked over to see

Cade, one of Silas' goons, cupping his face. "That asshole Gordon just tried clawing my damned face off."

"Get his ass," said Luke.

A second later, the two had shifted and launched themselves at where Presley had nearly calmed Gordon into retreating. After that, everything turned to chaos.

People poured from the barn, screaming and shifting as they ran.

Brawls broke out with everyone in various stages of shifting.

"Don't move," Oscar warned, shoving me flat against the barn wall.

He didn't have to tell me twice. More and more wolves filled the field, trapping me against the barn. I knew if I moved, they'd notice me, and there was no way I could talk my way out of a fight now.

It would be one against thirty.

"Ash."

I turned at the sound of the familiar voice behind me.

Kai stood against the barn just behind me, eyes blazing, chest heaving like he'd run here. His clothes were a little baggy, though, and I remembered the extras in the bed of that truck.

Oscar looked past me at Kai.

"She's a sitting duck," Oscar said.

"I'll get her out of here," Kai said. "Can you create a distraction?"

Oscar nodded. "Don't let anything happen to her."

"I'll keep her safe," Kai said.

He didn't look at me, but the way he said it...

Nope. Wasn't going to acknowledge the butterflies.

Oscar nodded, apparently satisfied. He looked at me, eyes blazing with whatever he was about to do.

"When they turn on me, you go," Oscar said.

"What?" My eyes widened in sudden worry. "No, don't—"

But he was already gone.

I watched as he threw himself at the closest wolf. "I challenge Silas!" he roared.

I gasped. "He can't," I said, but Kai was already grabbing my hand and yanking me toward the front of the barn.

I had no choice but to run or let Oscar's sacrifice be a waste.

19

Kai's hand was tight and warm in mine. I concentrated on that. And on the motorcycle I recognized as his, parked behind Oscar's truck. So, he hadn't come here as a wolf after all. My feet barely made a sound against the grass, but my breath? That came in loud, short gasps as we zig-zagged through the parked cars toward Kai's motorcycle. Behind us, I could hear growls and the occasional curse being yelled.

I tried not to think about what was happening. And to whom.

Werewolf hierarchy still confused me, but I was pretty sure Oscar challenging Silas would not end well.

My heart panged at the mental images.

Kai yanked me to a stop beside his motorcycle and grabbed the helmet. He didn't bother handing it over and instead shoved it onto my head and threw a leg over the bike without bothering to snap the helmet in place.

"Ash," he said urgently. "Ash, we have to go."

"Oscar," I said, the word sounding more like a desperate sob.

"He'll be fine," he said, meeting my eyes. "I swear it. But if we don't get you out of here, it's going to get ugly. Come on."

He was right. I had no choice but to trust him.

He started the bike, and I swung my leg over, wrapping my arms around his chest and clinging tightly. From somewhere out in the field, a wolf howled.

Kai kicked the bike into gear and pinned the throttle. We shot forward, and I gasped as the back tire slid left then right, looking for traction. Then we hit pavement, and the tires realigned as we sped off.

We drove for miles and miles.

Up winding mountain roads. Around curves that hugged guard rails.

I stopped waiting for any one of the wolves we'd left behind to appear from the woods beside us and started to relax. The adrenaline waned, and the fear turned to shock. My hands trembled and eyes burned with tears at what had happened. Or, more specifically, what could have happened.

If Idrissa hadn't come outside.

If Kai hadn't shown up.

If Oscar hadn't created that diversion.

By the time Kai pulled off at an overlook, I was a mess. Which, in Ash-talk, meant I was pissed at the world.

Kai cut the engine, and I climbed off the motorcycle, moving far enough away so that he couldn't bump into me when he climbed off too. I looked out at the open view that, in daylight, probably would have been gorgeous. Now, it was just a shadowy space where the mountaintop ended and the empty air beyond reached out to meet us. A guard rail separated me from the edge, and I stared at it, my thoughts jumbled.

In the silence, the night creatures melded into a

symphony of noise I'd come to find soothing. Kai's expression when I looked up, however, was anything but.

"I swear to God, Kai, if you say I wasn't supposed to be there, I will push your bike right over the edge of this mountain."

He smirked, and for some reason, that was worse.

"Don't look at me like that," I snapped.

"Like what?" he asked.

"Like we're friends. We're not friends. We're not even friendly. We're nothing."

"Nothing is a strong word for a guy who just saved your ass."

"Don't talk about my ass."

His lips twitched. "Got it. What can I talk about?"

"Oscar." My lip wobbled, so I bit down on it until I could trust my voice again. "Will he be okay?"

"Oscar will be fine."

"How do you know?"

"Because I've seen Oscar fight. He's going to kick Silas' ass."

"Really?"

"Really."

I exhaled.

"Can we talk about you now?"

"I don't know." My temper returned. "Can you say something nice?"

He smirked again, and I glared.

"Well?" I demanded when he didn't respond.

"You're really great at invoices."

"Ugh. I'm going home." I started for the road, furious. Asshole Kai was horrible. Silent treatment Kai sucked too. But teasing Kai could go right to hell.

Kai appeared beside me. "Umm, home is the other way."

"Not that home," I said through clenched teeth.

"Whoa. What?" Kai jogged in front of me and put a hand on either shoulder, stopping me in my tracks. His voice gentled. "Ash, you can't leave."

"Last I checked, it wasn't up to you." I yanked free and stepped around him, resuming my trek down the empty road.

Kai grabbed my hand, pulling until I was forced to turn and face him.

His expression was soft now. I hated it.

"It's not safe if you leave."

"Thanks for the concern, but I'll be fine."

"Ashes."

He was still talking in that soothing voice, and after getting the cold shoulder, it did something to me. Or maybe it was my near-death experience. I'd had a few lately. Either way, my insides stirred in a way that pissed me off even more. Why did Kai Stone have to be so damn yummy? And yet, so damn rude?

"Stop saying my name like that," I said. "And what is with the dumbass nickname, anyway?"

He hesitated, his brow lifting. "You don't know?"

"It's funny that you actually think anyone tells me anything in this town."

"Right." He looked a little sheepish. "I might have started it after you came in that first night with those bruises."

"You thought it was makeup," I remembered.

"Yeah. I might have told Silas and the others that it looked like you rubbed soot on your face."

I stared at him, not sure whether to punch him or leave him standing here. "Ashes. Soot. You're an asshole. Got it."

"Wait." He stared at me, his eyes full of moonlight. "I'm

sorry," he said, and out of all the things I imagined him telling me tonight, those words definitely hadn't been on the list.

"For what?" I asked warily. Maybe it was another trick.

"For treating you so badly before. You didn't deserve that."

I watched him carefully. "Just like that? You're sorry?"

"I know, my apology probably means shit. But I did save your ass. More than once. So, I hope you'll forgive me after tonight."

"Is this a trick?" I looked around, eyeing the woods with newfound worry. "Is Drake out there? Or Silas?"

"No one's out there," he assured me.

Then he stepped closer.

"It's just me. Asking your forgiveness."

"Okay, who are you, and what have you done with the real Kai Stone?"

He smirked again, and I found myself fighting the urge to lick where his mouth creased around that smile.

"I deserve that. I deserve all of it. I've been—"

"An asshole?"

"That's not the word I would have used but okay. I've been an asshole."

"And now you're not," I said tentatively.

"Now, I'm not."

"What changed exactly?"

He hesitated. "It's complicated," he said quietly then rushed to cut me off before I could unleash exactly what I thought of that answer. "But I am on your side, Ash. I hope you can believe that."

"I don't know what to believe," I said. "Everyone has their own agenda. Everyone wants something from me. None of it good. Most of it ends with my ass being kicked, killed, or worse."

I stepped back, dropping his hand. Mostly because I wanted to keep holding it, and that terrified me even more than Silas and Drake ever would.

"You told me I was yours," I said, "And then you acted like it never happened."

"Yeah, that was a dick move."

I snorted.

"Ash, that mark on your skin..."

"You don't have to explain," I said harshly. "I know I'm a threat to you. Idrissa told me everything."

His eyes narrowed. "What exactly did Idrissa say?"

"That if the curse is broken, you'd be alpha. That maybe you don't want the curse broken at all. Either way, I'm a threat to you. No wonder you kept me close. Pretended to like me. So you could keep tabs on me and make sure I didn't mess up what you have going here."

"Is that what you think?"

"What else is there?"

"More than you'd understand. Hell, more than I understand myself."

"Try me. You'd be amazed at what I can comprehend when I rub two brain cells together."

He didn't answer.

I growled in frustration. "That's right. I forgot; this town loves its secrets almost as much as it loves keeping me from discovering any of them."

I started to walk off again, but this time he didn't have to touch me to make me go completely still.

"My wolf wants to claim you."

Every muscle in my body froze as his words washed over me.

I didn't turn. I didn't even breathe.

"Is that enough of a secret for you?"

His voice rose, and I knew I'd pissed him off. I also

couldn't understand what he was telling me. Slowly, I turned around and studied his expression. Something dark and wild flashed in his eyes. But the softness he'd used with me tonight still remained.

"Claim me how?" I asked, even though I damn well knew that could only mean one thing to a wolf shifter like Kai.

"As its mate."

The words were soft, so low I almost missed them. My pulse stuttered, and I sucked in a sharp breath, trying to wrap my head around what he was saying. Part of me wanted to go to him, to wrap my arms around him and let it happen. But after the roller coaster that was Kai Stone, I hesitated.

"I thought finding your mate was impossible," I said. "The curse…"

He snorted. "Yeah, I thought so too. But here we are."

"I don't understand. Does that mean…the curse is broken?"

He shook his head. "If it were, my wolf would sense a pack connection, or at the very least, I think there'd be others coming forward with a mate claimed."

"So, this is just about you and me then?"

"I think so. It must have something to do with you being the curse breaker. Like, you're immune to the effects of the curse, and that's how we're able to recognize one another."

"Can I ask…what do you feel? I mean, how do you know I'm your mate and not just some girl you like?"

He laughed. "Fair question. Well, for starters, I feel pulled to you even when I'm not in the same room, though it's much stronger when I'm close enough to see you."

I didn't bother telling him I knew exactly what he

meant. That I'd been experiencing it since the moment I'd laid eyes on him that night at Oscar's.

"What else?"

"Aside from the fact that I want to rip out the throat of every male who comes within fifty feet of you?" He paused, and his amusement vanished.

"Devon," I said. "The day he came in and tried to flirt with me."

Kai's expression darkened, and I remembered how upset Kai had gotten. But how had he known to show up at that moment?

"How did you know to come out and stop him?" I asked.

He watched me carefully as he said, "I can feel what you feel, Ash."

"Like, you can read my mood?" I asked.

He nodded. "Something like that."

My eyes narrowed, and I tried not to think about how I'd been sort of doing that with him too. This shit was crazy. It couldn't be real…right?

"What am I feeling right now?" I challenged.

He cocked his head, studying me. "A little fear. Not for me but for what this means, I think. And excitement." A slow grin spread. "Pleasure." He stepped closer and whispered, "Desire."

He inhaled deeply.

"I've been able to smell that since the moment we parked," he added.

My cheeks heated, but I didn't deny any of it. How could I when he could sense it anyway?

"What about you, Ash?"

I took a step back, suddenly defensive. "What about me?"

"Can you sense my feelings?"

"Um."

He stepped closer, closing the gap I'd made between us.

My heart raced.

"I can tell when you're pissed," I said. "But that's not hard. You're always pissed."

He laughed.

"Fair. I've been seriously frustrated lately. What do I feel right now?"

I frowned as the awareness came over me. Had I really not noticed this strange ability before? Or was I chalking it up to my own overworked imagination playing tricks?

"You're worried about me," I said. "And you're trying to take this slow so I don't freak out."

He threw his head back and laughed out loud. It startled me. The sudden burst of joy I felt from him sent a wave of happiness through me, and I found myself smiling back at him.

This explained so much. Why my thoughts and emotions had been so consumed by him since the moment I'd arrived. Even in the middle of my grief, Kai had been a focal point. A beacon. And looking back, I realized he'd been the thing that had helped heal me too. When he was around, I felt better. Was that part of being someone's mate?

"Okay, you've proved your point," I said. "Although, I'm not sure how I'm able to feel you when I'm not even a wolf."

"You *are* a wolf," he said. "She's in there. Or this wouldn't be possible."

My smile faded. "But Kai, according to the curse, this *isn't* possible."

"I know." He sighed. "That's what I've been trying to figure out. Our wolves shouldn't be able to recognize a mate. It hasn't happened in almost twenty years now. At first, I denied it. Told myself it was a crush. Human lust. Whatever."

My cheeks warmed at the casual way he talked about it. I wanted to tell him I'd have settled for "human lust" as he put it, but the word "mate" kept ringing in my head, so I stayed silent.

"Then, tonight, when I saw you in danger, my wolf lost it, and I knew." His eyes blazed with anger, violence, and something more. "I left with you because, if I'd stayed, I would have killed every last one of those assholes who threatened you. You're my mate, Ash. I can't deny it anymore. But I also can't afford to let the others know. That's why I stayed away. If Silas or Drake or the others knew how I felt about you, it would make you an even bigger target."

"Is that why you didn't stand up for me the other day?" I asked. "With Silas and the others? You let them accuse me of being a witch."

"I nearly lost my shit when you told us about that asshole Vorack calling you and hunting you down," he said, his voice heavy with a growl that made me shiver. "It took everything I had not to show them how much I care about you."

"I care about you too."

Just saying the words made my heart pound in my chest. It felt too fast. But it also felt exactly right.

"I'm glad to hear it."

"So, being a mate. It's not a choice," I said slowly.

"It's definitely a choice, Ash. Don't think for a second I'd force you into anything," he assured me. For some reason, that made me relax.

"Okay, so the fact that we like each other…it's still our free will, right?"

"Absolutely. And it's much more than like. Mates are fated."

"Like destiny?"

"Yes, exactly." He hesitated and then said, "I don't call you Ashes for the same reason anymore, you know."

"Why do you do it then?"

His eyes flashed with barely restrained violence as he said, "The next person who touches you will burn to ash for it. Those bruises you came here with will be your last, that is a promise. Even if they kill me for it."

I thought of Silas and the others. Of what they'd tried to do. And what Kai would do to them if they succeeded.

"If they knew how you felt about me, they'd hurt me to hurt you," I said.

He nodded. "I'm so fucking sorry for the way I acted," he whispered, stepping toward me until we were so close I could feel his breath. "And if you don't feel the same, it's okay. But I needed you to know the truth. I never wanted to hurt you. I was protecting you the only way I knew how."

"Okay, I have to ask you something first. If I say I feel the same way, are we, like, married or something?"

He chuckled. "Not quite."

"Okay, because you had me up until human lust," I admitted. "After that, the mating stuff gets confusing."

His smile widened, and he wrapped an arm around my waist, pulling me closer so that our hips touched. "That's a good start," he said, his lips brushing my cheekbone. "A really, really good start."

He dipped his head, brushing his mouth over mine. Hot breath warmed my face, and my body responded. I wrapped my arms around his neck, pulling him close, and rose onto my tiptoes so that our mouths met again.

The kiss was slow. Sensual. Heat spread lazily at first

then faster until my body burned and my core ached. Kai's hands held me tight, and I was pretty sure it was the only thing keeping me upright.

My shirt rose, and Kai's hands brushed the bared skin of my hips as he tightened his hold on me.

His tongue worked like magic against mine, and I rocked into him, the heat building toward need.

"Kai," I breathed.

He made a sound deep in his throat and lifted me up, cradling me against him. I wrapped my legs around his waist, and he walked us back to where he'd left his bike. He sat down, straddling the seat while I straddled him.

My hips rocked against his, and he groaned. "Ash, you're killing me."

"You're the one who brought up human lust," I said.

He laughed quietly, his body shaking with it, and I couldn't help feeling thrilled at the sound. Kai's laugh felt like a rarity, something he only shared with a select few. I loved that I was one of them.

"You're right, but as much as I want to do this with you, I don't want the first time to be on the back of my bike at the Roan Mountain overlook."

"Sounds romantic," I said, nipping at his ear.

He leaned away, holding me so that I couldn't try for the other ear. "Not with the entire pack out hunting for you," he pointed out.

"Buzzkill," I muttered.

"Yeah, murder does that."

I sobered. "They would kill me, wouldn't they?" I asked, my hands still pressed against his shoulders for more reasons than just stability. "Silas, I mean. And the others. If they found me out here."

"No," he said firmly, his hand cupping my face as his thumb brushed against my jaw. "I wouldn't let them."

"That's not what I asked."

He scowled.

"Why do you stay here if the pack is so violent?" I asked.

This close, it felt like I could see every secret thought Kai worked so hard to keep hidden from the world. It was hard not to get lost in all that intensity.

"Because." He sighed. "It's not their fault. Without an alpha, their wolves are too strong. Their baser instincts are too dominant."

"You're making excuses for them, Kai. They're violent. Unpredictable. Dangerous."

"They're my family." He studied me. "You've never had family you stuck by, even when they became someone you didn't like?"

Yeah, he had me on that one. "Okay, I get it. But this is no way to live, Kai. They're going to end up doing something they can't take back."

Like kill me. Which I admittedly wasn't a fan of.

"That's why we're going to break the curse. Then we can all tether to an alpha, and their wolves will settle. No more chaos."

"Is that what you want?" I asked. "To break the curse?"

"Of course. Why would you even ask me that?"

"I don't know. I thought maybe you liked things this way. Wild. Independent. No one to answer to."

His expression darkened, and his gaze turned far away. "The pack needs order," he said. "We've run rampant for too long, and too many of us have been hurt by it."

I wanted to ask what he was thinking, but suddenly, his expression cleared, and his knuckles brushed my cheek. His voice softened, and I knew whatever memory had swept him up was gone. "We won't survive without it," he added.

I blinked, a little dazed at our closeness. His touch. The way he looked at me. Forcing my thoughts to focus, I took a breath.

"Okay," I said. "So, we break the curse. But…how?"

"I don't know," he admitted, and my hope deflated. "But I think I might know someone who can tell us."

One look at his face, and I knew exactly what he was going to say. An idea I'd been playing with for a while now. "Who?" I asked.

"The hexerei."

20

Kai hadn't lied. Oscar was alive and breathing and already waiting at home by the time Kai dropped me off. I closed the apartment door behind me and crossed to where Oscar stood at the counter, drinking a beer. Without a word, I put my arms around him and pulled him into a hug. He stiffened and then slowly brought his free arm around to pat my back. I pulled away, smiling at his awkwardness.

"Are you hurt?" I asked, looking him over.

He didn't have a scratch that I could see.

"Don't be ridiculous," he said with insult in his tone. "Of course I'm not hurt."

I shook my head. Of course, he'd be insulted over my concern.

"And Silas?" I asked.

"The fucker will live," he said darkly. "Which is more than he deserves."

I put my hand on his arm. "Thank you. For protecting me."

He shrugged me off. "What about you? Everything okay? No trouble with Kai, right?"

"No trouble with Kai," I assured him, my skin still buzzing from all the not-trouble we'd just had together.

"Good." He paused and then eyed me with a knowing glance. "He's a good guy deep down. Rough on the edges but has a good heart."

I stepped back and busied myself with getting a glass of water. Now I was the one avoiding. Kai had made me swear not to tell a soul about the mate thing. The fewer people who knew, the safer we were. I knew Oscar wasn't a threat, but a promise was a promise. And I was still getting used to the idea of it myself.

"Why exactly are you telling me this?"

Oscar just shrugged. "Just giving you some information."

I glanced over at him. "Right. Information. Thanks."

He grinned. "I can smell him on you, ya know."

I froze with the water glass halfway to my mouth. My cheeks heated, and I knew they were flaming red. "Seriously?"

"Hmm. Do I need to have a talk with the guy?" he asked. "Find out his intentions?"

"I— Uh..." I was a stuttering mess, and my cheeks were on fire.

Oscar laughed, loud and full and complete with a knee slap. "You're too easy to mess with, kid."

I scowled and drank the water, turning away from him in the process. When I lowered the glass, now empty, and looked back at him, Oscar's expression had sobered.

"Do you think it's a bad idea?" I asked. "Me and Kai?"

"As a matter of fact, I think it's a great idea."

"You do?"

"Well, I mean, I can't say I'm thrilled at the idea of you

with anyone. Kind of gives me weird inclinations to lock you in a closet for the next few years."

I snorted. "I think that time has come and gone."

"Yeah, you're an adult now. I'm a little late." He waved it off, but I couldn't help feeling a little warm and fuzzy, knowing Oscar felt protective of me that way. It had been so long since I'd been the object of parental concern, I'd forgotten the feeling.

"I've known Kai his entire life," Oscar said. "His dad was pretty rough on him so he spent a lot of time here. Kid's been working on motorcycles since he could hold a wrench."

He smiled, and it was easy to see the affection he had for Kai.

"You two are close," I said, and for some reason, that meant a lot to me. The two guys I cared most about in the world also cared about each other. It felt like…family.

"He's like a son to me," Oscar said. "He's got a good heart, but he's also tough as nails. Kai'll keep you safe," he added. "That's what matters to me."

"Thanks, Oscar." I fought the urge to hug him again. One hug a night was probably Oscar's max. But I did squeeze his shoulder as I passed him on my way to bed. Turned out, for all his gruffness, Oscar had a good heart too.

And, for the first time since discovering the truth about my birthmark, I actually wanted to break the curse, especially if it meant helping Oscar.

The next morning, Idrissa and Isaac were already waiting at the shop door when I came down to open up.

They wore matching expressions of guilt, which would have been funny. Except that I was still pissed about them lying to me.

"What do you want?" I asked.

"Can we come in?" Idrissa asked.

"Pretty please with a virgin cherry on top?" Isaac added.

I stepped back, allowing them inside, and crossed my arms.

Isaac held out a paper bag.

"What's this?" I asked, taking it hesitantly.

"Donuts. A peace offering," he said.

My brow rose.

"I would have brought alcohol, but you don't drink. And my shrooms dealer isn't awake this early."

I decided not to comment on that last part.

"We came to apologize," Idrissa said. "We should have told you about the fight happening last night."

"You should have," I agreed. "Instead, you lied. Just like everyone else has done to me." I glared at her. "I thought you were different."

"We *are* different," she insisted.

"What about your deal with Silas?" I asked.

"Silas is—" She stopped, and I gave her an expectant look.

"Silas is what? Trying to get me killed?"

She sighed. "It's not his fault," she said quietly. "Our wolves crave the pack ways. The fights, the challenges, always clawing your way to the top—it's not civilized, and he knows it. When the others aren't around, he's more reasonable."

"Silas is *reasonable*? Look, if you're going to keep lying, at least, make it believable."

"I was just trying to protect you."

"I appreciate that," I said, "But my entire life has been about others keeping secrets from me, all in the name of my own protection. I can't do that anymore, especially with people I consider friends."

Isaac took a dramatically large breath and said, "That's good because the secret you've been keeping is definitely starting to feel like a weight for me."

"*My* secret?" I looked back and forth between them. "What are you talking about?"

"We know," Idrissa said quietly.

"About your tattoo." Isaac's voice was a whisper that came out more loudly than his actual voice.

My jaw dropped. "Kai told you? That little ass—"

"Kai knows?" Isaac shrieked.

I glanced toward the garage where Oscar was setting his tools out for the day.

"Ssh," I hissed, turning to glare at Isaac.

"Kai didn't tell us anything." Idrissa cocked her head. "How long has he known?"

"Yeah, I guess you've been keeping two secrets." Isaac clasped his hands together and batted his lashes. "A tattoo on your body and Kai's name tattooed on your heart."

I groaned. "Okay, okay, first of all, I'm sorry. You're right. We've all been keeping things from each other."

"So, we're even?" Idrissa asked, brightening.

I glared at her, but I couldn't bring myself to hold it. Finally, I sighed and nodded. "We're even."

"Oh hell naw we're not," Isaac said. "Not until you tell us about Kai's giant—"

The front door opened again, and we all turned to look at Kai as he stepped inside. My expression turned to horror as I tried to decipher whether or not he'd heard Isaac's comment. But his face held only confusion as he glanced at the three of us.

"What?" he asked.

"Nothing," I said quickly.

Isaac snorted.

Idrissa smirked. "Your girl here was just bringing us into the circle of trust," she said.

Kai's confusion mixed with wariness. He looked at me. "Should I be worried?"

"They know about my mark," I said quietly.

His eyes widened in shock that turned quickly to distrust.

Idrissa held up a hand. "We're not going to tell anyone."

"Yeah, we've known for a few days and haven't said a word."

"A few *days*?" I repeated.

"That first day when you trained at the house," Idrissa said. "Your shirt came up."

Dammit. I knew it.

"You didn't say anything," I said.

She shared a look with Isaac. "We wanted to make sure it meant what we thought it meant," she said. "Before we said anything."

"And how exactly did you *make sure*?" Kai asked in a warning tone.

"Relax, we didn't go blabbing to the pack," Isaac assured him.

I relaxed.

Kai didn't.

"My grandmother kept a journal." Idrissa held up a small book. I hadn't even noticed it in her hand before. "She recorded some stuff from right after the curse was discovered. It mentions the wolf mark as a symbol of the curse itself—and the mark of the curse breaker. There's a whole section on a prophecy or whatever."

She held it out to me, and I took it, opening to the page she'd left bookmarked. Kai stepped closer to read it over my shoulder, and I had to remind myself to focus on the words on the page rather than the delicious way he smelled.

The handwritten words were scrawled in cursive that cut across the page like a blade.

"She met a hexerei," I said in surprise.

I looked up, and Idrissa nodded. "Met isn't the right word exactly. She captured him. Tortured him. And recorded what he told her."

I shuddered as I read on because Idrissa was right. And the woman detailed the torture. I skimmed over those parts until I got to the section where she'd written what the prisoner had told her.

"It says the curse can only be broken by the one bearing the mark and that a sacrifice must be made." I kept reading, nerves tightening my belly. "Death over a life. Life over a death. In the end, a wolf and a demon must choose each other."

I turned the page, hoping for more, but that was it.

I looked at Idrissa. "What does that mean?"

"No fucking clue," she admitted.

"Hexerei were referred to as demons," Kai said grimly.

I stared at him.

"I think you have to either kiss or kill a hexerei," Isaac said. "Or maybe both."

"Great," I said, handing the journal back to Idrissa. "Ending the curse involves a hexerei. Possibly killing one." I glanced at Isaac. "Possibly kissing one."

He shrugged. "It's just a theory."

I could feel the murdery vibes radiating from Kai. I had a feeling if I kissed a hexerei, they'd end up dead anyway.

"We need more information," Kai said.

Behind him, the door opened, and Drake walked in.

"What have we here?" he asked, giving us all a curious look.

"Morning," I called back a little too brightly. "Just sharing these donuts with my *friends*," I said pointedly.

He didn't even react to my insult as he squeezed past us toward the garage, and I waited until he'd shut the door behind him to speak again.

"I have to get to work," I said. "Customers will show up soon."

"We shouldn't talk about this here anyway," Idrissa said.

She looked at Kai expectantly.

"My place," he said. "Tomorrow. After work."

"Why not tonight?" Idrissa said.

I could feel her impatience, but Kai shook his head. He turned to me, his eyes gleaming in a way that made my knees weak.

"Tonight, Ash and I have plans," he said simply.

Idrissa nodded. "Fine," she said. "Tomorrow."

"Plans," Isaac said, pointedly raising his eyebrows at me. "Okay then." He looked way too googly-eyed for Kai's words not to mean something. I kept quiet, wondering what sort of plans he had in mind exactly.

"We'll be there," Idrissa said, shoving her brother and giving him a look. And then to me, "I'm glad we talked."

"Me too. See you tomorrow."

When the twins were gone, I looked at Kai. "They can help."

"I know."

"Then why do you look pissed?" I asked, careful to keep my voice low. The other techs had begun to arrive, and soon we'd have to put this conversation away, but I couldn't leave it alone until I knew where we stood. Especially after last night.

"I'm just thinking."

"About last night?"

"Well, yeah, I mean, I can't not think about that." A slow smile spread, and my stomach filled with butterflies.

"What exactly do you think about it?" I asked carefully.

His gaze sharpened, and he leaned in until his sexy eyes were just inches from my face, and his nose brushed mine. "I think you look beautiful today, and if these people weren't here, I'd take you in the back and show you how glad I am to see you."

I bit my lip, trying, and failing, to hide just how much I wanted that exact scenario. "I meant about the twins. And the curse. And the prophecy."

"Oh." He straightened, the frown from before firmly back in place. "I think it sounds dangerous, and I'm not interested in putting you at risk."

"Is that all?"

"Pretty much, why?"

I smiled. "Your thinking face looks pissed."

"Ha." He leaned in and stole a kiss, which, in turn, stole my breath. "Your surprised face looks turned on," he whispered and then walked past me and into the garage. "See you tonight," he called over his shoulder.

Asshole.

He wasn't wrong, though. I was definitely turned on.

21

Kai found me after closing time and motioned for me to follow him out the back. He'd pulled a baseball cap low on his head, and I started to ask about his terrible excuse for a disguise, but he held a finger to his lips. Silently, we wove our way through the empty garage and out the door. His motorcycle was parked right outside, but he walked past it and over to Oscar's truck.

"Get in," he said in a hushed voice, opening the passenger door.

I kept my mouth shut and did just that.

He came around and slid into the driver's seat, starting the engine and rolling out of the lot without a word.

We passed the front of the shop and then turned onto the main road. I watched while his gaze scanned the street.

"Okay," he said when we'd rumbled our way out of town and onto the back road that led further up the mountain. "All clear."

I exhaled.

"Does Oscar know we took his truck?" I asked. "Or are we adding grand larceny to our list of crimes?"

"There's a list?" he asked.

"Well, you and me being together right now feels pretty forbidden so, yeah." I shrugged. "I mean, it's not illegal but—pretty sure the pack would string us up."

"Good point." He winced. "I don't mean to force you to hide, but I wanted to spend time with you, and I don't think we're ready for having targets painted on our backs for it."

"It's fine. But your terrible attempt at a disguise is starting to make me question the whole badass criminal vibe you have going on."

"Hey. I'll have you know I'm a highly respected crime lord around these parts."

"Right," I said, drawing out the word.

"Fine. Busted. All my other disguises are at the dry cleaners. Robbing banks is messy business."

I laughed, my body literally tingling at the devious grin he shot me. Suddenly, I was very aware of the space between us and how, even with the distance across the bench seat, I could feel Kai's body heat.

"Where are we going exactly?"

He lifted a brow. "You'll see."

For the next twenty minutes, I simply enjoyed the view. The mountains rose around us closer and closer until the incline became steep and the truck's engine stuttered as Kai drove us upward. Finally, he slowed, and we turned onto a gravel road unmarked by any signs.

"A remote location where no one will find me. Hmm. Should I be worried?" I joked.

But underneath the humor, my heart pounded. I trusted Kai. More than I'd trusted anyone in a long time.

And that alone felt scary. Physically, I knew I was safe with him. But emotionally—that was a different story.

"Listen, don't laugh," he began, and now he looked nervous.

"Why would I laugh?"

"Because I wanted to take you somewhere special, but it's not like we can walk into town and have a fancy dinner."

"I don't need fancy," I said.

"I know. But you deserve it."

My heart warmed at that.

For a moment, our eyes held, and my heart stuttered for completely different reasons. The fear was gone. In its place was a yearning I'd never felt for anyone or anything—until now.

I wanted Kai.

I wanted to trust him. To give him parts of me I'd never offered to anyone else. And never would again. This was it, I realized. Whether supernatural fate or human love or something in between, it was Kai or no one.

Damn.

No pressure.

"I still don't understand why you think I'm going to laugh at you," I said.

His grin was crooked now. Sheepish.

"Because this place *is* special," he insisted. "To me, anyway. It's not exactly romantic though."

"Now, I'm intrigued."

He glanced over at me then back at the road. "Take a look."

I looked up, and my eyes caught on the glint of metal against the setting sun. The road had leveled out here, and the gravel became mostly dirt. The trees that had pressed in around us fell away to reveal more open space.

We were here.

Wherever *here* was.

Above our heads, a rusted metal sign read Crater's in faded lettering. We passed underneath it, and I heard the squeaking it made as it moved in the wind. I glanced to my left as we passed by piles of metal scrap and what was left of a vintage Chevy pickup. Just inside a chain-link fence, we parked beside a pile of rotting tires, and Kai cut the engine. I pushed open my door and hopped out onto the dirt, my boots kicking up a cloud of dust as I rounded the hood to where Kai waited for me.

"What is this place?" I asked, looking around at the graveyard full of cars, trucks, motorcycles, and even a few boats crammed together inside the chain link fence we'd come through earlier.

"A junkyard," he admitted.

"I see that," I said, more amused than anything. "But why?"

He took a deep breath, and I could tell already that this place really did mean something to him. And so did this moment.

"Crater was a friend of my dad's. I've known him since I was a baby." He looked away, staring out over the sea of broken cars. His voice dropped low as he went on. "When my dad's drinking got bad, especially once my wolf emerged, I'd run off and come up here and hang with Crater."

A shadow fell across his expression, his mouth twisting as some memory dug itself to the surface. "We'd sit and play cards. Or he'd teach me how to work on whatever he was fixing up at the time. Sometimes, we'd just sit and listen to the radio." He shrugged, his expression clearing as he looked at me again. "It was a safe space. And...well, I know you've been through a lot. And I thought you could use a safe space too. As glamorous as it is," he added with a smile.

"Kai," I began, but a booming voice interrupted me.

"Stoner, is that you?"

I turned to see a tank of a human walking toward us, his wide frame bulldozing its way past the car corpses and metal heaps. Okay, human was the wrong word. If I hadn't believed in supernatural creatures before, I would now. Just looking at this guy told me there was more to him than normal human DNA.

Kai grinned at him. "Crater. What's up, man?"

They did some sort of handshake-hug thing and then Crater turned to me. "Hi there, I'm Crater Row. You must be Ash."

"My reputation precedes me," I said, shaking his hand.

"Ah, don't worry too much about it." He winked. "Kai's pining is his own problem."

"Hey," Kai protested. "I bring one girl up here and you turn on me."

I laughed.

Crater was a monster of a guy—definitely not someone I'd want to meet alone in an alley, but I liked him already.

"One girl, huh?" I teased. "You sure you don't bring all your girlfriends up here to impress them?"

Crater laughed and clapped Kai hard on the back. "She's quick; I like her."

Kai glared at him.

"Relax, I meant as a friend," Crater added.

I hid a smile. It was funny, watching a guy like that back down to Kai.

Crater looked at me. "If you're here to visit your car, there's not much left of her, I'm afraid."

"My car? Oh, right. You're the one who towed it into town for me. Thanks again for that."

"No thanks needed. I didn't get much for the scrap metal, but Oscar said he'd pass it along."

"I appreciate it."

"Well, I'll leave you alone to give her the grand tour," Crater told Kai.

"You sure?" Kai asked. "You could join us. Give her the full experience."

"Nah. I'm headed out. Hunting trip." His eyes flicked to me, and I had a feeling his hunting wouldn't be done in human form. "Just lock up when you're done."

"Will do," Kai told him. "Thanks."

"Nice to meet you," Crater called to me. He waved as he walked to the vintage Chevy and got in. I watched him start it up, surprised to see the thing ran.

"Well, I guess we have the place to ourselves," Kai said as Crater drove off.

I grinned at him. "See? Romantic after all."

"Obviously."

"Are you going to show me around or what? I want the full experience."

I winked, a little shocked at myself. But Kai's answering grin made it worth it.

"Babe," he said, leaning in and brushing his lips over mine. "I promise that's exactly what you're going to get."

I shivered, and he leaned away again, grabbing my hand and tugging me along. "Come on. I'll show you where the magic happens."

I laughed and let him lead me into a junkyard.

Thirty minutes later, I'd visited "motorcycle mountain, V-8 Valley, and pickup parkway," as each section was apparently named. We'd even spotted what was left of my car which made me emotional in a way I hadn't expected.

But Kai was there, knowingly taking my hand and squeezing it in silent comfort. It meant a lot more than I knew how to put into words.

"I never knew junkyards were so organized," I said as we sat inside Crater's small trailer of an office.

Kai held out a bottle of water he snagged from the fridge.

"It wasn't always," he said. "I think I came up with the different names when I was like ten. And then Crater just indulged me."

I stared at him incredulously. "You mean he just... moved everything around to accommodate?"

"Yeah, basically."

I shook my head. "Why do I picture him just picking up entire cars and tossing them into their corresponding piles?"

He snorted. "Yeah, the guy's a beast. But relax, there's a crane out back. I mean, we're wolf shifters, not Superman."

"I was always partial to Spiderman anyway," I said. "Must be the animal lover in me."

He laughed.

I looked around, noting the vinyl wall paneling and thin as hell windows. It reminded me so much of the house I'd left behind. Not a home. Too temporary and toxic for that. But it was the last place I'd been with my father. The memory brought tears to my eyes.

"What are you thinking about?"

I blinked, forcing myself to refocus. Kai stood watching me curiously. I sighed.

"My dad," I admitted.

"Do you miss home?" he asked.

I tried to figure out how to answer that. "This trailer

reminds me of the one we lived in before— It was the last place we lived," I finished.

"You lived in a lot of places?"

"Yeah," I said with a laugh that contained zero humor. "You could say that." I looked up to see if there was judgment in him. But there was only curiosity. And caring. "Fourteen places in five years," I said. "Or something like that. I lost count."

He walked over to perch on the edge of Crater's desk right in front of where I sat in the wheeled chair. Our eyes met.

"I'm sorry about your dad," he said quietly. "I don't think I ever said that before."

"I'm sorry about yours too."

"Don't be. My dad's better off now. Hell, we both are." He cocked his head. "You miss the trailer?"

"I miss my dad. But I lost the version I miss a long time ago."

"Yeah, I know that feeling."

Silence fell, and I did my best to shove all the ghosts from my pasts into the back of my mind. What mattered was this moment. With Kai. And the next moment. And the next.

"This means a lot, Kai. Thank you for sharing it."

He blew out a breath. "It's a little weird, I know."

"It's yours," I said with a shrug.

He reached for my hand and pulled me to my feet. With the way he'd slouched down, we were eye to eye now. My breath caught, and I stilled, drawn into the sudden intensity of his gaze.

"I used to belong here, Ash. To this town. To Crater's. Oscar's. Not anymore, though."

Tears burned my eyes. I felt those words all the way to my soul.

"Where do you belong now?" I asked, my voice barely above a whisper.

"With you," he said simply, and the walls around my heart cracked wide open. "I know I was an ass about it, but I can't afford to risk you. To risk this. And the pack… they'd use you against me."

His stare was intent now as if searching for some answer he needed. Some sign.

"If that happened," he went on. "I'd burn it all to the damned ground. I needed you to see this place. To understand how much it means to me. Because I'd give it up in a second for you. And that scared the shit out of me before. But not anymore. There's only one thing that scares me now, and that's losing you."

"You're not losing me," I said.

But there was real fear in his eyes. A fear I knew too well. Especially since losing my dad.

"I'm not asking you to choose, Kai. You don't have to give anything up for me."

He shook his head like he was suddenly frustrated. "Maybe you should. Ask me, I mean. Because the answer *is* you. I choose you, Ash."

"I choose you too," I admitted.

He gave me a rueful smile. "Even after everything?"

"You're making it easier and easier," I said.

He laughed but turned quickly serious again. "I'm just… I'm tired of losing the people I love. I can't let that happen again."

"We've both lost people," I said. "And we've both been alone because of it."

"Not anymore," he insisted. "You don't have to do this alone. I'm here for you. I want you to know you can count on me. We're going to find a way to end the curse. And summon your wolf. And we'll either become part of the pack or we'll start our own. No matter what, we do it together from here on out. Okay?"

His words slid into the cracks around my heart, shattering the resistance until every single wall I'd left around it came crashing down.

"Okay." I nodded, a tear sliding down my cheek.

He reached up and pressed his thumb to the moisture, wiping it away. "You're my home now, Ash Lawson. You're my heart."

"My heart's already yours," I whispered. "Just don't break it."

22

Somewhere between my walking tour through Kai's childhood hideout and him telling me he'd choose me, I'd forgiven him. I hadn't meant to. In fact, there'd been a solid plan somewhere in my head to make him beg or grovel or maybe run naked through Ridley Falls to prove himself or something. But all of that had gone out the window the moment that tear had fallen and he'd wiped it away. I was a sucker for a hot guy acting as my Kleenex, apparently.

By the next morning, my heart had landed solidly in #TeamKai territory while my brain had remembered the whole "curse" conundrum and gone back to strategizing just how we were going to make that particular problem go away.

Tonight, the twins and I were all headed to Kai's to figure out exactly that, which basically just meant the workday dragged by slowly. Kai was in the garage most of the day on a customer job that made it impossible to get a minute alone.

Drake was especially watchful. More than once, I

caught him staring at me or Kai with a weird look on his face. Right after lunch, he went home early. Stomach ache, according to Oscar. I made a mental note to ask Kai what that dude's deal was, exactly, and then went back to my invoicing and scheduling. Anything to get this day over with.

The moment the clock struck five, I flipped the Open sign to Closed and ran upstairs to change.

"Where's the fire?" Oscar called.

He'd cornered me at lunch in between customers and phones ringing and the other techs coming in and out for their refrigerated leftovers. I'd denied anything strange about the conversation with the twins yesterday, but then I'd walked through the garage to talk to Mick about an invoice code and noticed Oscar and Kai in the corner together with heads bent and voices too low for me to hear over the air compressor.

After that, he'd looked equal parts stressed and resolved. Maybe even hopeful. And he'd made it clear he knew we were up to something tonight.

"I want to get to Kai's house before the rain hits," I said.

A storm had been rolling in all day. I'd never ridden a motorcycle in the rain, but I had a feeling it wasn't pleasant. Kai had already told me to hurry and gone to pull his bike around front.

Upstairs, I shed my work shirt, which was really just an old collared Polo that Oscar had outgrown that had the Twisted Throttle logo on the lapel. In its place, I threw on a tank top with my thrift store jeans and shoved my feet into my boots then hurried back downstairs again.

"Hey, kid," Oscar called as I headed for the front.

"Yeah?"

"You don't owe this pack anything," he said.

I stopped short, trying to figure out where this was coming from. "I know that."

"I'm just saying. If it's a choice between your safety and this damned curse, choose yourself. You got me?"

"I'm guessing Kai told you the plan?"

He shook his head. "He told me enough. I don't want details because then I'm culpable. You just make sure you come home in one piece because I'd hate to have to triple-murder all your new friends for failing to protect my niece."

I smiled and leaned over to plant a kiss on his forehead. "Don't go soft on me, old man."

"I'm tough as nails," he grunted, and I shook my head.

"See you later," I called as I left.

Kai stood at the curb, bike already idling.

"Not going undercover today?" I asked.

"The weather has everyone headed home early anyway," he said. "I think we'll be okay."

I stepped up to where he waited and let him slide the helmet onto my head then buckle it underneath my chin.

"One of these days, I'll have to learn how to do this myself," I said.

"Nah. That's not as much fun for me." He winked then patted the top of the helmet. "Ready?"

"Yep." I glanced up at the gathering clouds. "Think we'll make it?"

"Babe. I'm faster than you give me credit for." He threw his leg over and motioned for me to climb on behind him. "But you might want to hang on extra tight. We're going to take a back way so no one sees us."

I grinned, more than happy to do exactly as he asked.

The ride to Kai's house was a thrill of wind and gravity and the hum of my own body being pressed to his. By the time we arrived, I could smell the rain on the air, and not a single inch of sky could be seen through the gathering clouds.

"Impressed?" Kai asked as he parked and cut the engine.

I slid off the back, rolling my eyes at his smug smirk. "At your driving skills or your incredibly huge ego?" I shot back.

He grinned. "Is that what Isaac was asking you about when I came in yesterday morning?" His brows lifted. "My huge… ego?"

"Oh my god." I turned away, fumbling with the helmet's chin strap as the twins pulled up beside us in the Mustang.

They got out, and Idrissa hit the button to put the top back up.

"Isaac, just in time," Kai said.

"Ooh, what did I miss?" he asked.

I gave Kai a warning glare. "Nothing," I said pointedly.

Kai laughed, and both twins stopped in their tracks.

"What?" I asked, noting their stricken faces. I looked around, worried they'd seen or sensed someone else approaching.

"The song of the angels," Isaac said, a hand over his heart. "It's a miracle."

"Shut up," Kai muttered and started for the house.

Isaac looked at me. "Kai doesn't laugh," he explained.

"Okay," I said, drawing out the word. "I mean, I know he's kind of serious most of the time but—"

"No, not most of the time," Isaac corrected. "All the damn time."

"He's right," Idrissa said, falling into step with us as we followed Kai to the porch. "I think last time Kai laughed was senior year homecoming when Presley mooned the principal and the entire marching band all in one show."

"He. Doesn't. Laugh," Isaac repeated.

I let them pass me and file inside then stopped in front of Kai, who was holding the door open. Before he could say a word, I leaned in and kissed him on the mouth.

"I like your face," I said. "Laughing or grumpy, doesn't matter to me."

"Hey, I'm not grumpy," he protested as he followed me inside.

"Riiight," the twins said in unison.

Kai's house was surprisingly clean. We all hung out in the living room on two oversized couches while Kai ordered pizza, and then we settled in to work through how the hell we were going to figure this all out. Kai pulled me down onto the couch next to him and rested his hand on my thigh. My skin tingled through my jeans, and I focused on breathing like a normal person.

Not that I was normal.

Far from it, apparently.

"So, can we talk about this whole curse-breaking thing?" Isaac asked. "Because I have to say the idea of Ash saving us all is kinda hot."

"You think everything is hot," Idrissa shot back.

"Yeah, but Ash is extra hot." He grinned at me, and Kai's hand on my leg tightened.

I put my hand over his and squeezed. The twins didn't know Kai and I were mates. And we really needed to keep it that way for now. One impossible situation at a time.

"First, I have to know we're all on the same side," Kai said.

"Of course we are," I said. "That's why we're here."

He looked at Idrissa. "In the past, we haven't exactly seen eye to eye."

"That's because you chose to align yourself with Drake and Silas and your band of assholes."

Kai didn't answer.

"Ash is important to me," Idrissa said. "I'll kick ass to protect her." She smirked. "Actually, I already have."

"I've saved her more than once already," Kai shot back. "I think I've made it clear where I stand."

"You've run away with her," Idrissa corrected. "Not the same as standing and fighting."

"I'll do whatever it takes," he snarled.

I tensed.

Were they seriously going to argue over who was more committed to saving my life?

I shot Isaac a pleading look.

"You two used to be friends," Isaac said before it could escalate. "We all did. Let's just call it tequila under the bridge and start over."

"Uh, I think it's water," I pointed out, but Isaac just shrugged.

"I can if he can," Idrissa said. "But that would mean him turning his back on the alphahole club." She cocked her head. "Can you do that, Stone? Is Ash that important to you?"

"Ash is all that matters to me," he said quietly, and Idrissa's expression relaxed.

Isaac looked like he wanted to gush, but I shot him a look, and he buttoned it up.

"Let's get down to business," Idrissa said. "What do we know about the curse and how to break it?"

"We don't really know much more than what was in that journal," I admitted.

"Your parents never explained anything to you about your tattoo?" Isaac asked.

"No. And it's not a tattoo. It's a birthmark."

"Whoa, you were born with it?" Isaac asked.

"It looked more splotchy when I was younger. Then,

when I was twelve, I woke up one day, and it was this." I gestured to the mark hidden by my clothes.

"You think puberty maybe triggered the formation coming together?" Idrissa said.

"No idea. My mom got really weird when she saw it." I blinked away the painful memories. "She left soon after that."

"You haven't seen her since?" Idrissa asked.

I shook my head.

"And your dad never said anything?" Isaac's voice was full of sympathy.

"After Mom left, everything changed. My dad got really paranoid. We moved a lot. And he started drinking. By the time I was old enough to really demand answers, he wasn't sober enough to give them."

"Damn, Ash. That's horrible. I'm sorry," Isaac said.

Kai's thumb rubbed soothing circles against my leg. The others were quiet. I could feel all their eyes on me, and while I knew they all meant well, I couldn't stand this pitiful sympathy party they were all having for me.

"I managed," I said, shrugging it off. "The point is I don't know any more than you do. I didn't know there was a curse or that my mark meant I could break it until Kai told me."

Kai's hand squeezed my thigh in silent comfort.

"Okay, let's just talk about that for one second," Idrissa said. She looked at me then him. "You told her," she repeated. "That shouldn't be possible. I mean, technically, neither should this conversation. I've said the word curse like fifty times already."

Isaac's eyes lit. "Good point. If this were a drinking game, we'd all be sloshed."

"I have a theory about that," I said, and they all turned to me. "I think once you see my mark, it breaks whatever magic keeps you from talking about it." I looked at Idrissa and Isaac. "That day in the garden, you hadn't seen my mark yet so you couldn't say anything. But Kai saw it when we were—I mean, when he got me out of there."

Isaac smirked. I could feel Kai's emotions shifting at the memory of our make-out session against that tree.

"And then, I showed it to Oscar, and he was able to talk about it too," I finished.

"Girl's got a point," Idrissa said. "It makes sense. I mean, she's the curse breaker."

"Okay, so, one mystery solved," Isaac said. "Now we just need to, you know, actually break the curse."

"That journal entry wasn't much help," I said.

"The problem is there are too many stories and not enough verifiable facts," Kai said. "My old man used to tell me the key to breaking the curse was killing all the hexerei."

I winced at that. No way could I massacre an entire people. Not even for Kai and the twins.

"And our dad thinks the curse will be broken when the original caster returns to remove it," Idrissa said. She looked at me. "What does Oscar say?"

"He has no idea either," I told her.

"None of the elders or originals actually know anything," Isaac said.

Idrissa sighed. "Which begs the question: Can we even trust the stuff in Gran's journal?"

Isaac frowned.

Kai didn't answer.

"I think she had one thing right," I said.

Everyone looked at me. Kai hadn't said a word about it since we'd all sat down, but I couldn't think of a better idea than the one he'd already proposed.

"Which is?" Isaac prompted.

"The hexerei," I said. "Your grandma went to the source, which is exactly what we should do."

"You want to talk to a hexerei," Idrissa said, her tone making it perfectly clear she thought I was insane.

"It's the only way to know for sure," I said.

"And you want to what?" Isaac asked. "Just drive over to their land and knock on some doors? Have tea? Baby girl, I don't think that will go well for us."

"Actually," I said, "I was thinking we talk to the one staying right here in the Falls."

"Whoa, you want to make a social call to Silas' prisoner?" Idrissa said.

"He's already here. I mean, why not?"

Kai's emotions shifted suddenly, and he looked at me sharply. "That's why you were protecting him. Before. You'd already thought of this."

"No, I was protecting him because he doesn't deserve what the pack was doing to him," I said firmly. "But I have wondered if he knows anything about the curse."

"Why do you look guilty?" Isaac demanded, and I blinked, surprised he was able to read my thoughts.

"Kai suggested the idea last night, but to be honest, I had already thought of it before. I would have gone to see him already, but I don't know where he's being kept."

"It's a damn good thing too," Idrissa said. "You would have been caught and hauled in your damn self." She leaned forward. "You do know he has a twenty-four-hour guard, right? And the cabin they have him locked up inside is on Silas' family property."

"I could have figured it out," I said defensively. She looked ready to argue, so I added, "My point is, we could go together now."

I waited to see if she'd argue or tell me I was insane for

even bringing it up, but Idrissa's eyes gleamed with the idea.

Isaac whistled. "Damn, that might just be crazier than paying the hexerei tribe a visit. If Silas finds out—"

"He won't," I said.

"If Silas finds out, I'll deal with him," Kai declared.

Idrissa nodded approvingly. "Fair enough, but Ash is right. We need to make sure Silas doesn't find out."

"I can handle him," Kai said.

"I'm not doubting it," she replied dryly. "But we can't afford for any of them to figure out what we're after." She nodded at me. "Or about Ash's mark. It's best if we go about this covertly."

Kai nodded and glanced out the window. The clouds were sagging low, and the wind had picked up. Rain was inevitable. Not just rain. An epic storm.

"We go tonight," he said.

"Whoa, crazy boyfriend say what?" Isaac said.

Idrissa nodded. "Use the weather as cover. The rain will mask our scent."

"It's a start," Isaac admitted reluctantly. "But we need more than a thunderstorm to throw Silas off our trail."

"Isaac's right," I said. "Anytime I've deviated from where I'm supposed to be, they always find me."

Idrissa frowned. "I can distract Silas. The others, not so much."

"How?" I asked.

Isaac's expression lit with understanding. "Oh, shit, sis. No way."

He looked more amused than worried, but still, my nerves twisted.

"Idrissa," I said.

She sighed. "Remember how I told you I made a deal with Silas to keep you from fighting for a little longer?"

"Yeah."

"Well, if he held up his end—" She hesitated. "—I promised him a date."

"A date," I repeated. "With you?"

"Yes. Ugh."

She made a face, and my eyes widened.

"Silas…likes you?"

"Oh, gross, don't say it like that," she wailed.

I pressed my lips together to keep from laughing. But watching Idrissa freak out was sort of like watching Isaac have a normal day. Super dramatic and entertaining.

"You don't have to do it, sis," Isaac said. "We can find another way."

"Yeah, but this way is more entertaining," Kai said, trying to hold back a laugh of his own.

Without lifting her head from the couch cushion where she'd buried it, Idrissa flipped Kai off.

He snickered just as the doorbell rang.

"Pizza's here," Isaac said.

Kai got up and paid for the food while Idrissa pulled herself together so she could call Silas and plan their date.

Kai returned a moment later with pizza in one hand and a soda in the other. Isaac pouted at that.

"No beer?" he asked.

"In the fridge if you want it," Kai told him.

Isaac and Idrissa both disappeared into the kitchen for drinks.

"Here," Kai told me. "Someone told me you don't drink."

"Thanks." I took the soda and noticed he'd grabbed one for himself too. "None for you either?"

He shook his head as he cracked his can open. "My dad and yours have that in common," he explained. "Looks like so do we. Cheers?" He held up his soda, and I did the same, clinking our cans together.

"Cheers," I said, feeling strangely bonded by our matching drink choices.

Afterward, we ate pizza and plotted exactly how we were going to do this mission in the middle of a thunderstorm that bordered on hurricane and with Idrissa trying not to throw up during her date-slash-distraction.

When the food was gone, the rain started.

I looked at Kai across the table just as lightning flashed through the window behind his head. "It's time," I said.

He nodded, the look in his eye criminalistic yet panty-melting. "Let's do this."

23

I stood in the open doorway and watched through the rain as Idrissa drove off. She was headed home, to change for her date and the rest of us needed to get to our assigned spots, too. But the rain was relentless. In the end, I simply stepped outside. There was no point in running. The rain soaked me through the moment I cleared the doorway. Kai stepped out beside me. He looked over at me, water running in wide streams onto his hair and down his angled jaw.

"Ready?" I called over the thunder.

"Babe," he said, reaching over and grabbing me by the waist. He pulled me against him in one smooth move. I gasped as my chest pressed against his, and suddenly the cold rain felt hot between us. My nipples had never been harder. I wondered if Kai's wolf shifter senses knew that. "You have no idea. Let's break this curse so I can make you mine."

He kissed me like this was it, and for a second, my body forgot all about our dangerous mission to befriend a hexerei. All that mattered was Kai's mouth on mine.

"A-hem." Behind us, Isaac cleared his throat loudly. "You two wanna save it for the victory lap?"

Kai grinned. "Only because it would be weird if you watched."

"Not for me," Isaac shot back.

Kai chuckled and took off at a run for the aging pickup truck parked at the edge of the yard. I glanced over my shoulder to see Isaac staring after him open-mouthed.

"What?" I asked.

"Did your boy toy just make a joke?" he asked incredulously.

I just laughed and ran after Kai.

An hour later, we'd parked off the main road on what Kai explained was an old hunting trail. The pickup was tucked out of sight behind some trees that bordered Silas' land—not that we needed the cover. The storm made it impossible to see beyond a dozen or so yards ahead. No one would notice us here unless they knew where to look.

Rain came down in sheets against the windshield, and Kai had the heat on to help ward off the chill, thanks to my soaked clothes. In the quiet, Kai's fingers were drawing patterns against my arm. Even after we'd dropped Isaac off to borrow his mom's car for recon, I'd kept my spot beside Kai on the truck's bench seat. He hadn't let go of my hand the entire drive over. My skin hummed at the contact, but my thoughts wouldn't quite let me forget what we were here for.

"Shouldn't Idrissa have called by now?" I asked, turning my phone over and over in my other hand.

"Relax. I'm sure she's just waiting until we're all clear."

He was right.

But I still couldn't settle. Not until this was done.

"What would Silas do if he knew I was the curse breaker?" I asked.

Kai frowned, thoughtful. "I don't know," he admitted. "But I don't want to find out."

"He's your best friend," I said. "Right?"

"Yeah."

"Is this hard for you? Deceiving him?"

"It might be," he admitted. "If I wasn't doing it to protect you."

"Was he always like this?" I asked. "I mean, growing up together, was he always so . . . cruel?"

"No, Silas was actually one of the nicest guys I knew."

"Seriously?" I couldn't picture it. "What happened?"

"He went camping one weekend after graduation. The rest of us were all busy doing our own thing, so he headed out alone. He'd done it plenty of times before, so no big deal, we thought. He was gone for a couple of days, and when he came back, he was just different. Angry. Restless. Always looking for trouble."

"You think something bad went down on that camping trip?" I asked.

"No idea. He won't talk about it. But it doesn't matter, does it? Now, he's just like the rest of us. The longer we remain untethered to an alpha—unmated—the closer we get to becoming our beast permanently."

I thought of some of the wolves I'd seen at the barn the other night. The energy coming off them was raw and primal.

"I think some of them wouldn't mind that," I said.

He didn't look thrilled as he said, "I think you're right."

"What would Drake do if he knew I was the curse breaker.

Kai didn't even hesitate before answering, "He'd kill you before you could do it."

"You sound sure."

"Drake isn't like the rest of us," he said. "He showed up here three years ago, bloody and wounded and barely hanging on. Said his pack turned on him. We took him in, and when he was well enough, he fought for his place. He's wild like us, sure, but there's something else in him too. His wolf doesn't want to tether."

I shuddered. Drake was bad news—even to a pack of rogue, criminal wolves. That said a lot about the guy.

Before I could answer, my phone rang. Isaac's name lit up the screen. Well, actually, it displayed the words "Main Dish" since I hadn't yet changed it from Isaac's initial entry.

Kai looked up at me with raised brows.

"Don't ask," I told him and then hit the button to answer the call. "Hey," I said, putting it on speaker.

"The eagle has left the nest. I repeat, the eagle has left the nest."

I rolled my eyes.

"No one's listening to this conversation, Isaac," Kai said. "You can drop the spy talk."

"You don't know that for sure," Isaac hissed. And then louder, "I've got eyes on the target. Asset's secure. You may proceed."

Kai shook his head.

"What about Drake?" I asked.

"My sources say he's on a barstool at Bo's bar right about now. Three beers deep to Presley's four. We're a go, people. I repeat, Operation Hex-'em is a go."

"You did not just call it that," I groaned.

"It's brilliant, I know. Mother Hen over and out."

I looked down at my phone and saw Isaac had hung up.

"Mother Hen?" I repeated.

"Terrible code name," Kai said. "Come on. Time to get wet."

He winked, and I laughed. "You did not just say that to me."

"Punish me later, gorgeous." He got out and turned around to offer me his hand. I took it and slid out of the truck and into the pouring rain. Flirty Kai could convince me of anything, including standing out here in the worst thunderstorm I'd seen in years. When he looked at me like that, wet didn't even begin to cover it.

Kai slammed the truck door shut, and together, we ran through the woods toward the tiny cabin.

By the time Kai pulled me to a stop, I was soaked through and blinded by the rain in my eyes. I had no idea how he could see, much less know where we were, but he apparently did. When I stopped, he leaned in close to make sure I could see him and held a finger to his lips.

I nodded.

This was the part of the plan that excited me.

Kai backed up a few paces and then, like he'd done it a thousand times before, he shifted.

The defined arms and broad chest became front paws. Kai Stone, the human, was gone. In his place was the same black wolf I'd seen in the woods the night of the full moon.

He was even larger than I remembered. And his eyes were completely aware of me. His fur matted with the rain which he kept shaking out as if the wet annoyed him.

I remained perfectly still just as he'd coached me to do earlier.

But instead of marching off to complete the next part of the plan, he walked over to me and rubbed his enormous body against my hip. My hand fell to his head and trailed down his back as he slid past. Then he turned, and our eyes met.

My breath caught.

Kai was gorgeous and amazing—in any form.

And he was mine.

I smiled at him, holding out my hand, palm up.

Kai approached and stuck out his tongue, licking a trail across my open palm. I yanked my hand back, laughing at the way he wrung himself out again.

He looked at me uncertainly.

We were about to sneak into a heavily guarded cabin, under the threat of real danger, and he was worried what I thought of his wolf's wet fur?

"You look fine," I told him, reading his emotions, which was weird and exciting all at once.

Clearly satisfied, Kai turned away and disappeared into the trees ahead. I waited, crouched against a tree for cover, and listened. The thunder masked most of the noise, but I caught a grunt and then a yell and then nothing.

A moment later, Kai's wolf reappeared.

I let him lead the way into the clearing. Just ahead sat a small cabin. I started toward it, and my eyes flicked to something on the ground near the door.

A body.

I recognized Vinny, the werewolf from Bo's that Idrissa had knocked out my first day in town. My chest tightened, but when I got close, I saw the rise and fall of his chest. Alive.

Damn. Apparently, Vinny had a habit of being in the wrong place at the wrong time.

Kai's wolf gave me a look that said he knew what I was thinking. Then he ducked out of sight. I knew he'd stay close and keep watch to make sure we weren't disturbed.

I crept up to the cabin, slipping inside quickly, mostly to escape the damned rain. Outside, thunder shook the walls, and I stood for a moment, dripping all over the dusty wooden floor while my eyes adjusted to the dim lighting.

The cabin was empty except for a gas stove in the corner and a single chair against the back wall. Tied to the chair and gagged with a gross-looking rag was the hexerei.

He stared back at me with wary curiosity, eyes swollen but open.

His clothes were dirtier than I'd last seen. More stained with blood. As was the rest of him. His face and arms were covered in cuts, some fresh, some scabbing already. My heart ached at what they'd done to him. I took a step forward, and the man growled at me through his gag.

I stopped and cleared my throat. "My name's Ash. I only came here to talk. I promise I won't hurt you."

I waited, and when he didn't make another sound, I took another step.

No growl.

Progress.

I stepped up to the man and reached out, pulling down the gag with as little contact as possible. Drool, dirt, blood. The thing was disgusting. The moment his mouth was freed, the man sucked in raspy breaths then started coughing.

"Are you okay?" I asked.

"Water," he said quietly.

I shook my head, irritated I hadn't thought to bring any, but he nodded at a jug in the corner. I grabbed it and uncapped the top, doing my best to feed it to him without drowning him in it.

When I lowered it again, I gave him a rueful smile. "Sorry about that. Looks like we're both the same amount of soaked."

He grunted, looking me up and down with suspicion. "I'm not going to talk, and you can tell the rest of them sending in an innocent girl won't change that."

"The others don't know I'm here," I said.

"Huh." He eyed me with renewed interest. "What do you want?"

"I'd like to ask you about the curse."

He blew out a breath, instantly stone-faced again. "Like I said, I don't have anything to say—"

"Do you recognize this?" I peeled the waistline of my jeans away to reveal the wolf mark on my hip.

The hexerei stared at it then finally looked up at me. His eyes were wide with disbelief and something else. Wonder.

"I don't understand. She said you'd work with us. But you're here with them."

"Who said?" I asked. "Who am I supposed to work with? Your people? Can you tell me what I'm supposed to do?"

His eyes narrowed again. "This isn't how it's supposed to be."

"Well, then, tell me how it *is* supposed to be," I said. "A life for a death, is that it? Am I supposed to defeat someone or something? Or kiss someone? That one is definitely a weirder option, but I'm willing to do what needs to be done. Well, except for murder. I don't think I can do that. But kissing a weird stranger, I guess, is doable."

He shook his head. "I don't understand. You're the savior we're waiting for. And you think you have to kiss someone? This isn't Snow White."

"Good, because if a bunch of dwarves show up, I'm out. This is all very witches, werewolves, and what the fuck. You know what I mean?

He stared at me. "You don't know about any of this, do you?"

"No," I admitted. "I was hoping you could help me with that."

"But you have the mark."

The impressed look he'd given me before was gone. Now, he just looked annoyed. Impatient. That made two of us.

"I do have the mark, but I didn't even know what it meant until recently," I said. "All I know is that I can supposedly break the pack's curse. Give them back their humanity. Let them choose an alpha and mates and hopefully settle them the hell down so they stop trying to kill me. But how?"

"Humanity." He curled his lip. "The wolves cannot regain what they never had."

I frowned. "What does that mean?"

"That curse belongs where it is."

"But the mark—"

"The mark bearer is our chosen one. It signifies the power you hold. The wolves will know who rules them, and it will not be one of theirs."

"I don't understand. Your chosen one? You think I'm the chosen one of your tribe? Why?"

He shrugged. "The mark chooses its champion, and we must honor it."

"If I break the curse, am I still your champion?" He didn't answer. "Answer me," I demanded. "If I set the wolves free, what then?"

"The lupin are beyond saving." He closed his eyes, his expression anguished. "The only peace that awaits the lupin is on the other side of their destruction. The curse will accept nothing less for our sworn enemies."

I huffed. The guy either talked in riddles or not at all. And we were running out of time. My phone buzzed in my pocket, but I ignored it and leaned closer.

"Tell me how to break the curse, and I'll let you go before Silas comes back," I said.

He looked at me, considering.

Outside, a wolf howled, and I knew we were out of time. But I couldn't leave without an answer. There was no way I'd get this chance again.

With my heart pounding, I grabbed a fistful of the hexerei's disgusting shirt and shook him. "Tell me," I repeated.

"The magic demands a sacrifice," he said.

Damn. Okay. Apparently, that part was non-negotiable.

Outside, the growl and clash of wolves rang out between rolls of thunder that grew farther away with each new rumble. The rain had nearly stopped from the sound of it. The storm was passing. We were out of time.

"What sacrifice?" I demanded.

"Like I told your friend before, it's a yin and yang. A hexerei and a wolf must become one. No more separation." His eyes flashed with renewed hate. "But he reminded me why that will never happen. I will not help you anymore. He saw to that."

"Who? Who did you talk to? Was it Silas?"

"No. His name is—"

Behind me, the cabin door crashed open. I released the hexerei and whirled in time to see a very classy-looking Silas barreling through the open doorway, his tie tossed over his shoulder. He glared at me and closed the distance, grabbing me before I could slip past.

"Hello, Ashes."

I pulled against Silas' hold, but his grip was like iron.

"Don't even try it," he snarled at me, and I knew, this time, there'd be no talking my way out. "It's time to prove yourself once and for all. It's time to fight."

24

Silas dragged me outside, and I hurried to keep up so I didn't land on my face in the mud. My boots squished over the soft ground, and I surveyed the scene that had changed drastically from when I'd entered the cabin. Vinny was no longer lying unconscious. Now, a brown wolf stood in that same place, a lump clearly forming on the top of its head. When he saw me, he growled.

And he wasn't the only one. Several more wolves lined the perimeter, and I sensed them closing in behind us as we made our way farther out. But then my eyes caught on something ahead, and I stared in horror at the two wolves wrestling violently near the trees.

Silas gave a shrill whistle, and they broke apart and looked over at us.

My stomach dropped as I recognized Kai's wolf huffing breathlessly as he looked over, first at me, then at Silas' hand on my wrist. Beside him, the other wolf looked at Silas expectantly. His cream-colored coat and sharp eyes were strangely familiar.

Presley, I realized.

Kai had fought Presley. For me.

My heart warmed at what he'd just given up for the sake of protecting me. At the same time, worry and sadness speared through me. I hated seeing him have to choose like this.

"We have a traitor in our midst after all," Silas yelled.

At the sound of his voice, more wolves emerged from the trees.

I swallowed hard at the sight of them coming slowly forward. As they passed Kai, they growled in warning. The warm feeling Kai's protection had given me was quickly replaced by cold fear.

Shit.

There were too many of them.

This wasn't going to end well for either of us.

Behind them, two human figures raced out of the trees toward where I stood. Isaac and Idrissa—both with matching expressions of fury and determination.

My chest swelled as Idrissa screamed at Silas.

"Stop this now," she called.

But he ignored her. To the wolves, he said, "Kill him."

They raced past us and into the cabin.

"No!" I wrenched away from Silas. Or tried to. But all it got me was a sharp pain up my elbow and a tighter grip. I winced both from my own pain and from the sound of the hexerei's screams that rose then abruptly cut off.

I stared at Silas in horror.

"You didn't have to do that," I said, my voice cracking as I imagined the wolves ripping the man apart. He'd hated them, and they'd just proven him justified. It was horrible.

At the sound of the screams, Idrissa and Isaac stopped short. They stared past me at the cabin with wide eyes.

Kai appeared between them, back in his human form. I hadn't even seen him shift, but now I couldn't look away.

He stood completely naked and completely unconcerned about that fact, glaring at Silas with raw murder in his dark gaze. If I hadn't feared for my life, maybe I could have appreciated the view. Instead, all I could think about was who Silas would order the wolves to attack next.

"Let go of her now, Silas."

Kai's tone was the only warning Silas would get. We all knew it.

Silas loosened his grip but didn't let go.

"I won't tell you again," Kai said.

"You've gone too far," Silas snapped at him.

Isaac pulled a pair of shorts from his back pocket and held them out to Kai. "Here, dude. No sense blowing in the wind while you kill this asshole."

Without breaking eye contact, Kai snatched the shorts and pulled them on. "Good point. I won't be using my wolf for this," Kai said. "I'd rather feel the air slip from his lungs through my own hands."

He took a step forward.

"What the hell, man," Silas demanded. "You would throw away our friendship for this?" He shook my arm.

Kai bared his teeth. "You threw it away when you touched her."

"Whoa, dude." Presley stepped up beside me. He wore a tiny pair of shorts and nothing else. Blood coated his throat and mouth.

I looked away, my stomach twisting at the mental images of what he'd just done in that cabin.

"She was helping the hexerei," Presley said. "She's a traitor."

"I wasn't helping him," I protested.

"Prove it," Silas snarled.

He released my arm as the rest of the wolves joined us, surrounding Kai and the twins and me. I saw Kai's gaze flick to them and back to me. Even without Silas holding me down, we were trapped.

"If you're one of us, fight and take your place," Silas said. "It's the only way we can trust you. Otherwise, you become our prisoner and are subject to interrogation."

"Silas, don't make me kick your ass like I did in the seventh grade," Idrissa said.

"It's pack rules," Silas said.

"It's bullshit," she shot back. "Stop letting your asshole of a wolf run things and be a human fucking being. She's not trying to bring us down. She's a friend."

"Well, now we know where you stand," Presley said. "If you're not with us, you're with her. And that's a bad place to be right about now." He looked at Kai. "What's so special about her, anyway?" He grinned. "Is it her ass? Because I do agree she's got a killer ass."

Kai growled and started forward. Isaac grabbed him and hauled him back again, but Kai's eyes glowed yellow, and I knew his wolf was way too angry to calm down now.

Shit.

This was going from bad to worse.

I bit my lip and then turned to Silas. "Okay," I said. "I'll fight."

"Ash, no," Idrissa said, her expression filled with horror.

"It's the only way," I said.

"Ash, don't," Kai said through clenched teeth.

"I won't let you get hurt because of me," I told him.

The look in his eye made my heart ache, so I turned away. "I'll fight," I told Silas firmly.

"Baby girl, this is a bad idea," Isaac said.

"It's fine. Silas is going to pair me with someone equal," I said, relieved when my voice came out sounding even. I gave him a look that hopefully appeared braver than I felt. "Won't you?"

Silas nodded. "Rules are rules." He paused, and for a moment, I actually had myself convinced I stood a chance. "Unless, of course, someone challenges you directly. If that were to happen, I wouldn't be able to step in."

"No one's stepping in," Idrissa began through clenched teeth. "And no one's fighting. She's going home." She pinned Silas with a look, and I watched as her form began to shudder. "We had a deal. If you're backing out, you're going to pay for it."

"I challenge her."

Drake stepped forward, and I could only stare in shock at his naked form currently too covered in blood to even make out.

"What?" Isaac screeched.

"This is insane," Idrissa said. "Why would you challenge her? She's not a threat to you at all."

"She's strong," Drake said. "I can sense it. And my wolf feels the threat." He stepped closer, eyeing me. My mouth twisted in disgust at the blood coating his skin. None of the others were this much of a mess. It was like he'd done it on purpose. Like he'd enjoyed the kill. "My wolf needs to secure its place in the pack, or who knows what it'll do," he said, the lie so obvious, it made me sick.

"Give me a fucking break," Isaac said. "Your wolf has lost its fucking grip, man." He looked at Silas. "You have to stop this."

"Rules are rules," Silas repeated, and it was such a cop-out, I wanted to claw his tongue off.

"Fine," I said, heart pounding. I looked at Drake. "Let's fight."

"Oh, I don't plan to fight *you*, sweetheart." His expression was colder than I'd ever seen. The look in his eye far surpassed anything Silas had ever said or done. "My wolf would rather hit you where it'll hurt the most."

He swerved suddenly, shifting as he twisted his body—and slammed into Kai.

I screamed.

Drake's claws raked over Kai's body, drawing ribbons of crimson across his skin, and I lost my grip on reality as the two went rolling. Somewhere along the way, Kai shifted, and then they were both wolves. Both murderous. Each clearly trying to kill the other one.

Someone grabbed me, and then everyone was moving at once.

A sharp pain stabbed at the back of my thigh, and my knee buckled. I went down just as Isaac appeared next to me, hauling me back up again. He carried me toward the trees, back in the direction of Kai's truck, but my body screamed with each step.

I sucked in a ragged breath as fire spread from my leg up to my chest and all the way down to my feet.

"Something's wrong," I heard myself say.

All around us, wolves growled and surged to where Kai and Drake continued to fight. A few watched us, but none approached as Isaac continued trying to back me away from them.

"Isaac." My voice broke, and I nearly fell again.

"Shit, Ash, you're bleeding." Isaac's voice sounded far away. Black dots laced my vision. "Driss!"

Isaac screamed for his sister, and a dark brown wolf tore itself away from the throng pressing in around Kai and Drake. She streaked toward us and stopped, sniffing at my leg with concern in her eyes.

She looked up at Isaac and let out a whine.

Isaac lowered me to the ground, studying the wound more closely.

"Motherfucker…she's bitten," Isaac said grimly.

He didn't sound quite as concerned as he should, considering my insides felt like they were about to burst through my skin. The sensation built until I couldn't stand it any longer.

I screamed, and my body just…exploded.

Cracks and pops echoed around me as my bones literally broke and reformed. I squeezed my eyes shut against the pain, and when I opened them again, gagging and gasping for air, I saw fur.

Fur where my arms should have been. Fur for legs. The ground was closer. Too close.

What the hell.

I looked up and met Isaac's wide eyes.

"Holy shit," he breathed. "Ash, you're a—"

Somewhere farther out in the muddy field, Kai howled.

I had no idea how I knew that sound belonged to him. I just did.

Tipping my head back, I let out a howl of my own. It was reflexive. Something I didn't even know was happening until the sound escaped me.

And then I knew what Isaac was trying to tell me.

I was a wolf.

25

The animal inside me felt both foreign and familiar. Like a piece of me that had always existed and was just now making itself known to the rest of me. And the first thing I knew for sure was that my wolf side was a bossy bitch. She didn't use words, per se. More like urges. Feelings. And I knew instinctively how to let her exist alongside my human self. My mind sort of just…made room for her.

And the moment I did, her instincts took over.

The need to protect rose so strongly that I didn't even have time to question my actions before I was up and shoving past Idrissa and Isaac. My paws felt clumsy and strange against the soft mud for about three seconds. After that, the speed and senses of my wolf took over, and I flew past the other wolves, shoving my way through their ranks with an ease that surprised me.

My wolf sighted Drake and Kai and went straight for its prey.

Opening my mouth, I leaped the final few yards and closed my canines around Drake's furry shoulder, yanking him off Kai's wolf in a quick and violent move. Drake yelped, and I felt the moment his flesh tore. His blood filled my mouth, but I didn't let go.

Drake's wolf writhed against my grip, but I held fast.

The asshole would not hurt my mate again.

Mate.

My wolf held no hesitation as she thought the word.

If anything, she strained harder in her urge to protect. To hurt. To kill if necessary.

That last thought was enough to make me finally release my jaw and let Drake up again. He twisted away and rolled to his feet, whining. When he spotted me, his wolf eyes narrowed, and he crouched low, ready to attack. I could feel him about to spring, and my wolf welcomed it.

Bring it, asshole.

Before Drake could leap, another wolf stepped between us. Then another.

Silas and Presley. My wolf seemed to recognize them somehow. Smell maybe? God, this was weird.

A third wolf brushed my shoulder, and I jumped, then settled when I recognized Kai. He brushed me again, and this time, I pressed in closer.

My wolf didn't take her attention from Drake, though. She still wanted his blood to run. I could feel it and feel my own disgust at the same time. At least, she wasn't quite so in control anymore, and I held my ground beside Kai while Silas and Presley pushed Drake farther and farther away from me.

Idrissa appeared, her wolf form graceful, lithe, and deadly as she helped to block Drake from where I stood.

Finally, I watched as Drake shifted back to his human form. Naked and bleeding, he stood in the mud. His hair had fallen into his eyes, and he made no move to brush it back again. His gaze wasn't on the wolves standing before him. Instead, it was on me.

I'd never seen a person look more cruel.

"You're going to pay for that, you little bitch," he said to me.

My wolf bared its teeth at him.

Fucker.

Beside me, Kai growled and edged forward.

Silas and Presley shifted back, and they both gave Kai a warning look then turned to Drake.

"You fought and she won," Silas said.

My wolf was not impressed with the sight of their naked asses aimed in my direction. All she wanted to do was spill Drake's blood and then run off with Kai into the woods. My human side was pretty much okay with the latter but the blood spilling…not so much.

Gross.

"Dick move using Kai as a proxy," Presley said.

"It's not against the rules. Besides, it's obvious Kai's protection of her makes him a traitor too," Drake spat. He glared at me again. "But you're right. I should have just killed the bitch outright and been done with it." He shifted his glare to Idrissa, who had circled around to flank him, still in wolf form. "I thought you said she couldn't shift."

"Someone bit her," Isaac said from behind me.

My wolf had scented him coming, which was the only reason she didn't turn and attack him for sneaking up on me.

With a wary glance at me, he stepped just a little closer to where I stood, clearly aligning himself with me and Kai. "The bite signaled her wolf and forced the change." He glared at Silas and Presley. "I told you she's not a witch."

"Who the hell did it?" Silas demanded.

"One of you is obviously responsible," Isaac accused.

"It wasn't me," Presley said.

"I didn't fucking touch her," Silas snapped. Behind him, Drake growled again.

Silas looked back at Drake. "Fight's over. Go home."

"Fuck that. She cheated."

"No rules for the fight," Silas said. "You know that. Besides, you're the one who attacked Kai like a dumbass. If anyone cheated, it would have been you."

Drake didn't answer. I could feel his wolf rising to the surface, and my wolf welcomed the idea of another round. All she wanted was to shut him up. For good.

"Ash is one of us now," Isaac said. "Now, get your asses over here, and welcome her to the pack."

A few of the other wolves inched closer, and I dropped my head to growl at them. But the intent rolling off them wasn't to harm. Isaac was right. They were coming to welcome me.

"You attack her now; you go against the pack," Isaac warned. He pinned Drake with a challenging glare. "You want to go against all of us, be my guest."

Drake spit out a mouthful of blood, glaring at Isaac then at me and Kai. "This isn't over," he said and then slowly turned and walked away.

I watched as he disappeared into the trees, but my wolf didn't relax until all trace of his scent had faded.

The other wolves approached me slowly. I tensed, but Kai stayed close. He didn't seem too alarmed by them so I forced my wolf to remain still.

One by one, they walked up and dipped their head at me in acknowledgment. My wolf watched in confusion, then curiosity, then satisfaction. She seemed content with their recognition of her. Meanwhile, I wanted to flip them all off. How could they think we were friends—just like that? Wolf customs were going to take some getting used to.

After that, they dispersed, most of them not bothering to shift back as they padded silently into the trees and disappeared.

Silas and Presley were the last to leave.

They stood a healthy distance from us, eyeing my wolf with interest and what she perceived as respect. It was the only reason she didn't try to attack them outright. Their nakedness didn't bother her. Me, on the other hand … yeah, this was awkward.

"Look, Kai," Silas began.

He pulled his lips back and growled at them.

Silas sighed. "You know how our wolves get," he said. "But I didn't bite her. And you know I won't condone it if Drake tries to come at her again."

"Yeah, dude. She's one of us now," Presley said.

Isaac snorted. "Just like that?"

I huffed. Took the words right out of my mouth.

"She fought," Presley said with a shrug. He eyed Kai. "And she's important to you."

It wasn't a question, and somewhere in the back of my human brain, I knew that was going to be a problem. But Kai merely pressed himself closer to me, confirming Presley's words as true.

"Drake wants to be the top," Silas said.

"That's nothing new," Isaac said.

Silas frowned, his gaze flicking to me. "He won't stop now that he knows your weakness." He looked back at Kai again. "Watch your backs."

Then he turned and headed for his house.

Presley followed.

When they were gone, Isaac and Idrissa pressed in around us.

My wolf inhaled their scents and noted how they dipped their heads, Idrissa as a wolf, Isaac as a human. Both acknowledging my wolf as part of their group.

No, not group. Pack. I was part of a pack now. Wow. I had so many questions. Mainly, how in the hell did I shift back again?

"Okay," Isaac said, "It's just us, baby girl. Time to give up the beast."

I stared up at him.

"She probably doesn't know how," Idrissa said as her wolf shimmered then receded until she stood before me as her human self—naked as a jaybird.

Wow, Idrissa was kinda hot. If I was into that sort of thing.

But then Kai rubbed his furry neck against mine, and I forgot all about Idrissa and Isaac and everyone else, for that matter. My wolf only cared about him.

"Why don't we give them some space," Isaac said. "Come on, sis. I'll race you home."

"We can't leave her here. What if Drake comes back?"

My wolf stiffened at that.

"He won't show until that wound is healed," Isaac said. He chuckled. "Baby girl whooped his ass."

Idrissa grinned at me. "Hell yeah, she did." She glanced out at the woods. "Okay, we'll head out." Then back at me and Kai. "But call us when you get her home and back on two legs."

Kai made a grunting sound that I assumed was an agreement. Then Isaac and Idrissa left.

Kai's wolf prodded me, and I found myself looking directly into his dark eyes. My wolf acted before I knew what she was going to do.

In a quick move, she reached out and licked his nose.

Kai blinked.

My wolfy jaw dropped in complete surprise at my own behavior.

Kai let out a growlish laugh, and I stared back at him. Could wolves laugh? Because I was pretty sure my mate just did.

Then he was turning and trotting toward the trees, and my wolf needed no more invitation than that to join him.

I fully expected Kai to try to convince me to shift back to my human form, but he did the exact opposite. For the next few hours, we ran together, exploring the woods, wading through streams, and making our way up to an overlook at the top of the mountain.

Not just any overlook.

Roan Mountain overlook.

The same place where he'd told me I was his mate.

There, Kai's wolf pressed in close, his paws intertwined with mine. When I looked over at him, he licked my nose and then cuddled against me.

If wolves could be romantic, Kai had just won "most swoony."

My she-wolf was hooked.

If she hadn't recognized him as her mate before, she damn sure did now.

I settled in close, and we passed out.

Later, I woke to the sound of leaves shuffling, and when I tried to move, I groaned at the stiffness in my legs.

Legs!

I lifted my head and looked down to see my human form had returned. Clothes, however, had not. Beside me, Kai's wolf pressed in close, keeping my bared skin warm with his massive fur-covered body.

He stirred and looked up at me, noting my human body.

I started to tell him to look away. I wasn't exactly a prude, but waking up next to your wolf boyfriend with morning breath was one thing. Waking up nude and covered in mud and twigs and someone else's blood was entirely another. But before I could utter a word, Kai moved away and shifted.

Our eyes met, and there was no trace of awkwardness in his tender expression. He bent down, lifting me into his arms and tucking me in against his bared chest.

"Hey," he said.

"Um. Hi."

"Are you okay?" he asked quietly.

"Yeah, I mean, I think so," I said, wondering how long I could milk this because my current position wasn't something I ever wanted to give up. Kai's broad chest and rippled abs were enough to make the whole shifting-and-trying-to-rip-Drake's-throat-out completely worth it.

"How do you feel?"

"Naked," I said.

"No complaints from me." His chest rumbled with a deep chuckle.

My nipples hardened. It was getting more and more impossible not to notice all the hard parts of his body currently pressing against me. My wolf stirred, urging me to give in and make use of the moment. Her best idea yet.

My hands tightened around Kai's neck, and he sighed, his warm breath washing over my forehead.

"Actually, you're wearing more than you think." His eyes flicked to my chest, and I lifted my hand, brushing my fingers over the pendant my father had given me.

Strange.

"It shifted with me," I said.

"Looks like it. Where did you get it?"

"My father."

"Huh, must be wolf magic or something."

"Must be," I agreed.

I became acutely aware of the fact that we still had exactly zero pieces of actual clothing on between us.

Through our bond, I felt Kai aware of that very same thing.

"We should get you home," he said.

"Or we could stay here and—"

My stomach grumbled loudly, and I scowled at my own body's attempt to cockblock me.

Kai laughed. "Looks like your baser needs are prioritizing themselves differently than you'd hoped. Come on. You definitely need calories after all that running."

He didn't wait for me to answer. Instead, he stood, lifting me into his arms with ease, and headed down the trail.

"I can walk," I protested.

"Suit yourself." He set me down, and the moment he did, my knees buckled. He barely caught me, once again lifting me easily into his arms.

"Indulge me," he said wryly, eyes twinkling with what felt like amusement.

This was a different Kai for sure.

Happier.

Lighter.

It was really weird. Good, but weird.

We walked in silence down the mountain trail, and after several minutes, I was surprised to see Kai's backyard just ahead where the woods ended. Had he brought me to the overlook because it felt like home to him? Somehow, that meant more than just some random hideout he'd chosen.

He carried me inside the back door and down the hall to a bedroom.

The entire space smelled like him, but it was strongest here. His bedroom, I realized as he set me down against the soft gray sheets. I grabbed the blanket and pulled it up to cover me.

Best to keep the mystery alive and all that.

His lips twitched knowingly.

"The shower is through there," he said, pointing toward an adjoining bathroom. "Get cleaned up, and I'll leave you some clothes to borrow."

He started for the door.

I sat up quickly, still clutching the sheet to my chest. "Where are you going?" I asked, suddenly uncertain about having him venture too far from me.

He returned and sat on the edge of the bed, facing me. With a gentle hand, he reached out and tucked a strand of my hair behind my ear. "I'm going to make us some food, but I'll be close enough to hear you call me if you need anything."

I let out a shaky breath, feeling silly. "Okay."

"I know you have a lot of questions, but let's eat, and then I promise to answer them all. Sound good?"

My stomach growled again.

Kai laughed. "I'll take that as a yes." He leaned over and gave me a quick kiss that stirred me in other ways. "Hurry up, little wolf. I want to get past the questions and on to dessert if you know what I mean."

I grinned. "Dessert's my favorite."

He left, and I padded across the room to the shower. The hot water and pine-scented body wash were a balm to my senses. The mud and dirt and blood washed away, leaving me feeling much more human by the time I was finished.

Except I wasn't human.

Not entirely.

When I was clean and dry again, I inspected the bite on my leg. The skin had already scabbed over, making the wound look days old rather than hours. I marveled at how quickly my body was healing.

A perk of being a wolf, I supposed.

It was one of the questions I intended to ask Kai.

In the bedroom, I slipped into the sweatpants and tee Kai had left out. They both smelled like him, which was a comfort, considering all the questions swirling in my mind right now. My wolf felt the most settled when she sensed Kai nearby.

Following the sounds of cookware and the smell of bacon, I walked into the kitchen. Kai looked up from the bar where he'd just plated a few pieces of bacon next to a pile of scrambled eggs.

"This smells delicious," I said.

"I hope so. I'm not much in the kitchen."

"Lucky for you, I'm a great cook," I said, and then my cheeks heated at how presumptuous that sounded. But Kai leaned over and pressed a kiss to the corner of my mouth.

"Damn right I'm lucky," he said and my embarrassment settled. "Here. All yours." He grabbed a fork and set it on the plate before me. Then he motioned to the bar stool. "Sit."

Manners might have dictated I wait for his food to be finished, but my gnawing hunger won out, and I dug in, scarfing the food. Kai offered me a second helping of each and then joined me with enough food on his own plate that I couldn't possibly be embarrassed by my own portions.

When I could think past the hunger, I set my fork down and sighed in contentment. "That was amazing," I said. "Where'd you learn to cook?"

"My dad passed down his one-meal cooking repertoire to me, I guess. Don't get excited. Breakfast is the only meal I can cook without burning," he warned.

"Noted," I said, leaning down to scratch at the scab on my leg.

Kai frowned. "Can I take a look?"

I pulled my pant leg up and showed him the wound. He inspected it closely, running gentle fingers over it and leaving goosebumps on my skin.

"Already healing nicely," he said. "It'll be good as new by tomorrow."

I shuddered, and he straightened again.

"So, healing is a perk then?" I asked.

"Usually. The more severe the wound, the longer it will take, but yes, we heal faster than humans as a rule," he said. "And especially if we can shift into wolf form to do it."

I thought of my dad. If he'd been able to shift, would he have healed from that gunshot?

"Hey, where did you go?"

His voice was gentle, and I blinked, noting the concern in his expression.

"Just thinking. Is that why you didn't try to get me to change back last night? So I'd heal?"

"Partially."

"And the other part?"

"My wolf really wanted time with yours."

For some reason, my cheeks heated at that, and I ducked my head.

"Your wolf is gorgeous," he added.

I felt weirdly embarrassed yet flattered at his words. "Thanks. She thinks the same thing about you. In fact, she had quite a few thoughts about you last night."

He grinned. "Oh, really? Like what?"

"That you're okay," I said, feigning indifference.

"Just okay?"

"I mean, she was distracted by Silas' ass but—Hey!"

I shrieked as Kai grabbed me and tossed me over his shoulder, running into the bedroom and dumping me on the mattress.

"Whose ass were you looking at?" he demanded.

"Just yours," I said, batting my lashes in mock innocence. "And maybe Idrissa's," I added.

He launched himself toward me, and I shrieked, rolling away as he tried to tickle me. I struggled against his impossible hold and, in the end, resorted to fighting dirty. When I grabbed his nipple, he yelped and backed off.

"I should have expected your dirty tactics," he said with a laugh, and the reminder of what I'd done to Drake sobered me.

"Stop beating yourself up," Kai said. "I can see it written all over your face. What happened last night wasn't your fault. Drake provoked it on purpose."

"I didn't even think I could do something like that," I said quietly. "Do you think he's okay?"

Kai sat back, giving me space to sit up too.

"He'll be fine," he assured me, his expression flashing with fury. "Not that he deserves it after that shit he pulled."

"Do you think he'll try again?" I asked.

"That's not something you need to worry about," he said. "I won't let him or anyone else hurt you."

My insides warmed at the protectiveness in him. And my wolf practically drooled for him.

"The hexerei," I said. "They didn't have to kill him."

Kai sighed. "The hexerei have been trying to find our weak points for a long time. Ten years ago, there was a pretty bad skirmish on the border of our lands and ever since then, the pack has made it a rule to take no prisoners. None of it was your fault."

He was right. I knew I'd walked into a war that had existed before me. But I still felt badly for the way it had turned out for that guy. He hadn't done anything except be what he was.

I had to change the subject before I let the guilt tear me apart.

"Kai…my wolf—she called you her mate."

His eyes filled with intensity. "As did mine."

"Does that mean… Do you think the curse is broken?" I asked, hopeful.

He shook his head. "Recognizing a mate doesn't mean you've become so. You still have to complete the bond, and even then, there's a mental connection that happens when you've recognized your one true mate that hasn't shown up for us. I was hoping last night would trigger it, but…"

"But it didn't," I finished, shoulders sagging.

"It's not the end of the world," he assured me. "Most mates don't feel that connection until after they've completed the mating bond anyway."

"Well, how do you complete the bond? Maybe we could do that and see what happens."

His expression changed, and the way he looked at me had my entire body tingling. "The bond is completed through physical mating," he said in a voice that seemed to rake over my skin. "Joining our bodies," he added, leaning in closer.

My heart pounded as his words registered.

"Well, I think it's worth a try," I said, nearly panting with my need for him. "Don't you?"

His eyelids lowered, and he looked at me with an

expression of pure desire. "I've wanted nothing else since the moment I laid eyes on you, Ash Lawson."

My mouth went dry.

Did I want him? Hell yeah. Did I also melt a little when he called me by my rightful last name?

Damn straight.

I reached for him, pulling him down on top of me.

"Me too," I whispered. "Kai, make me yours."

"Ash, you need to be sure about this. It would be forever. Wolves mate for life."

"I've never been more sure," I told him.

He looked at me like he still wasn't convinced.

"Kai, listen to me. My mother left a long time ago, and my dad might as well have. He checked out mentally, emotionally, in all the ways that mattered. He never told me the truth, and he wasn't there for me when I needed him. You've been there for me more times than I know what to do with, and I know you'd never let anything happen to me. You're my family now. I don't even want anyone else."

His lips twitched. "Not anyone? Not even Oscar?"

I punched him lightly. "Not the same, jackass."

He grinned, and the desire in his gaze made me shudder with the intensity of it as he leaned in close again.

"It goes without saying, but I'll say it anyway: you're it for me, Ashes. Always. Forever. Til death."

"Til death," I echoed.

He made a sound like a growl and crushed his mouth to mine. His hands were on me then. Fast, firm. Demanding. His tongue prodded my lips apart and delved into my mouth, teasing my own tongue in a way that made my core ache for more. His fingers roamed over the shirt he'd given me, sliding it up and running his rough palm over my hips and up to cup my breast.

When his fingers rolled my nipple, I arched into him.

"Kai," I said, breathless and completely at his mercy.

Between my human desire and my wolf's need, I'd never craved anything as much as I craved Kai Stone right now.

Without a word, Kai stripped my shirt off and then did the same with my sweatpants. He sat up and looked down at my naked body. This time, there was no embarrassment. The look on his face was pure awe and raw desire as he raked his gaze over my skin.

"You're so fucking beautiful, Ash."

He ran his hand gently over the bite wound on my leg then stood up and stripped out of his own clothes. I sat up on my elbows and looked him over, openly appreciating the rippled abs and hard angles of his broad chest.

"You're not so bad yourself," I said with a smirk.

His lips curved and he crawled across the mattress until he was directly above me. Slowly, he lowered his body against mine and kissed me. This time, there was no urgency. Only lazy perusal. His tongue slipped inside my mouth and stroked me with a steady rhythm that made me impatient for more.

My hands slid up his chest and over his shoulders, gripping him and pulling him closer. When it all became too much, my hips rocked against his, and he groaned.

"Patience," he rasped.

"What's that?" I asked and grinned when his eyes narrowed.

"Is that how you want this to go?"

His words were a challenge that sent a thrill racing down my spine.

"You're the motorcycle rider," I said. "I thought speed was your thing."

"Hard and fast, sure," he said, his eyes narrowing in a way that made me shiver at what was to come. "But this won't be quick if that's what you mean."

I reached up and nipped his bottom lip. "Prove it."

He snarled as he kissed me and when his hands and lips landed against my body, there was nothing gentle about it. Pleasure speared through me. His mouth, his tongue, his hands—they all knew exactly how to touch me and make me come apart.

When Kai slid inside me, the entire world tilted. As it righted again, the universe itself changed for me. My wolf rose up so close to the surface I had to concentrate to keep her from taking me over. No way was I shifting now and giving this up. I was so close now. Right on the edge.

Kai's teeth scraped along my skin. He hesitated, but I pressed up and into his teeth, inviting him to do more. With a soft growl, his mouth closed over my skin, and he bit down gently.

My wolf howled inside me, and the emotion that welled up swirled between us—moving, merging.

I hissed at the sudden pain, but it was gone quickly as Kai's teeth released my skin. He kissed and licked at where he'd broken my flesh, and I shuddered in delicious pleasure.

Something between us locked into place. A bond that could never be broken.

"You're mine now, Ash," Kai said against my ear, and that was all it took for me to let go.

My orgasm ripped through me, and I bucked, hanging onto Kai like a lifeline. And I knew, from this moment on, that's exactly how it would be for us.

"Can I bite you?" I whispered.

Kai's expression darkened, and he exhaled sharply. "Yes," he managed, his hips rocking against mine faster now.

My wolf reacted instinctively. I reached up and bit down against the soft spot on his shoulder. Kai shuddered, and I felt his orgasm rip through him. My tongue tasted blood, and my wolf seemed to hum in what felt like relief and ecstasy. This. This had been what I'd needed all along.

Kai was right.

This was our destiny.

Kai buried his face against my throat, and we both rode the last wave of his release until all that was left were our joined bodies and quiet breaths.

Finally, Kai lifted his head and looked down at me. His hands stroked my cheeks, tucking my hair away from my face.

"Are we mated now?" I asked.

He grinned. "We're mated," he said. "For today. We might have to do it again tomorrow though just to be sure."

I grinned, my entire body humming with pleasure and satisfaction. "You're on." Even as I said the words, I could feel him hardening again already.

"Although, why put off tomorrow what we could do today?" I rocked my hips gently against his, and he smirked.

"Good point. I—"

Outside, a car door slammed shut, and I froze.

Kai stilled, his body tensing.

We both listened as another door slammed, and then footsteps sounded on the sidewalk. Kai scrambled off me and shot to the window, barely moving the blinds aside so he could peek out. His expression twisted, and his eyes flashed with suspicion and concern.

"What is it?" I asked, sitting up on my elbows.

My mind raced. If Drake had returned to finish this, I—

"I don't know. Never seen them before," Kai said, and my brows pinched in confusion. "They're carrying though."

He stepped back and headed for the door.

"Carrying what?" I asked, scrambling to grab my sweatpants so I could go after him.

"Guns," he said grimly. He paused in the doorway and looked back at me. "No matter what happens next, stay in here. Do you understand?"

"Kai, you can't just—"

But he was already gone.

I yanked my pants on and then hurried to the window. Boots fell in heavy steps as whoever it was climbed the porch steps to the front door.

"Ash Langford, or should I say Ash Lawson, I know you're in there," called a male voice that was so familiar and so horrifying that I went cold with fear. "Come on out now, and no one gets hurt. Or don't, and it'll end just like it did for your dear old daddy."

Vorack.

He'd come for me.

And if I didn't do something, he'd kill Kai for getting in his way.

26

I had no idea how Vorack had found me, but right now, that didn't matter. What did matter was Kai. If he got hurt because of me, I would never forgive myself. Fumbling out of fear, I grabbed my shirt and yanked it over my head.

But it was too late.

The front door opened, and I heard Kai's voice ring out, low and full of warning.

"Get the fuck out of here now, and I'll let you live."

"Is that right?" Vorack drawled, clearly unconcerned. "And just who the hell are you?"

"Time's up. I'm the one who's going to kill you."

There was a loud click, and I jumped toward the bedroom door just as the gun went off. A thunderous shot echoed through the house, ringing in my ears and sending terror into the pit of my stomach.

My wolf rose swiftly, and by the time I reached the living room, I was about two seconds from shifting. But the scene before me stopped me cold.

Kai stood on four legs, his black wolf bloodied and

crouched beside Vorack, who lay motionless on the floor in the entryway. Through the open front door, I saw another man lying on the porch. Frank. The one who'd messed up my face. Both of their throats had been ripped out. I couldn't even bring myself to summon a reaction to the carnage. All I cared about was Kai.

I stepped over Vorack's dead body and crouched down beside Kai. He looked back at me with dubious eyes, and I reached out, laying my hand against the blood coating his fur. With careful fingers, I ran my hands over his fur, checking for wounds.

"You're not hurt, are you?" I asked.

With a grunt, Kai scooted out of reach and shifted.

When he was human again, he rose and pulled me to my feet.

"Are you hurt?" I asked again, panic lacing my voice.

"I'm fine," he assured me. "It's their blood. Not mine."

I exhaled in relief. "Thank goodness." The hesitant look didn't leave his eyes, and I frowned. "What's wrong?"

"This is the guy who killed your dad, isn't it?"

"Yes. I don't know how he found me, but—"

A wolf ran into view and onto the porch. I gasped then relaxed as the coat and eyes registered as familiar. Idrissa shifted and stared back at us with concern. Behind her, a second wolf arrived. Isaac shifted, rushing up to the porch.

"Are you okay?" he asked. "Is she okay? What happened— Oh, shit."

He stopped short at the sight of Vorack and his henchman lying in pools of their own blood.

"We're okay," I said.

The sight of them naked was a bit easier than the first time. Still, I kept my eyes averted as they both stared back at us with shocked expressions.

"How did you know?" Kai demanded.

"Silas called me," Idrissa said. "He's on his way too."

"What did he say?" I could hear the rage mounting in Kai's voice. Someone had led Vorack here. And I hated to think about what would happen when they found out who did it.

"Drake ratted Ash out," Isaac said.

"Drake?" I blinked. "How did he even know to call them?"

"I told them Vorack's name," I said, stunned and panicked. "That day the hexerei tried breaking into the Throttle—" I broke off and gripped Kai's arm. "Oscar," I said.

"He's fine," Isaac assured me. "We went there first."

I exhaled.

"Whoa, holy shit." Isaac's eyes widened, and he seemed to be studying me more closely. "No way. Is this real life?"

"What?" I asked.

Kai was silent.

"Drissa." Isaac motioned for his sister to come closer.

"What?" she asked.

"Do you smell that?"

She leaned in and sniffed, and then her eyes widened too. "You two are…mated?"

The disbelief in her voice was laced with excitement.

"Yes," I admitted.

She and Isaac lit up. "No way," Isaac crowed. "This is amazing. It's—"

"Later," Kai snapped. "We don't have time."

"Right." Isaac frowned. "Sorry."

"Tell me about Drake," Kai said flatly.

"Apparently, he's been looking into Ash," Idrissa said, still glancing between us but clearly back to business.

"Silas went by his place, and I guess the asshole's got a whole Criminal Minds pin-up wall dedicated to her."

"Why?" I asked.

Her gaze flicked to my hip where we all knew my mark was inked.

"Shit," I said.

"Drake knows. That means Silas does now too," Kai said.

"How?" I wondered.

"Does it matter?" Isaac said. "The point is he knows. And so do the others. And when they get here, the first thing they'll find are the dead bodies you're using as Welcome mats."

"Dammit," Kai muttered.

"This is bad," Idrissa said, looking down at the bodies. "I mean, the elders and town police turn a blind eye to a lot but dead humans?" He looked at Kai. "They're going to shit a brick."

"We can worry about that later," Kai said. "Right now, we need to figure out how to handle the mark."

My eyes narrowed at that. Suddenly, I'd been reduced to a permanent ink stain.

"I'm a person, actually," I said. "And I'm standing right here."

"I know." He sighed. "I'm sorry. I just meant we need to protect you. Drake obviously wants you dead rather than let you break the curse. And we don't know if Silas agrees. It's not safe here."

"I can take her home while you talk to Silas," Idrissa said. "He's your friend. Maybe he'll listen to you."

"Maybe." Kai shook his head. "But they'll look for her there. And I'm not leaving her side until we know she's safe."

"Our house?" Isaac suggested.

Kai shot him a withering look.

"Right. Also obvious," Isaac said.

"I should leave," I said, shaking my head. "Get out of town until this is figured out—"

"You're not going anywhere," Kai said. "Not alone." He looked down at where Vorack lay at our feet, but I couldn't bring myself to do the same. "We'll take his rental car. Go to Franklin."

"What's in Franklin?" I asked.

"Nothing. That's the point," Idrissa said.

"It'll give us some time to figure things out," Kai told me.

"I don't have any clothes," I said.

"We'll buy clothes."

I nodded, shaky and feeling a million things at once. "Okay."

"Good. Isaac, can you go get my truck from where we left it last night? Lead them in the wrong direction for a bit?"

Isaac nodded. "You got it."

"Thanks, man."

"I'll stay here," Idrissa said. "Intercept Silas."

"Thanks," Kai said.

She didn't look happy, and when Kai darted into the bedroom to put on clothes—again—she grabbed me. "Call me when you get safe," she said.

"Is that wise?"

"Buy a cheap prepaid cell and then toss it when you're done with it," she said.

I nodded. "What about…them?" I asked, gesturing to Vorack.

"I'll take care of it," she said.

I hated to think what that meant. "Thank you," I told her. "Oh, Oscar. I have to tell him—"

"You can't tell him anything," she warned with a shake of her head.

"But—"

"When they can't find you two, he's the first person they'll ask," she said gently. "Don't burden him with the truth."

It made sense. Didn't mean I liked it. Oscar had been good to me since day one. I hated the idea of just abandoning him.

"Okay." My eyes burned with tears. "Just watch out for him, okay?"

"I promise," she said, squeezing my hand.

Kai returned then, and after a quick hug with Isaac, I was climbing into Vorack's car with Kai as we headed out of town.

"Talk to me," Kai said gently.

"I don't know where to start," I admitted.

"What happened back there..." He trailed off, glancing over with concern. "It's okay to be upset. I never wanted you to see that but I couldn't let them hurt you again."

"Is it weird if I don't feel bad about it?"

"Not at all. That guy was going to hurt you, worse than he already had."

"I think it's more about what they did to my dad." I squinted my eyes, forcing out the mental images of my father's body lying bloody and broken. Fitting that Vorack was now also lying dead just inside someone's front door. I couldn't bring myself to be sorry about it either.

"I'm sorry about your dad," Kai said, squeezing my hand.

"Thank you," I told him.

After a moment, I turned to look at him, emotion clogging my throat. "It's ironic, you know? I wanted to leave so badly before, and now, all I want to do is stay."

He reached for my hand. "We'll be back," he said. "This is your home now, Ash. And no one will ever take that away. We're going to break the curse and then we can—"

The windshield exploded, and my ears rang with the sounds of a crash. Glass flew in tiny shards into every space, nicking my skin, tangling in my hair.

Kai yelled something I couldn't make out.

Someone screamed.

Probably me.

I shut my eyes and put my hands over my face to shield it from the glass flying. The car spun, the world outside spinning round and round until we came to an abrupt stop again.

I lowered my hands and saw a van parked in the center of the road. Not parked. Stopped. Its front end had been smashed into the dashboard.

I blinked, my thoughts clicking into place clumsily.

My body felt heavy. Too heavy to move.

As I stared ahead, a man got out of the van, stumbling a bit as his feet touched the pavement.

"Ash," Kai said.

I looked over and saw him leaned against the seat, blood leaking from a wound on his head.

"You're hurt," I said. Or tried to. The words came out in a mumble of pain. It hurt to talk.

I reached for his hand and winced. It hurt to move.

"Ash, run," Kai rasped, and my panic spiked.

The man from the van was headed this way, and nothing about his expression looked friendly.

"Is it her?" someone called out. A female. Her tone was harsh, no-nonsense.

I tried to crane my neck to see behind us, but my muscles wouldn't obey. Everything felt...stuck.

"Ash, don't let them take you," Kai whispered.

There was desperation in his eyes now.

He fumbled with his seat belt as my door was wrenched open.

The man from the van peered in at me.

"It's her," he called to someone over his shoulder.

"Get her in the car."

The female again. She didn't sound nice.

The man grunted and reached over to unbuckle my seat belt. Kai grabbed his wrist, baring his teeth at the man.

"Don't touch her," Kai warned.

That calmed me. Kai would shift, and then they'd all be sorry.

But the man ripped out of Kai's grasp much easier than should've been possible. He glared at Kai. "What are you going to do to stop me, lupin?" he taunted.

Kai didn't answer.

"That's what I thought. Your wolf's just a little too beat up to join us, isn't he?" The man grinned in victory and then clicked the button to release my seat belt.

The moment I was no longer held by it, he grabbed me and wrenched me out of the car. A small tattoo on his neck caught my eye, and I sucked in a breath.

Hexerei.

This man was a witch.

"Ash." Kai's voice was desperate. But weak. "Don't let them put you in a cage."

The words rang out like a gong in my own memory. My father had said those same words as he'd died. I thought of the other hexerei, the one Silas had killed, and how they'd caught him trying to break into Oscar's apartment. My apartment.

They'd been after me all along.

Which meant they'd been the ones my father had been running from.

Kai's eyes fluttered closed, and his head lolled to the side.

Terror gripped me as I realized Kai wouldn't be coming to my rescue after all. I called on my wolf, but she'd receded too far, thanks to my current state of pain and disorientation. So, I did the only thing left to me. I punched my abductor in the nose.

He howled and let me go.

I landed hard on my back.

My head slammed against the pavement, and I barely had time to cry out before everything suddenly disappeared into darkness.

~

Want to find out what happens next?
Book 2, Wolf Captive, is available now!

THE LONE WOLF SERIES
WOLF CAPTIVE
HEATHER HILDENBRAND

ABOUT THE AUTHOR

Heather Hildenbrand was born and raised in a small town in northern Virginia where she was homeschooled through high school. She's only slightly socially awkward as a result. She writes paranormal and fantasy romance with plenty of abs and angst. Her most frequent hobbies are truck camping with her doodle, talking to her plants, and avoiding killer slugs.

You can find out more about Heather and her books at www.heatherhildenbrand.com or shop her store online for special editions at www.heatherhildenbrandbooks.com.

ALSO BY HEATHER HILDENBRAND

A Glamour of Smoke & Shadow (a prequel)

Kingdom of Briars & Roses

Prince of Secrets & Shadows

One Dark Spark

Two Blazing Hearts

Three Scorched Kingdoms

Dark Wolf Soul

Deadly Wolf Bite

Broken Wolf Heart

Protect Me (Immortal Vices & Virtues)

Hunt Me (Immortal Vices & Virtues)

To Hunt A Wolf

To Kiss A Wolf

To Keep A Wolf

Midnight Cursed

Midnight Hunted

Midnight Bound

Wolf Cursed

Wolf Captive

Wolf Chosen

Wolf Revealed

A Witch's Call

A Witch's Destiny

A Witch's Fate

A Witch's Soul

A Witch's Prophecy

A Witch's Hope

Twisted Tides

The Girl Who Cried Werewolf

The Girl Who Cried Captive

The Girl Who Cried War

The Winter Witch

The Spring Witch

A Witch's Heart

Midnight Mate

Goddess Ascending

Goddess Claiming

Goddess Forging

Kiss of Death

Knock Em Dead

Death's Door

Dead to Rights

Dead End

Shop for signed books at www.heatherhildenbrandbooks.com.

www.ingramcontent.com/pod-product-compliance
Lightning Source LLC
Chambersburg PA
CBHW020339310726
48979CB00015B/2430/J

* 9 7 8 1 9 6 1 4 5 5 0 1 6 *